BLOOD DEBT

A ROGUE WARRIOR THRILLER

IAN LOOME

INKUBATOR
BOOKS

Published by Inkubator Books
www.inkubatorbooks.com

ISBN (eBook): 978-1-83756-245-9
ISBN (Paperback): 978-1-83756-246-6
ISBN (Hardback): 978-1-83756-247-3

PROLOGUE
EVANSTON, INDIANA - AUGUST 14, 1991

The boy had been on the hunt for hours.

He pushed through the overgrowth gingerly, sometimes slowing to just inches at a time, pushing light branches aside, avoiding clumps of leaves and brush, steering clear of anything that might create noise.

Though he was just eleven, he was well practiced at bushcraft, at tracking and snaring small game. His father had taught him well.

But it was three in the afternoon, and the two had been stalking one another since just after eight that morning.

The woods near the family home were ideal, a few square miles of closely knit pine and elm trees, narrow passages through them perfect for ambushes, bushes and shrubs offering ground cover. Camouflage gear and rubber knives were the order of the day.

"Remember," his father had told him over fried eggs and sausages for breakfast, "that your goal is to be as close as possible without being seen. If your prey is at a disadvantage and you can use the element of surprise, it's a major strength."

The boy had eaten his eggs and nodded. He was inquisitive and clever, with dark eyes that seemed to look through his subject. He didn't always understand his father's lessons, or their importance, at least. But he liked that, at least in this one area, the old man knew he existed.

His father would spend each week selling insurance – after a decade in the military – and then he'd spend the weekend teaching Bob how to shoot, how to build a shelter, how fend for himself if he ever had to survive in the wild.

Weeknights, they'd spar in the dojo his father had built behind the farmhouse. It was contact karate, but he knew the old man went easy on him.

But in the woods, the rule was simple: kill or be killed.

He checked the compass inset into the pommel of his knife. The sun streamed through the gaps in the sugar maple trees. By his reckoning, he'd looped around and was back close to where they'd entered the woods.

The wild was alive with strange sounds. Bird calls, mostly, but occasionally a shriek or chattering call, something bestial he couldn't recognize. He paid close attention, checking tree tips to see if they'd been bent or broken, watching the dirt ahead for footprints or debris. The wind gusted, rustling choruses of leaves and intertwined branches.

Their first trip out there had come when he was seven years old. His father had given him his tent, his knife, a disposable lighter, some fishing line with a hook, and a can of beans for dinner. Then he told him he'd come back in the morning.

The sounds had terrified him, left him sobbing. He'd

known there was nothing out there he couldn't handle, short of running into a bear. But the dark crept in like a stranger, seeping into the surroundings of the campsite, swallowing up his ability to see the clearing, to judge it safe, enveloping him in unfamiliar territory, engulfing him in vulnerability.

The first time.

THE SECOND TIME, he'd known what to expect and had mustered the courage his father demanded of him. "Your grandfather didn't die on the Normandy beaches defending this country so that you could grow up to be a coward," he'd said on the second trip, this time leaving Bob with everything but the can of beans.

After he'd slammed the truck door behind him, his father said, "I'll see you in two days."

At first, he'd let the fear and self-pity take over again. But after about an hour, he'd set up camp and started making snares out of the fishing line and tree branches.

After finishing the snares, he'd gone fishing at the creek on the other side of the woods. He'd come back with lunch, an eight-pound pike that had had more bones than Bob had thought possible in a fish.

But it had also provided bait for the snares.

Proud of himself, he'd waited around the campfire well into the night, the stars and moon clear in the sky above his clearing.

When he'd checked the snares... they were all empty.

The second day had been harder. He'd been nervous all night. Despite the risk, he'd left the fire burning to ward off anything mean. Compromising, he'd created a rock wall around it, stacking them two deep to prevent sparks from kicking out.

By nighttime, the snares had still been empty. He'd run out of fish.

His sleeping bag had been warm enough, but the sounds of the woods had been frightening once again: padded foot-falls close by that broke twigs and crushed leaves; hoots and hollers and the occasional howl; the gusting wind billowing the sides of the tent.

In the morning, he'd woken just after dawn and gone to check the snares.

He'd stood, mouth wide open in shock, staring at the baby deer as it lay bleeding to death.

The snare had caught its foreleg.

Unable to extract itself, it had attempted to chew through the line and only succeeded in making the wound much worse.

The dark-stained soil around it suggested it had been bleeding for quite some time.

He hadn't known what to do. He'd been hunting with his father but hadn't shot anything yet. He hadn't had a gun, anyway, just his hunting knife. He wasn't going to stab the poor creature to death. But he knew he couldn't just leave it.

He'd tried to get close, to try to cut the line. But it had kicked and panicked, frothing at the mouth.

So instead, Bob retreated to the camp and waited for his father to arrive at nine o'clock. When he had, he'd showed him what had happened.

His father calmly walked back to his truck, found his rifle, and put the young deer out of its misery. The crack of the rifle had seemed different this time, and Bob had winced, as if taken back by its accusation.

"Now," he'd said as he returned, rifle carried low in one hand, "you're going to help me dress it."

"Dress...?"

"That creature deserves a better purpose than dying in an accident. It has good meat on it, so we're going to recover that meat. I'll flip it onto its back and cut it open from its sternum to its stomach and remove its internal organs. Then you'll skin it."

"I'll..." The boy felt numb. He'd barely been able to look at the animal when it was wounded. The idea of it lying there, splayed open...

He'd felt his stomach turn.

His father knelt down to his level. "Consequences, Bobby. It's one thing to make a mistake. But it's a worse sin to not own up and fix it."

It seemed almost inconceivable that he'd remove an animal's hide. "How do I...?"

"You start by slicing around its ankles, creating an initial separation point. Then you slice up the inside of each leg up to where my gutting incision begins. You repeat the process with a starting cut around the base of its neck, then its forelegs. I'll show you how, so don't worry. Then we peel off the skin like taking off clothing, basically."

"And then we can go home?"

"No. Then I butcher the deer for its meat." His father clapped him on the back. "Get comfortable. It's going to be a while yet."

The drive home had been mostly silent. Bob listened to the road noise, the woods flitting past the passenger window, the sun still low in the sky.

He'd felt lonely, isolated. He knew his father cared about him, but father was an adult, in a different world, grand and separate. His mother taught him his lessons; his father taught him how to survive. But sometimes, he'd see the other kids in the town near their rural home and wonder what it would be like to have them around.

"Pa... why don't we have friends?" he'd asked.

Brian Singleton, Marine Sgt. Major retired, had looked over at his son and scowled. Then he'd returned his attention to the road.

Bob wasn't sure why or where it came from, but he'd felt a stirring sense of resentment. It was the sense of being... dismissed. Sometimes, it felt like his father saw him as a tool, a means to an end. Or maybe a project.

His father broke the awkward silence. "You okay last night?"

"It was scary," he'd said. "You didn't leave me a rifle. You didn't leave me a rifle, so I couldn't protect myself, and I couldn't kill the deer."

His father had let that sit, as if concentrating on the empty ribbon of scarred asphalt ahead of them.

Eventually, the man said, "You know why I didn't leave you a gun? Because I thought you'd just fish. That was my fault. Always consider the other options, the potential consequences. The smartest people you'll ever meet can become dumb awful quick by jumping to conclusions, assuming they know better than someone with experience, or that it's always better to wing it. Figure things out properly. Do research, read, practice... and always consider your options. I didn't do that. I taught you to trap, and you just did what came naturally. But there are always consequences to actions we don't consider. You have to try to see those things ahead of time if you want to make smart decisions. You hear me, boy?"

"Yes, Pa," young Bob had offered as the truck bounced along the pockmarked road.

"I knew you'd be scared. That was the point. In life, we're all scared sometimes. Overcoming that fear is the most important thing you can do, sometimes more important than the task or goal itself. Now, you know you can."

Despite everything, that made Bob smile just a little. There was honesty in what his father was telling him: that he wanted him to survive, to make it.

To never be defeated by fear.

Now, four years later, he'd learned his lessons. And while he hadn't found his father after five hours in the woods, the old man hadn't caught him, either.

Ahead in a thicket, he heard a rustle. It was quick, but too heavy to be a rabbit or fox. He jogged over to the thicket in a crouch, trying to keep his footfalls short and silent.

Bob looked over the coarse thatch of bushes just in time to see an arm's-length tree bough snap back into place.

I'm behind him.

I'm behind him, and for once, he didn't spot me.

He felt a rush of energy, the thrill of the hunt, and of knowing it was almost his to win. He crept quickly past the spot. A makeshift trail led past more bushes, the lower strands broken by a weighty object passing.

He sneaked by them, then passed a large tree trunk. A small clearing was on the other side.

But his father was nowhere to be seen.

Bob took a step into the clearing... and the ground gave way, the thin layer of mulch and leaves covering the small pit collapsing under his weight. He plunged six feet to the bottom, landing on his backside.

He looked up.

"Remember what I told you when we drove out today?" his father asked, looking over the edge.

"The best fights are the ones you avoid having," Bob muttered.

His father reached down into the hole and offered him a hand. Bob allowed himself to be pulled up over the lip. He got up and dusted himself off. "I almost had you, Pa."

"I let you think you did, and you walked into a trap as a result. If it looks too easy, it is. Don't be cocky! You spent five hours walking around in circles. I walked a hundred yards and dug a six-foot pit. You gave me a manner in which to avoid the fight completely by taking you out of the picture."

They walked back to the truck. It was nearly four, both men hungry. "Can we try again tomorrow?" Bob asked.

"Nope, blowing up tree stumps tomorrow," his father said. "But I'll start teaching you how to use explosives carefully."

"Really?" Bob exclaimed.

"Really. I'll tell you something else, son: when you can't avoid a problem? Sometimes it's better to just blow that sucker up and start over."

1

NEW ORLEANS

The Rev. Donald Green leaned forward, both fists resting on the table ahead of him. Taped to its front edge, a hand-drawn sign declared:

Community Garage Sale for Charity.

His expression appeared anything but charitable.

His niece, Denise, tugged on the edge of his blue jeans. A lithe young woman in her early twenties, she was seated behind the table, looking worried. She followed his line of sight across the road.

The front yard of an old A-frame house was busy, a handful of burly men enjoying a party, hazy smoke rising off the barbecue, the half-sized hedge not enough to cut off their view.

They were loud, blasting rock music, beer bottles everywhere. Each of the men wore a leather rocker vest featuring a head-sized patch on the back. It was a skull, a dagger protruding downwards through one eye socket, a snake slithering out of the other. Stitched letters above it read "The Damned M.C.," while those below it read "New Orleans."

A row of motorcycles was parked at the curb: Harleys and choppers, teardrop gas tanks emblazoned with flames and skulls, high-backed seats, struts stretching out as if chewing up the road ahead.

"Uncle, please... they're going to see you staring." Denise worried.

"They see the collar, but they don't respect it," Rev. Green declared. "They know they're scaring folks off, but they don't care. They don't care that this street is mostly older folks, just trying to hang onto their homes. They sure don't care that this money could help Mrs. Jessup save her house from the bank."

He raised his voice so that he could be heard across the street. He was happy Denise had driven up from the Ninth Ward to help her family out, but upset she was being subjected to the display. "I suspect they don't give a damn about anything but themselves."

"They probably wouldn't worry much about laying a beating on you, neither," Denise suggested. "Please, Uncle... sit down before you rile them up any more."

"I ain't afraid of those punks," the aging pastor said. "I survived two tours in the Vietnam jungle being stalked by the Cong, I would have you know. Compared to that, these dudes ain't nothing." He raised his voice again. "You hear that, you no-good troublemakers!"

If they did, the bikers did not care to respond. They continued laughing. One crushed a beer can and tossed it at his friend's head.

Green looked to his left. At the next house over, old Mrs. Summerlea's place, three tables of small goods sat just ahead of a neatly trimmed yard. It was filled, in turn, by the unwanted contents of a dozen garages and attics.

Basements were a dangerous proposition in the neighborhood. It had been under water three times in twenty years from hurricane flooding, as it sat just north of downtown and just off Lake Pontchartrain. So storage space was at a premium.

Any chance to free some up and raise money for the church relief fund was bound to be popular.

But the women at the knickknacks table looked despondent. No one had stopped in an hour, since the bikers began partying. It might have seemed a small inconvenience, but it was bigger than that, Green knew.

They were making a habit of imposing themselves on community events. They'd shown up outside a wedding, ruining it. They'd intimidated kids coming out of school.

He wondered what they were up to. They'd bought three houses on Colbert Street: the pair across the road and another two-bedroom A-frame a few blocks down. He figured they might also have bought two on Louisville Street, a block east.

They were quiet for the first month, but had since become a blight: partying all night, attracting other criminals, accosting residents drunkenly and, in one case, mugging them.

Police didn't seem to care. That didn't surprise Rev. Green at all. Lakeview was sedate compared to much of the city, not a priority like Saint Roach or Central City, where gangs warred, stole, and destroyed with impunity.

"This is disastrous," he muttered. "I'd hoped that between the karaoke machine being so cheap and the free hot dogs, we'd attract enough sales to pay the ticket on Mrs. Jessup's house this month."

There were fifteen homes on the block, eight on one side, seven on the other. Three had been for sale for nearly six months, beautiful homes, declining in price now by the month. He knew the possible outcome of the street getting a bad reputation. Between the hurricane rebuilds and the changing population, property values were already sliding.

A week earlier, their problems had deepened when a consortium bidding on the new highway bypass had proposed running one leg parallel to Interstate 630. They proposed an eminent domain grab, with the city or the contractor paying "fair market value" for the nearest homes.

What value? If this continues, we won't be able to give homes here away, let alone rebuild the street.

It had to end. Someone had to stand up to the bikers, make it clear they had outstayed their welcome. "I'm going to go talk to them," he declared.

"Uncle, no!" Denise demanded. "How do you think Wanda would feel if you got hurt? Besides... you spent five years helping me get a degree, and I am not going to graduate without you there. That's not going to happen if you end up in the hospital, or worse."

He'd married Wanda a decade earlier. She was widowed, too. She was mourning the loss of her son during a military training accident – or that was the official story. She was tormented by the notion the government was lying to her.

Pastor Green had understood that was probably just grief, Wanda clinging to the notion that maybe Jon was still out there somewhere. He remembered comrades lost in Vietnam, their families maintaining the same sense of denial.

It had taken years for her to put it all behind her. She'd welcomed the move from Phoenix to New Orleans. They had a good life, a good parish and congregation to minister.

Then the biker gang moved in.

"Can't be helped, baby girl," he said. "These gentlemen may not respect us, but they're not stupid enough to beat on a servant of the cloth in plain daylight, with multiple witnesses."

Denise looked across the road again. One of the bikers was spraying a garishly made-up woman in a white T-shirt with beer from a shaken can. "I... wouldn't be so sure, Uncle. I suspect none of these gentlemen has a fond relationship with logic. Please..."

He was showing off a little, the pastor supposed. But the girl needed to see someone being strong, standing up for what was right. There was never a white knight, a guy on horseback, coming to the neighborhood's rescue. Don had always liked westerns, figured they had a lot to say about the human condition. But people always forgot the Magnificent Seven were drifters, not lawmakers. They were bums who did the right thing, not people with money and power, who seemingly never could.

And most of them died in the end.

His nerves fluttered slightly as he approached the gate. *Be strong, Pastor. Because that's what the job requires.*

"Just... don't you fret!" he told her. He rounded the table and headed across the road. "I'll be right back, none the worse for it."

. . .

ACROSS THE ROAD, Deacon Riggs sat in a director's chair.

His silvery locks and short-cropped beard marked him as older than most of the group. His beefy, tattoo-covered arms were crossed as he stoically watched his brethren having a good time. They arm-wrestled, told jokes, downed beers and spread old lies for the tenth time.

To Deacon, the brotherhood part of being in a motorcycle club was greatly overstated.

He watched as Booker Harris, a six-six giant, poured a warm beer over his brother's head. Booker had the emotional depth of a three-year-old and the brain of a fourteen-year-old, he figured. When he wasn't giggling like a girl and wasting beer, he liked to hurt things: people, small animals, family members. Whatever.

Rick "Diesel" Hauser was rolling a joint, his pale skin burning in the late summer sun. Diesel loved his nickname, even though he'd gotten it because of the rumor his mother drank diesel gasoline before he was born.

Michael "Dirty Carl" Napier was shotgunning a beer at the other end of the picnic table, the burly biker's head tilted back while his woman poured the beer down a greasy oil funnel.

Morons, ever single gol' darn one of them, he thought. *Without the club, they'd be lost. They'd be in prison or dead.*

But that's why I'm the leader. Got to have at least one functioning brain cell paying attention to the details. They don't have to worry about shit, really. Nobody wears the fucking crown but this guy.

The project was moving smoothly, and they deserved some time to cut loose, he'd decided. *Couldn't make the dumb motherfuckers any dumber.*

At the table, Diesel put the finished joint behind his ear for safekeeping. He reached across the table and grabbed a can of beer from a plastic ring of six. He popped the top and took a sip, promptly spitting out a foamy mouthful.

"Shit! Warm as fuck..." Diesel muttered. He tossed the mostly full beer can onto the ground.

Deacon's gaze narrowed. "Pick that shit up," he said.

"What?" Diesel asked.

"Pick that shit up and drink it."

"But... it's hot, Deke... Beer's been sitting in the sun."

"I don't care. I don't like waste. Pick it up and drink it."

Dirty Carl leaned across the table to interject. "Oh! Hey... it's okay, boss, it's my beer. I don't care..."

"Did I fucking ask you?"

Dirty Carl averted his gaze.

Diesel hesitated.

"Well? What're you waiting for? Pick it up," Deacon demanded.

Diesel did as ordered.

"Now drink it. Every fucking drop."

Diesel recognized the tone was not one of a man offering options. He began to tip back the hot beer, his face contorting slightly. After a few seconds, he lowered the can and burped, then crushed it and set it down on the table.

"You know why you just drank that?" Riggs asked him.

Diesel shook his head.

"Because I fucking said so. That's why."

Riggs turned his attention back to Booker and the road beyond him.

Point made. The average jerk on the street, he got caught up early, brainwashed by some lame-brained sheep of a parent into worrying about other people. Deacon had no time for that shit. The shrink at Angola penitentiary had gone on and on about "emotional growth," about how people like him were "arrested" and didn't grow feelings for others properly. *What a bunch of shit.* The world was a cold, hard shithole, from birth to death. The only way to come out on top was to make sure it was colder and harder for the other guy.

Sure, the boys deserved to cut loose. But it was good practice to remind everyone who was in charge.

An occasional loud party served an excellent secondary purpose: scaring the locals. They had a garage sale or some similar crap going on across the street. The old guy running it had been staring daggers at him all day.

Speak of the Devil.

The man was shuffling his way across the road.

Riggs noticed the priest's collar.

Church hypocrite. Even better. He remembered how the women at the mission had lectured his mother when she was working the streets, how they'd made her pray for her supper.

Riggs hated them for that.

His crew had yet to see the man coming. Riggs drained the last of his can of beer, crushed it, then threw it at Booker Harris. The six-foot-six, bearded mountain of a man laughed as it bounced off him.

Riggs nodded towards the road. Harris turned to look. He was so large that the rest of the crew noticed, and they turned, too.

The pastor looked up and saw a dozen or so men staring his way. But he didn't seem worried.

He should be, Riggs thought.

He rose to his feet. "Booker, see what he wants."

The pastor approached the front gate. The behemoth walked over and obligingly opened it for him.

The pastor looked the group over. His gaze settled on Riggs.

He knows a leader when he sees one.

The pastor ignored the men closing around him as he made his way across the small front yard. "You in charge of this mess?" he demanded.

Riggs crossed his arms. "I don't remember sending out neighborhood invitations, so you must've decided to crash our party."

"This is a good street, with fine people living on it," the pastor said. "You know who I am?"

"I do."

"Then you know most of these folks come to my church every Sunday."

"I do."

"I am responsible for ensuring they're happy, healthy and right with God..."

"You didn't answer my question," Riggs said.

The pastor frowned. "I didn't hear none."

"I asked if you were crashing our party."

"Sounded more like a statement." The pastor crossed an equally beefy pair of forearms. "I'm not here to 'party.' I'm here to ask you, politely, to stop scaring off folks whenever we have a get-together. That sale over there... that's to raise money for an elderly woman trying to keep her home of forty years..."

Riggs looked unimpressed. "Do I look like I'm wearing a 'Care Bears' T-shirt or something? Why should we give a fuck about some old lady? In fact, maybe you'd better explain to me why I shouldn't let Booker here whip your ass six ways to Sunday for bothering us."

The pastor looked over at the towering man. "Bigger men have tried," he said. "And the Lord is on my side. You want to be judged unworthy of grace in the next life, that's your look-out, son. But don't tangle with the Lord... and don't make the mistake of thinking folks here are soft. Nobody's going nowhere."

"Nobody 'cept your old lady friend, I guess," Riggs said. He nodded to Booker Harris. "Booker, chuck his ass out on the street."

Booker grinned. "You got it, boss man."

He turned the pastor's way. Riggs figured Booker weighed close to three hundred pounds. Added to his height, it made him look like some kind of mythical giant.

The pastor squared off, setting his feet apart slightly and raising his two fists in a fighter's guard.

The bikers began to laugh. "Oh... so you're a boxer now, are you?" Riggs said.

"Not no more. But once." The pastor was bobbing and weaving ever so slightly, as if the tension of the moment had him revisiting old habits. "Once I was a different kind of fighter."

Booker's expression shifted to annoyance. The bear swung a giant fist at the pastor, but the smaller man – a solid six-two and two-twenty himself, Riggs figured – bobbed out of the way easily.

Booker looked angry. He took a half-step forward to throw a punch but was greeted with a crisp jab to the mouth. It snapped his head back. He shook it, trying to ease the sudden cobwebs from the hard shot; but before he could recover, the pastor threw another jab, then another, snapping Booker's head back twice more. The giant stumbled back a step.

He didn't get a chance to right himself. The clergyman stepped in and threw a thundering right cross, catching the bigger man on the side of the chin, crushing the mental nerve. Booker's legs instantly turned to jelly. He collapsed to the ground, dazed.

Almost as quickly, he was trying to right himself.

The other bikers stood in stunned silence for a few seconds.

"I told you I was a fighter," the pastor said. "Heavy-weight Golden Gloves and former Angola Prison champion. Anyone else wants to take a shot, they'll get the same."

Riggs eyed him coldly. "I thought you church types were supposed to turn the other cheek and all."

"I thought you biker types knew that sometimes fighting for what's right means defending yourself from violence. Now, are you going to end this party, or what?"

Riggs nodded to his friends. "I don't think they appreciate the welcome wagon being so surly." He reached into the back of his waistband, where a speed holster was clipped to his leather belt.

He drew his Ruger .357 Magnum.

"Let's just skip past the bullshit where you try to knock out a dozen of my men and get your ass kicked, and just go right to the point where I deal with the problem."

The pastor began to raise his hand hesitantly. "Son... you don't want to make a foolish choice, now..."

Riggs strode over to him and pressed the barrel against the pastor's forehead. "I ain't your son, you crazy old sum'bitch. Now, you'd better say you're sorry to Booker and my friends for being so inhospitable... or they're going to be picking your brains out of chain link for the next week."

From the other side of the fence, by the road, another man sounded matter-of-fact about the situation.

"You really don't want to do that."

2

From the sidewalk, the situation looked fluid and dangerous. Bob clocked ten men, mostly large, all in denim and leather. The rocker patches suggested a biker gang.

He'd watched from his car down the block as the older pastor had crossed the road. His garage sale table had been in front of 5780 Colbert Street, the home of Donald and Wanda Green.

That meant the man about to get into a tussle was probably the late Jon Rice's stepfather.

It had taken longer than he'd expected to make it to New Orleans, three months of ducking traffic cameras, hanging out in small-town diners and motels. Avoiding Team Seven – the former CIA unit that had employed him – had been a matter of survival. The trip south from Chicago had been labored, a jagged route connecting tiny dots on the map. Wayne City Missouri gave way to McKee, Kentucky, which in turn led to Marlon, West Virginia, which led him to Chapin, South Carolina.

He'd been in New Orleans for less than an hour, and already something was going wrong.

It wasn't like the Greens lived in a bad neighborhood. The lawns were neat and manicured, the houses one- and two-bedroom family classics, some a single story, others two. They were fronted by porches, wrapped in wood siding tinted shades of blue, white, yellow and green.

Appearances, apparently, were deceiving. A conflict had clearly escalated. When the pastor impressively cleaned a giant biker's clock, Bob figured they'd been bound to get worse.

So he'd hightailed it down the block at a gentle trot to say hello.

He assumed the guy now holding the Ruger GP100 revolver to the pastor's head was some kind of leader.

I'm guessing that's chambered in .357. A guy like that thinks stopping power is important.

The man risked a quick glance Bob's way. "Everybody's real keen on telling me what to do this morning," he said. "And who might you be?"

"Me? I'm Bob," Bob said. "Old family friend."

"Yeah? You picked a real unfortunate time to visit, Bob," Riggs snarled. "I'm about to kill this big fucker where he stands. Trespassing is a justification for self-defense in the State of Louisiana, and he already done assaulted one of my friends..."

"From where I was sitting, it looked like your friend threw the first punch..."

"Protecting my property, is all," Riggs said. "How do we know this dude is a pastor? What I have in mind is maybe he's just some kiddy diddler come to scope out the house, see if there's some kids to lust after."

"Yeah... I don't care about any of your bullshit justifications," Bob said. "What I do know is that if you pull that trigger, I'll be forced to draw my piece... and then the only thing you'll have in mind will be a large bullet hole."

Riggs kept the gun raised and steady. He flitted a quick look Bob's way, his hand flexing on the gun's grip as he weighed the threat. "You're bluffing."

"I've never been known to," Bob suggested calmly. He opened the gate and walked into the yard.

He was past a half-dozen men before Riggs gestured their way. "Frisk him; take his piece if he really has one—"

"Can't allow that," Bob warned. He nodded back towards the garage sale. "You realize as soon as you drew that gun at least two or three people were calling the cops, right?"

Riggs scoffed a little. "Y'all think they're going to ride to your rescue? Typical response time around here is ninety minutes or some shit. They're not going to save your ass."

"No, but they'll arrest yours. Lots of witnesses, lots of love for the pastor over there, I'm sure."

Booker was rubbing his sore jaw. He took a step closer to Bob. He waved a friend over. "Diesel, check his waistband."

The other biker was big and round, with frizzy hair, his mustache and goatee both braided, eyes hidden behind black Ray Orbison sunglasses. He ran towards Bob.

Bob let him get within an inch before stepping to one side and dodging the clumsy charge. He pushed down hard on the passing biker's back, Diesel's forward momentum carrying him crashing to the ground.

From his left periphery, Booker swung another meaty fist, so slow that Bob could practically step around it. As the punch continued past him, he pivoted on one heel, using the momentum from the turn to ram an elbow into the biker's shoulder joint.

Booker crashed to the ground next to his friend. Diesel scrambled to his feet angrily. His hand came up from his waistband, a snub-nosed .38 revolver gripped between meaty fingers.

Smith and Wesson 642, punchy .38, walnut grip, no-snag trigger. Tight pull.

Before it was even fully raised, Bob stepped forward, a palm punch catching the small bone in the man's wrist, something snapping. The biker yelped and dropped the gun.

Booker tried to rise to his feet and intervene, but Bob's foot came up hard, catching him across the jaw, dazing him. The biker rolled onto his back.

Bob advanced on their leader.

"All right, enough bullshit," Riggs declared. He straightened his gun arm and leaned forward with purpose. "Come another step and I'll..."

If he'd expected Bob to screech to a halt, the biker was in for a shock. Bob's hand shot forward, jamming a finger into the pistol's guard, behind the trigger. Riggs tried to turn his way, to rip the gun free, but was greeted with a headbutt to the bridge of his nose.

Blood began to stream out. Bob ripped the pistol from his grasp, his foot coming around to sweep Riggs's feet out from under him. The biker crashed to the ground.

Everyone froze, stunned by the new arrival's ferocity.

"Fucking get him!" Riggs bellowed. "Kick his ass, you chickenshits!"

They barreled towards him, but before any had moved more than three steps, Bob raised the Ruger and cocked the hammer. "Uh, uh, uh, gentlemen, unless you want a more perforated version of your boss. Hands high; nobody reaches for a piece. Not a good idea."

Keeping his eyes raised, he took a few steps back until he was next to the preacher. "Now, my friend Pastor Green here is going to come with me, and we're going to move our business to the other side of the street."

Riggs leaned up on one elbow. "You... you're going to regret this..." he threatened.

"If you think I'm the only capable friend he has, think again," Bob said. It was a lie, but one that might buy them space and time, at least for him to assess how the Greens got into the dispute to begin with.

Maybe there was a way to diffuse it all. He hadn't come to Louisiana to get into another fight.

He kept the gun level as he backed towards the pastor. "Head on out, sir, I'll keep you covered."

"I didn't need no help... but I sure appreciate it," the older man said.

Bob backed out of the yard after him. "Gentlemen, if I said it had been interesting, I'd be lying. If none of us ever talk again, we'll all be happier for it."

Booker had risen to his feet and was rubbing his sore shoulder. "Think... think it's dislocated," he whined. He looked up at Bob. "Mister, you are one dead motherfucker. You just don't know it yet."

Bob closed the gate behind him. "On the contrary, big man. I'm well aware that I've been dead for years. But that's your problem, not mine."

He backed up to the road before turning to cross, glancing over his shoulder until he was standing next to the pastor on the other side of the street. He gestured towards the sales tables. They were empty, the women having gone inside. "Looks like your sale is going to be a bust," Bob said.

"Yeah... but we'll be here to do it again on another day," the pastor said. "I'm real grateful for what you did."

"Don't mention it."

"I take it you're Bob?"

"I am."

"They going to stay there, across the road?"

"We're not on their property, so their legal justification is gone. Most criminals don't really want police attention; it's bad for business."

"They're not going to let that go, though," the pastor suggested.

"Probably not. But we can figure that out."

"Well, okay then. Come on, come inside, and we'll fix you a coffee. You can meet my Wanda, and I can explain this sorry mess."

3

Pastor Don Green's house was as modest, neat and tidy as the rest of the street, neighbors across the street excepted.

Past an immaculately neat front garden fronted by wooden boxes filled with sunflowers, a path ran up to a narrow, whitewashed porch and front door.

"It really is a nice little neighborhood," Bob offered.

"Best in the dang state, you ask me. Still affordable, but also safe, busy, lots of families, decent homes. Lots of rebuild from the flooding, mind."

He led Bob up the front steps.

"Wanda was real surprised when you called this morning," he said. "Not that it wasn't pleasant, mind. She said Jon had a lot of nice things to say about you back in the day."

He let them in. The house was warm, well-lived in. Family pictures lined the front hall. From its far end, a woman's voice called out: "I'm in the kitchen."

Green led Bob there. "Wanda! Honey, our visitor's here a little early."

Wanda Green was seated at a Formica-topped breakfast table, working on a crochet pattern. She got up right away. She was short and had to throw her arms upwards to get them around Bob for a hug.

"As I live and breathe, Mr. Singleton, I never thought we'd get a chance to meet."

Bob felt his cheeks flush red. "Jon spoke fondly of you often, ma'am," he said. "I'm just sorry I didn't bring him back to you."

"Well, now... it's been a long time," she said, releasing her grip. "I do still think about Jon every day. You don't ever get over losing your baby, no sir. But I do take comfort from the fact that he loved what he did and that you looked out for him. You come to terms, uh-huh."

He withdrew a folded-over envelope from his jacket pocket and handed it to her. "Here. Jon left this in Virginia before Tehran. Couldn't be seen wearing a cross there..."

Wanda opened the envelope. The chain she withdrew was thin and delicate, a silver crucifix hanging from it. "Oh!" She fought off tears. "Oh my. I gave this to him for his communion when he was eight." She smiled softly, the memory of him more real in the moment. "Thank you." She held the tiny cross close to her body for a moment and closed her eyes, as if taken back in time. Then she put the chain around her neck. "So that I can keep him close."

She meandered over to the counters while her husband sat down. "Grab a chair there, Bob, and I'll get us some coffee," she said, "if you're so inclined..."

"He had a run-in with our new neighbors," Pastor Green noted. He didn't mention the gunplay, which Bob figured was a hedge against scaring his wife. "They've got some sort of party going across the way, scaring everyone off the sale."

She returned with two mugs of coffee and offered them each one before retrieving her own, along with small pots of cream and sugar. "Now you know my feelings on that, Don..."

"Leave it to the police, I know," he said. "But you know damn well they don't spend a lick of time worrying about what happens around here. Not enough crime."

Wanda sat down. "It's a sad, sad state of affairs, I tell you what... People just want to go about their business, and instead, they have to put up with being harassed and bullied."

"Bob made a couple of them look real foolish. I do wish you hadn't jumped in like that, although I do appreciate it," the pastor said. "They're going to be trouble long after you're gone."

"And then?" Bob asked. "If I'm not here next time..."

"Those were some pretty slick moves," Pastor Green said, trying to shift the tone. "Wanda said you and Jon were in ordnance and supply, something like that."

"More... service provision," Bob said. "Flexible solutions to complex problems."

"Uh-huh," Green said, skeptical. "That backward-elbow thing looked more like black-belt karate or some such, some of that Bruce Lee mixed martial arts business. They teach everyone in the Marines to fight like that? 'Cos I don't remember nothing like that in Army basic training."

Bob knew the pastor was digging for an explanation. Wanda, on the other hand, sipped her coffee obliviously.

"You pick things up here and there," Bob suggested. He hung his head slightly. They deserved more honesty, but he had to weigh it against letting them know too much, giving the wrong people reasons to visit them. "We... got into

some dangerous situations in the Middle East,
Afghanistan..."

"I never did like hearing about that stuff," Wanda said,
interjecting for the first time. "He'd be all calm whenever he
was on leave from duty, but if anyone brought up where he'd
just been, he'd tell us as much as he could about the place,
but never a word on what actually happened there. He knew
how the risk, the threat to him every day, he knew how that
affected me."

"He was considerate," Bob said. "That was rare on the
team. He didn't talk a lot about his personal life, I'll be
honest. He did mention how happy he was he could help out
by sending some money home after his father passed..."

"Jon was our lifesaver," Wanda said. "I had immobilizing
inner-ear problems, couldn't get up without my head swim-
ming. So work was problematic for several years. He never
complained, sent home a lot of money, pretty much everything he made."

Probably not, Bob thought. The team was well paid, but
they took care of their own living expenses. Jon had a place
in DC, traveled in his time off. He had resources. Still... there
was nothing wrong with her remembering a slightly better
version. Every mother deserved that. "He was a great kid,"
Bob said.

"I last saw him four months before he passed. He came
home, brought a friend with him from his unit..." Wanda
lowered her coffee, holding it just ahead of her, elbows on
the table, casting her mind back. Her face brightened. "Oh
my! I just had a thought! I have a photo Jon left behind once
when he was on leave..."

She rose and walked over to the other side of the living
room. A small wooden chest with metal strappings and a

large keyhole sat next to the sideboard. She crouched slowly and opened it, then returned with a photo in hand. Wanda passed it to Bob and sat down.

"He said they took this in training overseas somewhere, maybe Damascus?"

Bob looked at the image. There were four of them, standing side by side in khaki camouflage, desert and dunes behind them. Jon Rice, Tyler Gaines, Elliot Azadi and Bob, each carrying an M16 assault rifle, aside from Gaines, who had a Winchester .30-30 slung across his shoulders.

"Yeah... Damn, this would've been training for the Tehran mission in Israel, early 2006." Bob couldn't believe how young they all looked, tanned, sleeves rolled up and smiling...

Wanda looked back at the metal-banded wooden chest. "All my keepsakes of him fit in that one box, unfortunately. I wish I had more. Wish I had him, really."

Bob felt her pain, the harshness of losing her only son revisiting her with haunting clarity. Her voice seemed smaller and quieter suddenly, timid.

"They said his Jeep flipped in Tikrit, on the way back to base. But it was so long before we knew anything." She looked up at him, her expression suddenly determined. "Is that what it was, Bob? Did Jon just die in a stupid accident?"

So, straight to it, Bob thought. He knew she'd probably weighed and reconsidered her son's death throughout the fifteen years past. Jon Rice had been just twenty-four when the Tehran mission went askew. He felt grim, knowing nothing he said would make it okay.

She deserved better. "He died a hero, Mrs. Green. It wasn't in any accident. It was a mission. And Jon wasn't an ordinary soldier. Like me, he undertook special missions for the CIA, in dangerous places."

Her eyes widened and began to well with tears. She held her hand to her mouth, shocked. She lowered it abruptly, lips pursed as she tried to maintain her composure.

"I knew it," she said softly. "I always knew Jon was working on something bigger. He didn't do all that training, spend all those years becoming a fighter, only to work in requisitions. I knew they weren't telling me straight."

"We had a mission in Iran to help a nuclear scientist defect. It went wrong. Jon was shot in the process of trying to rescue his teammate, and died at the scene."

She began to cry gently, tears rolling down her cheeks at her son's memory. After a moment, she turned her head slightly, as if embarrassed. She drew a Kleenex from a box on the table and wiped the tears away, then composed herself. "He paid for this place, you know. We were able to buy outright because he paid off our mortgage in Bisbee. He was so good. Such a good boy."

"He made everyone who knew him proud," Pastor Green intoned.

Wanda wiped her eyes once more. She sighed a little and clutched her Kleenex ahead of her. "When... when he was a boy, he made me this sculpture in art class at school, a bright red-and-white polka dot mushroom, like they had on the Smurfs cartoon he used to watch. That was the last thing of his that I had..."

Her husband nodded back, towards the front street. "It was in the front yard, in the small rock garden. Our new neighbors smashed it the first night they moved in, or so we figure."

Bob frowned, but held in the sudden burst of rage,

seething inside over the idea of anyone mistreating this poor woman. *Hold it in; suck it down deep. Nurse Dawn wouldn't be impressed if you started losing your temper, now would she?*

He looked out the front window, across the street. "I don't get it. Why would they set up shop in Lakeview? It's practically the suburbs. I mean... I know it's not fancy or anything, but there have to be much worse places, gang territory, places where their ilk fit in better."

Pastor Green sipped his coffee, then placed the mug on the table. "I wish we could tell you," he said. "The neighborhood is generally nice, even if this is the cheaper section of it. Colbert is a pretty quiet street, normally. Noise from the interstate, that's all. But..."

"But?"

"But we don't rightly know. They bought that house across the way about six months back. They bought the house at the north end of the block a week later, then the house next door to the one across the road when the owner decided he'd had enough."

"He just left?"

"Folks here are older," Pastor Green explained. "He was planning on retiring to Jacksonville anyhow, to be nearer his grandkids. But he let the place go for nothing. We were hoping someone nice would take it, but the bikers let it be known that if anyone else bid on it, they'd see trouble."

That didn't make sense either, Bob thought. Bikers usually made their money selling drugs, prostitution or protection. All three worked better when they weren't attracting attention.

On the other hand, homes next to each other made sense: one could act as a decoy home, that when searched by police, would come up empty, even though it seemed as if that's where the foot traffic headed. In fact, customers would be led around the back to the other house – which, with no foot traffic, was unlikely to be eligible for a police search warrant.

So perhaps it was someone's idea of seizing an opportunity. But... there were no customers there, no wellspring of poverty and addiction upon which to capitalize.

"It's strange," he admitted finally. "It's not how that type usually behaves."

"That's what we thought," Pastor Green said. "We thought maybe they were trying to get in on the freeway money..."

"Freeway money?"

He nodded. "The city has a proposal to build a new bypass route. One of the options is to run it directly adjacent to the interstate. Some folks think they're going to strike it big when the city buys their house. But my understanding is that under eminent domain, they can't get more than the market says it's worth. And the market here has never been that strong."

"People are fooling themselves, then," Bob suggested. "That doesn't sound like the kind of mistake a criminal gang would make. They're not inclined to gamble with investments when they can just take what they want."

"But if it ain't that," Pastor Green wondered, "what else is there? Since when did bikers get interested in cheap real estate?"

Wanda shrugged. "No matter. I'm sure all this will pass."

Bob held in his discomfort. He wondered if, in intervening, he hadn't just made things worse.

4

The man behind the expansive walnut desk was dressed immaculately. He was backdropped by dark gray wood shutters, tall and stretching nearly from floor to ceiling.

The slate-gray suit was tailored, the navy-blue tie the finest spun silk, the cuff links platinum with diamond studs. If he'd stepped out from behind the desk, the shine on his thousand-dollar brogues might have blinded Deacon Riggs.

He hated reporting to Denny Roulette. The lawyer's office in the French Quarter was stylish, full of antiques, gilt mirrors in the lobby and offices. It smelled of books and money, the latter before you'd even gotten through the door.

It was the domain of an altogether different, more duplicitous form of predator. Criminal types – lowlifes of all variety – made Riggs comfortable. The kind who stole your shit by signing a document while leaning on a mahogany masterpiece? They made him nervous.

"I told you I didn't want you coming here in daylight

hours." Roulette was twirling a capped fountain pen between his pudgy fingers. "We have a reputation to protect."

"Too real for you, counselor?" Riggs pulled one of two chairs ahead of the desk slightly to one side and plopped himself down in it. He put his cowboy-booted feet up on the corner of the workstation and withdrew a toothpick from the top pocket of his leather vest, placing it between his teeth and chewing it. "Way I figure it, you're not the one taking the risks."

Squares like Roulette, they always liked to be adjacent to the danger, Riggs figured. They liked the rush of knowing someone who lived by their own rules, but they themselves tried to appear saintly, justified and civil. He hated the hypocrisy of it, wanted to grab the man by his sandy hair and smash his chubby little face into the desk.

But business was business.

"Your people are being paid handsomely, with more to come. But you know full well the person I represent has only so much patience for failure. And get your damn feet off my desk!"

The lawyer was professionally genial while in court or on TV. But with Riggs, his expression never changed: a sour, stern look, like a jailer.

"We haven't failed at shit," Riggs insisted. He took his cigarettes out and removed one, along with a Bic.

"Don't even think about lighting that thing in here," Roulette said. "Jesus H. We expected twice as many listings by now. You've been on Colbert Street for eighteen months."

Riggs put the cigarettes and lighter away. "These people are old and stubborn. Most of them have lived on that street since the days of drive-ins and jukeboxes. They're not going to run at the first sign of trouble, and you don't want us to get physical, so..."

Roulette pinched the bridge of his nose and squinted, tension eating him up. "You can't threaten them directly for the same reason I didn't want your merry band of idiots to mug that old lady last month: if people *feel* threatened, nobody gives a shit about their problems. If people *are* threatened, we have to worry about police, politicians, outside attention."

"Police? In this town—"

"They ever put the touch on you?" Roulette asked sternly.

"Nope."

"Then maybe you should figure you're a little low-rent for them. They're the most corrupt fucking police force in the country. But they don't want your money, Riggs. What does that tell you?"

"Well, shit..."

"Damn right. They think bikers are low-life pieces of shit. Guys like Sammy Habsi, on the other hand, they respect. And Mr. Habsi doesn't like outside attention."

"It might be too late for that already," Riggs said. "That's why I'm here. We have a complication. Jesus Christ, Denny, I need a fucking smoke, okay? It's been a hell of a day."

Roulette leaned forward slightly and wagged an index finger at the biker boss. "Not. A fucking. Puff. I hate the smell of that shit. You can wait the five minutes I'm willing to waste on you and do it outside. Now: what's the deal? My assistant said you sounded panicked when you called."

Riggs hesitated. He wasn't used to admitting fault or vulnerability. He'd learned that from his old man long before any of his repeated prisons stints. That kind of weakness got strong men killed. Roulette was a suit, and suits weren't to be trusted, even when they were the ones paying you. Maybe especially then.

"Out with it," Roulette demanded.

"We had a couple of white knight types this morning. Local pastor and a friend of his."

"So? I give a shit *why,* exactly?"

"So, they were tough. The pastor's some sort of ex-champ boxer. He knocked Booker's head in. Then his friend shows up and starts pulling some Muay Thai martial arts shit or something."

Roulette sighed deeply. "Riggs, why are you here? What do you expect me to do?"

"Take the cuffs off!" the biker implored. "You don't want us to hurt anyone, or start real trouble. But this dude today, trust me... I know the type. Sometimes..."

"Sometimes what?"

"Sometimes, you meet a dude who says very little, but manages to speak fucking volumes, okay? When it's in a bar or the joint, he's the guy who's quiet until he has to speak up, and even that's just to try to cool shit off, avoid the situation completely. But he's never the guy who seems the most nervous. You dig? He's the confident guy who walks out of the room every time without a speck."

Roulette scoffed gently. "I figured that was you. That's why we hired you."

"That guy gets to deal with problems directly, not like some corporate weasel, all intimidation without wanting to get his hands dirty. All talk, no action," Riggs said. "You want me to resolve this particular problem, you just say the word."

The lawyer was silent for a moment, his gaze shifting to his desktop as he weighed his options. "Do whatever you have to... but it's on you. I don't know about anything. I don't condone anything. Solve the problem."

"Oh? Just like that, then."

"Exactly." Roulette leaned forward. He twirled his pen thoughtfully for a moment. "Look... you and I both know Habsi doesn't belong here. He's not old New Orleans money. He's some Middle East mongrel with a trust fund. Even twenty years ago, he wouldn't have gotten a foot in the door."

"Damn straight."

"But we live in the here and now, Riggs, not twenty years ago. And right now, he's also the guy with the money, the connections. Men like him always win in New Orleans. Here, the story in the paper is never 'man bites dog.' Here, the big dog always bites the man, and the man stays bit. And Habsi is one of the big dogs. So... yeah. Solve it, however you have to. I don't want to know."

That was as much as he could expect, Riggs realized.

It was enough.

He rose and took his cigarettes out, lighting one as he walked out. "Pleasure doing business with you, counselor."

RIGGS RODE his Harley down Canal Street, twin triple lanes separated by tram lines, in the heart of the city. The buildings were low-rises, art deco with ornate scrollwork, four or five stories typically, with awnings at street level to front the shops and restaurants.

He kept his speed down and an eye out for evening partygoers. They tended to drink a few too many and then wander into the street, or out from behind one of the tall palms that lined the boulevard. He'd almost killed some young couple jaywalking a week earlier, after his attention was caught by a blonde in a Ferrari, outside the Ritz Carlton.

He kept an eye on his wing mirrors, wary of police. Rollers would stop him just to rack up points, find any excuse to issue him a ticket. They'd crack his taillight or mirror, mud up the plate. Anything to justify issuing him a citation or, if they really hit the jackpot, to call the wrecker truck.

Riggs had never met a cop he liked. His father, who split when he was twelve, had been a career criminal. His uncle, who molested every kid he could get his hands on, had died in Angola Prison, near Shreveport, beaten to death by his cell mate on the first day of his second term of confinement.

His mother had worked part-time as a stripper, then as a prostitute when the dancing dried up. After they were gone, with Riggs a teenager, he'd taken care of himself until a robbery had gone too far, and he'd done his own time at Angola.

Police arrested people. It was basically all they did, as far as he could tell.

It was Friday, which meant most of the guys would be at The Purple Bird. They'd be playing eight ball, smoking weed, tipping back jugs of draft. It was a dependable life, one of their own making and control.

Riggs had never had much else. He'd been lieutenant to the former boss now serving a dime at Angola for heroin distribution. Before that, he'd been a petty criminal, two decades spent running a stolen auto chop shop in Orleans Parish.

When he'd been elected leader, he'd promised the club members they'd work less, party more. He'd guaranteed them a steady source of income from weed in an underserved part of the city – and one of the few ideal for drug houses. As long as they made their share and kicked up, everyone was happy.

Lakeview was away from the action, but its back alleys, rare in New Orleans, were ideal for entrances away from prying eyes.

That had been eighteen months earlier. Denny Roulette had provided serious cash, not just to work for him but to buy two homes, which they got to keep and use for at least a year, maybe two or three. So far, Roulette and his boss had delivered everything he'd promised and more.

In return, the gang had managed to harangue at least a dozen homeowners across four blocks into selling cheap and moving.

But Riggs knew their mere intimidating presence wasn't enough; eventually, they had to escalate their efforts to drive the old folk out.

It took another ten minutes to navigate through the evening partygoers. He parked the bike at the end of a line of Harleys, on Perdido Street, behind The Purple Bird. Booker's Softail, with its distinctive dreamcatcher hanging from the Plexiglass windshield, was missing.

He was probably hurting, Riggs figured, humiliated twice, including by a man in his sixties. He pitied whoever ran into the giant gangster on that particular night.

He used the narrow laneway between buildings to walk to the front of the bar. Their puppet "owner" kept reminding them that going through the rear kitchen could invalidate their insurance, and they'd finally broken the members of the habit.

They'd taken up the back corner of the main level. He counted nine fully patched members. The Damned MC had four chapters in Louisiana, three in New Orleans. But they barely mixed in each other's business. His crew were mostly men he'd grown up with, served time with.

Diesel was leaning on his pool cue, waiting for his chance to shoot. "Boss," he acknowledged. "Look... I fucked up, I know..."

Riggs shook his head curtly. "The dude was an unknown quantity. The old guy brought backup. Nobody would have expected that. Don't sweat it."

"You talked to the suits?"

A waitress walked by carrying a black plastic tray. She removed a glass of draft beer from it and handed it to Diesel.

"Thank you, darlin'," he enthused.

"Yeah, we got into it. They don't want to know, they just want it dealt with."

"That's good, right? Go crack some skulls, get shit done."

"To a point. We don't know nothing about this guy, this new arrival."

"Bob."

"Eh?"

"He said his name was Bob."

"Yeah. We need to figure this dude out, what his weaknesses are. Get your phone out, give Dirty Carl a call. He's minding the store at the bayou cookhouse. Tell him to get back to Lakeview, get eyes on the pastor's place. Chances are this Bob dude is staying there. If he goes anywhere, we follow him. If he talks to anyone, we find out who and why. Maybe this guy can work for us. Maybe if we make an example of him, the others will fall in line."

5

WASHINGTON, DC

A motor whirred as the suspended paper target began to move away from the shooting gallery counter. Eddie Stone held down the red button beside the counter until the target was thirty yards away.

He raised the .40-caliber Glock 19 until he was looking down its sights. Even adjusted, they tended to be off a millimeter or so to the left, the square reticule too large to properly center with his dominant eye.

He compensated automatically and squeezed the heavy-pull trigger smoothly, letting the gun's kick surprise him, his spare hand supporting the butt. He repeated it three times, his hand vibrating slightly from the recoil.

He lowered the smoking barrel of the gun. It felt right: balanced, in line, smooth. He'd had the recoil spring replaced recently after a jam, but otherwise, he'd become accustomed to it. He'd taken a revolver to DC; that had been a mistake.

He'd always been responsible about re-qualifying and practicing. He liked to shoot, so it wasn't a hassle.

But since the incident at the graveyard, when Singleton had caught him with his guard down, he'd been back almost daily.

First, Singleton had knocked him cold.

Then Gerald Dahlen had shot him in two places.

Six weeks later, he was still limping, the wounds still healing and painful. But his pride hurt more. Stone had been a field agent for decades, a black ops specialist trained to kill a man in seconds. Singleton had tossed him around like...

Like a seventy-year-old man? That's the reality of it, isn't it, Eddie boy? You're old and past it. Doesn't matter how many bullseyes you hit if you can't see the other man coming.

He sighted the target and carefully took one more shot. He lowered the gun, laying it on the counter, then held down the little red button.

The torso-shaped target drifted methodically back to the counter. He unclipped it. The first three shots had struck it in the head. He felt a surge of embarrassment at his anxiety. He'd been trained to shoot center mass for decades, but his nerves had prompted a more lethal response.

The fourth was dead center where the chest would be, perfect. *Got it together at the end*, he told himself.

He took off his earmuffs and carried the target back to the front desk. He handed it to the range attendant. "Store that one with the rest, Mike."

Mike studied the grouping. "Working some shit out, Ed?"

"Something like that. We live in interesting times."

Mike chuckled at that. "We do indeed, sir, we do indeed."

His phone rang.

"Stone."

"It's Alpha."

Stone remained unconvinced by Michael Murphy. Of all the attack dogs at the CIA, he'd been the most qualified to take over as the team's most prolific operator. But there was something off about him, a need to impress. He'd survived in the job for several years, which suggested it was a bad call on his part; nevertheless, he sometimes wondered if he wanted the man to get it over with and fail.

"Make me happy, Alpha."

"Wish I could, boss. Not a sniff in Miami or Fort Lauderdale. We've turned over half of Florida at this point. If I had to guess—"

"It sounds like you do."

"I'd say he's heading for San Diego. That's the guy, right? Azadi?"

"It is. Well... his cousin and great-aunt, that is. The rest of the family are out of the picture, other than the uncle in Palm Beach."

"They're all dead?"

"It's a long and sad story, but irrelevant to the mission at hand, Alpha. I'll get our friends at the NSA working on a domestic profile for sig ints."

"Roger."

Stone sighed gently. "We'll end up spending millions on signals intelligence, all to catch a man who just wants to be left alone," he muttered. "If he'd just stayed dead..."

"Sorry, boss?"

"Don't worry about it. Company politics."

"What about local law enforcement?" Alpha suggested.

"Not a chance. Singleton has gone to the press before, about Gerald Dahlen. We thought he was dead for a decade; there's no telling what intel he's sitting on to potentially expose the program. That's discounting past operations and failures that he might suddenly decide to talk about publicly. No, we have to put this dog down."

"So what next?"

"We'll keep looking. But either way, the team won't go green at this point. Too much flak for us to handle this internally; too much risk of being caught breaking the non-domestic mandate. If we spot him, we'll get an outside contractor to bat cleanup."

"There are only two other leads in the south, in Arizona and Texas, and both are lesser players in terms of the fallout from Tehran."

Stone smiled ruefully at the notion that Bob Singleton might take the "normal" route to anything. "Stay tuned, Alpha. I know the way he thinks, and he's probably closer than you realize."

"Roger that."

Stone ended the call. Whatever was shaking his confidence, he had a feeling dealing with Singleton would end it.

6

They ate early, the six o'clock news just underway as they finished up.

After, Wanda insisted on doing the dishes without them, kicking the men out onto the porch. The pastor took a seat in one of the wicker chairs and Bob the other.

Don reached forward to the coffee table. He looked both ways down the street.

He was reaching under the table to retrieve something when a car pulled up to the curb outside with a slight screech of brake dust.

The driver's side door opened, and a young man in a pale gray suit climbed out. He rounded the car quickly and jogged up the front path to the porch.

"Don!" He looked worried. "I heard what happened."

Pastor Green gestured the man's way. "Bob, this is Derek Bevan, my associate pastor. Derek's six months out of Bible College, but he's already quite the hit with the lady parishioners. Bob's an old friend of my late stepson, just visiting."

"Well, it's a pleasure to meet you, sir," the young man said earnestly. He leaned in with an open hand; Bob shook it. "I was just on my way home for the night – I live about four blocks thataway." He pointed north. "I stopped at the corner store for some briquettes, and Jerry mentioned you'd had trouble."

"Nothing we couldn't handle, son," the pastor advised. "But I do appreciate you stopping to check."

Bob was distracted. "That suit... the cut is perfect for you. Tailored?"

Derek nodded sheepishly. "My father has some money, and he got it for my graduation. It's a little rich for my taste, to be honest, but..."

"He has good taste. Designer?"

"Pardon?" Derek asked. "I don't quite get what you mean..."

"Is it a designer suit?" Bob asked. "You know: Bill Blass, Burberry, Armani?"

"I... I didn't really pay attention. Yeah, I think it's Bill Blass," the young man said.

"Hmm. Yep, pricey," Bob said.

"Now, Bob, be nice to the boy. You're making him uneasy and such."

Bob held up two palms. "Not my intention. Apologies."

Derek nodded back towards the road. "Well, I guess I'd better get home and make my cat Lucy dinner, or she's going to be righteously ticked off. Just so long as you're okay, Don."

"I am, son, I am. Good to see you."

The young pastor headed back down the steps to his car. "Good night, y'all," he called out. He climbed into the car. A moment later, he drove off.

"Good boy. Eager," Green said. "He's got a dream of being

one of the big ones one day, maybe have a TV or radio show."

He reached under the table and retrieved a quarter-smoked cigar, as well as a green Bic lighter. "Mind you, if he'd come two minutes later, I'd have been busted. You can be sure Wanda's told him to snitch on me if he catches me smoking."

He tried to light the stogie, but the Bic was dead. "Well... dang. Now what?"

Bob retrieved his own disposable, which he'd been carrying since Chicago. He'd learned long ago it paid to have a lighter on hand.

He reached over and flicked the flint wheel. Pastor Green leaned in and took a few puffs before leaning back again. He blew out smoke. Then he took a sip from his coffee. "Ahhh... that's good."

The pastor noticed Bob's amused stare. "What? Oh, I know. Church says smoking's a sin and all. Crucially, the Bible does not."

"So that's your one vice?"

"It is. Well, this and the NBA season. Pelicans are having a good year. Can't afford to go most seasons, but at least they're repping for the 504."

"The 504?"

"Area code." The pastor frowned. "You never heard that before?"

Bob shrugged. "I'm slowly coming to the realization that I've been out of the loop for too long to be even remotely cool."

The pastor chuckled at that, then took another long puff, the cherry glowing in the twilight. "You thinking of heading down the road tomorrow morning?" he asked. "Wanda mentioned you couldn't really stay. She figured you just wanted her to know about Jon, which was real nice of you."

"That was the plan, yeah. But..."

"What?" The pastor noticed Bob's intense look, like he was weighing serious matters. "You're not thinking about that foolishness this afternoon, are you? Don't be thinking about any of that nonsense, not on my account, anyhow."

Bob took a sip of coffee. He'd been off caffeine for two decades. Wanda had just assumed he'd want a cup. He figured it was polite to try. "You handled yourself surprisingly well," he eventually said. "You were a fighter?"

Pastor Green nodded. "I did a stretch for burglaries when I was nineteen years old. Just dumb, no schooling, looking for trouble, excitement. Money. They gave me four years in Angola State Penitentiary."

"Tough reputation."

"Richly deserved. I was lucky, in a sense, as my cell mate was a former coach to Larry Holmes, the great heavyweight. Figured I had a gift, so he taught me some."

"Taught you well. You clobbered that big guy."

"Yeah..." Pastor Green sighed. "The bad old days."

"I don't expect those guys are just going to leave you alone," Bob said. "I still think you should call the police."

"Why? It'll just make them resent us more. The cops are real fond of telling you how much the community depends on them, but the truer that is, the less they seem to come around. It's like there's two standards, one for the folks with money, one for those without. We're just average, working class. Not a priority. But I guess that's nothing new."

It was clear the Greens didn't want him getting into trouble on their behalf. Wanda had shown him pictures of Jon when he was a kid; Don had filled him in on some of the challenges in his role. Both had shied away from discussing the assault on the pastor that morning.

Eventually, Bob said, "There might be a few things I can do, just to ease the pressure on you a little bit. I have some... expertise with difficult situations."

"Out of the question!" Pastor Green insisted. "The idea of an old friend of Jon's getting himself in trouble – or worse, hurt – over our business... well, that's just not acceptable. No sir!"

"Whatever they're up to, it's a deliberate harassment campaign," Bob said. "It has to be. There are too many cheap tenements and collapsing dives that would better suit the drug houses, in neighborhoods filled with their junkie clients. Why come out here? Why snap up cheap housing, only to spend all day running to and from downtown?"

"I can't say I know those answers, but..."

"But nothing, Don! Why would they stop now? Because they got a little pushback today? If anything, your going over there in the first place set things in motion. Now they see you as a problem, and you can be darn sure they see me as one."

"All the more reason to hightail it out of here," the pastor suggested. "If something were to happen to you..."

"Oh... I can take care of myself, don't you worry," Bob said.

"Yeah... but according to Wanda, that's what Jon used to say. She'd say, 'Don't go back' to some war zone, or 'Don't go off to the Middle East or South America,' and he'd say 'I can take care of myself.'"

Bob was silent, collecting his thoughts. They'd already lost a loved one to trouble, and they related him to Wanda's dead son. They probably didn't understand that nothing or no one could've prevented Jon Rice from joining Team

Seven, that covert ops were in the man's blood. It had meant everything to him, right up until the end.

"You look like you've got the world on your back," the pastor said.

"I was there when he passed," Bob admitted. "I remember a lot of horrible things about that day. I have a lot of regrets, both about decisions that were made for us, and about some of our own."

"Uh-huh."

"But one thing I remember very clearly was the look of determination on Jon's face when he was trying to evac. We were supposed to rendezvous at this little park not far from the public square in Tehran where the operation went down. He was wounded, the odds already against him. But instead of crawling off to a hidden spot to see if he'd live or die, he headed for the extraction point."

He looked up to see if the pastor was paying attention. He was.

"Jon had a singular goal in life: to serve his country with honor as a warrior," Bob said. "But more than that, he recognized something a lot of folks in the military recognize: there's always a dirty job that needs doing, and there are some people built better to do it. A colleague of his needed saving, he waded in without concern for himself, and it got him killed. It was how I think he'd have wanted to go."

The pastor allowed himself a small smile at that. "He was fulfilled. You tell Wanda all that?"

"Not yet, no. She's a mother, even still. Not sure how much she'd want to hear—"

"She'd want to hear that."

"There's a message in there somewhere, too."

"I know. It's the reason I'm a pastor, Bob. To help folks in the manner Jesus said we should. I mean, I know what the young folks think about religion these days, and given how many men have abused it for power and wealth, I can't say I blame them."

"Not a 'prosperity gospel' guy, then?"

"No, sir!" Pastor Green declared. "I believe a certain book that said rich men will have a heck of a time getting into Heaven has more authority in these matters than the rich men themselves, whether they're playing 'man of God' or not. No, we're here to serve... which is why I should be dealing with this 'problem' myself."

He stared out at the biker house and rocked in his chair slightly, a subconscious nervousness coming through.

The pastor puffed at the cigar. He blew out a rich plume of smoke, then clipped the butt on the edge of the coffee table and returned it to its hiding place. "Wanda pretends she doesn't know, although I'm guessing I stink to high heaven of tobacco. Still, every so often she'll remind me how proud she is that I quit. The dark art of guilt application is strong with that woman."

He checked his watch. "Almost time for that singing show she likes so much." He rose to his feet.

Bob stayed put.

"You need a minute?" the pastor asked.

"Yeah... yeah, just collecting my thoughts," Bob said. "I'll be in shortly."

"Okay, then."

The pastor went inside.

Evening had set in, twilight giving way to darkness. Half the streetlamp bulbs were out, Bob noticed, worsening the gloom.

At the house across the road, a single bulb was lit and

visible through the front window. If they were home, they were being surprisingly quiet, he thought.

The caffeine had his blood up, his feet restless. Nurse Dawn probably wouldn't approve, but she was in Chicago.

Maybe time to take a look at the place, see what they're up to. See if I can't tip the scales back in the Greens' favor a little before things escalate.

7

A cross the road, Booker Harris sat near the back of the near-empty living room on an overturned milk crate.

A single unshaded lamp kept back the darkness, but he was otherwise alone. There was no television, just junk furniture and debris – empty bottles, pizza boxes, fast-food bags.

He stared at the house across the street. Occasionally, he'd see the faintest red ember glow. The old man was smoking a cigar, he figured.

The anger inside him was near fever pitch, a rage he was holding down as well as he could.

Booker had always had anger issues, for as far back as he could remember. His first assault arrest had been in grade school, beating a classmate who wouldn't share his pudding pops. His old man had been the same way, taking his frustrations out on his kid whenever he felt like hitting someone.

He'd solved that by shoving a pair of scissors between the old man's ribs one night. The cops had ruled it self-defense after his mother provided X-rays from their doctor showing the injuries his father had brought down upon him.

He wanted to deal with the pastor in the same permanent manner.

But the rules were the rules, and Deacon had made it clear: no one hurts the old folks without his go-ahead.

Didn't say nothing about their visitors, though. Didn't say nothing about some nosy carpetbagging Yankee. I lay a beating on him, that's fair game. Hell, I reckon I could kick that scrawny bastard to death, and technically, I ain't done nothing wrong.

He stared at the home, its lights all on, the elderly couple no doubt entertaining their guest, doing whatever normal, square folks did with their time: watching TV or darning socks or something.

He'd never been around civilized people, not for any prolonged period.

By now, most of the gang would be at The Purple Bird, getting three-sheets drunk on whiskey and ginger ale. That was what they did most nights, when they weren't enforcing the club's business.

He loved being in The Damned. They weren't modern bikers, like the Angels or Los Bravas. They weren't all off living normal-day lives with wives and kids and mortgages and business holdings. Most didn't even have day jobs, unless you counted selling the odd ounce of weed or gram of coke.

They were real rebels, still, living off what they could take, sharing communally, rocking the patch twenty-four seven.

Deacon had come to depend on him as his muscle.

Not no more. Not after today. Be lucky if he don't kick me to the curb. It made him so angry, his left hand curling subconsciously into a tight fist.

That the guy who humiliated him was sitting, free and clear, less than fifty yards away? That did not sit well at all.

That he had to spend his night slinging dope to the odd junkie who ventured as far as Lakeview made it even more demeaning.

They think those walls protect them? Only thing stopping me is what Deacon asked. Only thing...

Booker held the thought, a wry smile playing across his lips. *Doesn't want me to hurt the old folks. But he didn't say nothing about their house.*

He rose, wincing slightly. The old man's body shot had cracked a rib, while the punch to the side of his jaw had cracked the bridge holding his lower teeth together.

He wandered into the kitchen next door. A bottle of vodka sat, half-drunk, on the counter. He picked it up, feeling its heft. He put it back down on the counter. He opened the cupboard above it and rummaged around until he found the small rectangular can of kerosene, which had already been in the lamp-strewn house when purchased.

Booker unscrewed its cap and poured three fingers into the bottle of vodka. He screwed its cap back on momentarily and shook the bottle, ensuring the kerosene helped coat the glass. Then he unscrewed the cap again and rummaged in a top drawer, withdrawing a hand towel. He twisted the hand towel into a makeshift wick, dipping one end into the kerosene before inserting the other end into the bottle.

He hefted it again, ensuring it had enough weight to be easily tossed through a window.

Didn't say nothing about their house, and now it's going to burn.

He put the Molotov down on the counter and reached up to the shelf beside the fridge, grabbing an old bottle of brandy that had gone unfinished. He repeated the process, then carried both Molotov cocktails back into the living room and checked the house across the road again.

They'd be in bed soon.

Once the last light went off, he'd go to work.

He'd throw it through a glass windowpane to make certain they didn't stay sleeping and accidentally burn up along with everything they owned.

Booker rolled a joint. He lit it with his Zippo.

The back door buzzer sounded twice. The first was short, just a blip; the second longer. That meant a customer.

BOB CLOCKED motion in the room opposite, a body moving laterally. *Heading into another room?*

It gave him a moment of leeway to change positions himself. He slipped off the porch and jogged quickly across the street.

Then he headed north, past two adjacent wood A-frames. He looked for any signs of a guard dog or alarms before hopping a fence and heading between two houses.

As he'd suspected, the back alley and backyards were unlit, dark save for the faint outline of shapes in moonlight. The barest glow blushed out of a kitchen window; the odd naked bulb above a back door cast short, stocky shadows.

The bikers' house was three doors down. He followed the alley to their fence. The backyard was sparse, the grass long dead, a handful of cut logs used as benches, a firepit.

Bob tried the gate. The latch was unlocked. They probably weren't expecting problems from the seniors whose homes surrounded the crash pad. He followed the yard to the rear windows and peeked through.

The kitchen appeared empty, a light above the stove ensuring he could just make everything out. There was no movement, no sign of life. He could hear music playing gently, possibly from a front room. But there were no conversations, no signs of other potential opponents.

They've left one person behind to look after the place. That might be an opportunity. If he could determine where they kept the dope and disable whoever was watching it, they'd be stuck there when the police arrived.

Something moved in the next room, a shadow. Whoever it was seemed huge, the shadow creeping up the wall and partway across the roof.

The big guy, Booker, the one Don decked.

It was probably penance. His friends had gone out on business or to party, and he was paying for his earlier failure by being left behind.

To his right, something shifted in his peripheral vision.

It was the back door opening. Bob ducked immediately, dropping to his haunches, hidden by the shadows as he hugged tight to the wall, under the kitchen window.

A scrawny-looking young man walked out, just avoiding a stumble as he stepped from the doorway to the backyard, no stairs in place to help navigate the one-foot drop. He wore a string T-shirt and baseball cap, baggy shorts.

As he turned towards the alley, Bob saw the barest glimpse of the young man's face, the sallow, sunken pockets under his eyes. He had pipe-cleaner arms, his shoulder slumped.

An addict.

He ambled to the alley and stood there in the half shadows by the fence.

A moment later, the door opened again. Booker exited, hopping down the stairless drop to the yard with a practice that suggested he'd made the trek a time or two.

Bob edged his way backwards slowly until he could perch just around the south corner of the house, out of sight.

Booker walked over to the opposite fence, to the south side of the property. He pulled on a section of it, hinges on the other side giving so that it swung open like a gate.

He jogged up to the peeling wood back door of the seemingly derelict home next door and looked both ways without spotting Bob. A key ring from his pocket unlatched the padlock holding it closed. He opened the door, then leaned forward. A moment later, he opened a second, inner door, which creaked steel-on-steel hinges. He disappeared inside.

After a minute, he came out and reversed the process, the inner steel door slamming with a clang.

He returned next door, letting the gate swing shut. Booker handed the man a small brown paper bag. The skinny customer nodded a nervous thank-you and turned to head north, down the alley.

Booker returned to the bikers' place, slamming the back door behind him. He looked irritated.

The drug house is next door.

It made sense. They were using a traditional "trap" house. They'd isolated the product to a place that was doubtless in some patsy's name, so that if they were raided by the police, they'd have no probable cause to raid the crash pad next door.

They were never in the trap house except to get product,

so unless the police caught them in that small window, they were almost impossible to legally tie to it.

No one would be psychotic enough to rob the house next door to The Damned MC, and if they did, there was Booker or another colleague nearby at all times. They probably had closed-circuit TV set up. The inner steel door would have an inward hinge and be too heavy to pry.

Bob checked the alley in both directions. It was quiet and dark. He considered his walk there. The ends of the alley were three and four houses away respectively. Their customers weren't ever seen near the front of either home, just the side streets at the end of each block.

It was smart business. The seniors would never say a peep, even if they noticed the sudden influx of skinny, vacant-looking guys into the neighborhood. It wasn't a hill to die on.

Was that it? They found a quiet community and saw an opportunity to expand?

No. It wasn't enough.

Lakeview was nowhere near the heart of New Orleans, so the users probably had to bus it, or walk for miles, as many didn't own cars. If anything, it was inconvenient to foot traffic.

And why two other homes nearby? What had Don said? Possibly more they didn't know about? They were much too close to be practical, from a drug house point of view.

Tactically, it made even less sense. The more they concentrated ownership in one area of New Orleans, the more likely they were to draw police attention.

He moved back to the window, but flinched away immediately; someone was standing right in front of it as he peeked around the corner.

He let his mind blank for a minute and slowed his breathing to an even, steady pace. His pulse slowed, and he felt calm.

Had he been seen? He'd know in a moment. Booker hadn't seemed the subtle type.

A few blocks west, a dog barked. Traffic on I-630, a mile south, could be faintly heard as a rushing hiss, like wind through a narrow gap.

The door remained closed, the alley silent other than the nearby dog, who kept up his consistent complaint.

Bob edged back to the window and checked inside again. Booker was standing in front of the kitchen counter, next to the refrigerator, along the back wall.

He had a clear liquor bottle of some sort on the counter ahead of him, barely lit by the LED tube bulb under the shelves. Whiskey? It was a pale yellowish, almost too pale, like wine. He almost missed the piece of cloth extended from its open neck. It was almost the same cream shade as the wall behind it.

A Molotov. He's making Molotov cocktails.

Bob tried to put himself in the giant's shoes. His boss was angry with him. He'd want revenge against Pastor Green. It just went with the occupational territory. So far, they hadn't engaged any of the residents other than the incident that morning, when the pastor had walked onto their turf. That was probably by design, too.

Was the big biker sociopathic enough to ignore his boss? Would he try to argue that torching someone's home wasn't the same as attacking them?

Probably. Emotionally arrested scumbags lived on loopholes.

Why is it that everywhere you go, things just get worse?

Yeah... you know the pastor would rather you let this alone. He's already said so. It would be easier just to head down the road a mile or so, find a bar, have a few whiskeys. Those Molotovs are probably for some rival gang halfway across Louisiana. You're making trouble by getting involved, not solving it. Plus, you get to watch him waste good vodka...

Go have a drink.

Go on, Bob. You know that's what you really want. You feel that adrenaline creeping in, that liquid edge, that tension in the muscles. Stick around, and people will get hurt.

That's what you do. You hurt people.

Go have a drink, and everybody's fine.

8

Across the road, the Greens' living room light went out.

Booker sat by the front window, one hand on each bottle neck. They'd be asleep in a few minutes, he knew. He wanted them unconscious so that it was a shock.

Besides, if anyone was still awake and wandering around, they might manage to smother the flames.

Rouse them from sleep and they'd flee in panic, giving the house no chance of surviving. He was certain of it. Life was pretty predictable, Booker had always figured, and his momma had always told him how smart he was.

And he wanted the home to burn. Booker had only ever known one way to send a message, and that was by hurting whatever he figured hurt him, just worse.

Old bastard, acting like he's someone's daddy. Acting like he's got a point to prove.

Maybe they wouldn't wake up. Maybe that wouldn't be so bad; nobody was going to see shit at ten o'clock at night. These were old folks, usually snoring by the time *The*

Tonight Show came on. Most didn't even drive, and vehicle traffic there, outside of buses and bikers, was rare.

Maybe nobody would see shit, and they'd all burn, and they wouldn't be a problem again for nobody. And he could honestly claim to Deacon that it was an accident, that he was just trying to give them a scare.

He got up and put the Molotovs down on the coffee table. He checked his pocket and made sure he had his Zippo. He lifted his left jeans pant leg and made sure the knife was in its ankle holster, his preferred backup piece in a scrap.

How to go about it? Go out the front, right across the road, real quick?

No, too much risk of being seen coming from the house. If he walked up the block, on the sidewalk, chances were no one would pay attention. Put each bottle in a paper bag and it'd look like any drunk taking a couple of bottles home.

He went to the kitchen and found a pair of paper bags amid the junk under the sink. He placed each bottle in a bag. In the top drawer, by the cutlery, was a pair of scissors and scotch tape. He taped the paper bags around the necks to leave the wicks just exposed.

If there were any junkies in the alley, he'd have to give them a scare, make sure they hightailed it before he got down to business.

He looked over at the back door.

No point in waiting.

It's party time.

BOB FELT HIS HANDS TREMBLING. It broke him away from his introspection.

He hated that sensation, the shivering quiver that came when he thought about having a drink.

It had been weeks, just one little relapse on the way south from Chicago.

But it felt like it had been hours.

Keep your head in the game. Check your target.

Snap out of it, stupid.

He checked the window, his hand straying to his coat pocket out of habit, to ensure the .357 was still there – although its weight was hard to miss.

Booker was approaching the back door. He had a bottle in each hand, crudely disguised in brown paper.

Bob hustled past the door to stand on its other side. If Booker was true to form, his egress would be less than cautious.

The door swung wide, Bob using one hand to gently bring it to a halt.

On the other side, Booker's two sneakered feet appeared on the edge of the step down. He jumped down to the yard with a thud and took a couple of steps forward, as if checking the alley for traffic.

Bob stepped behind him and drew the disposable lighter in one motion, lighting the wick of the bottle in the big man's left hand.

Booker clocked the open flame in his peripheral vision. "AIHHH!" he shrieked squeakily. He shook the Molotov for a moment, the shock of it bursting to life replacing common sense, his urgent desire to put it out, his other hand occupied.

But the kerosene was doing its job.

Bob reached up and lit the other Molotov.

"Shit!" Booker exclaimed.

Bob stepped out from behind him, ducking under the giant's raised right arm and leaping a few feet forward for clearance.

"What the fuck!?" The biker stood there, frozen, framed by the wide-open doorway, a burning wick in each hand, a flummoxed look on his bearded face.

Bob snapped a high kick, his heel catching the big biker in the chest.

Booker stumbled backwards, tripping over the raised back step, the bottles flying back into the house behind him, smashing on the kitchen floor.

"Oh shit!" he yelped. "Shitshitshitshitshit..." He scrambled to get over the hearth and back into the house, not even thinking about his assailant.

Through the kitchen window, Bob saw the slightest lick of flame. The walls were probably spattered with grease, the vents, too.

Booker ran back out of the house. "Shit, shit, fire, fire!" he bellowed. He saw Bob and froze in his tracks, snapping back to reality. "You!"

He charged. Bob dropped low at the last moment, turning side on, allowing his right leg to come over the left so that he could catch Booker's shins in a scissor hold. The giant's weight and momentum slammed him to the ground.

Before he could scramble to get up, Bob rolled to the balls of his feet, then dropped an elbow down hard, into the back of Booker's head. The biker slammed face-first into the dirt and lay still.

Bob looked back at the house. Black smoke poured from the back door. Flames licked the windowpane.

He didn't have much time.

He rifled the big man's pockets, finding an old Zippo, which he pocketed, and a cell phone.

The password screen came up.

Not essential, but worth a try. He pressed 1-2-3-4-5-6.

The phone unlocked.

Here's to the amateurs.

He dialed 911.

"New Orleans Emergency Dispatch, who am I speaking with?"

"Yeah... Hi. I'm Booker." Bob used his best bass-infused New Orleans accent. They'd be taping the call. "Got a bit of a fire going in the kitchen here... I'm at 5781 Colbert."

"Booker, are you still in the house? If so, you need to hang up for now and get out. Is there anyone else home?"

"No."

"Okay, then you just get out now. I've got a crew on route, okay? Y'all need to go to your neighbors and call your family while we handle this for you, okay?"

"Yeah, sort of out of control now, climbing the wall and stuff... I need to go get some drugs... Some cocaine and heroin that I sell, in the bedroom. I'm a drug dealer. Most of it's in the derelict house next door, but we keep some on hand for partying."

"Uhh... okay. Did I hear that right? Did you say..."

"Got to go now," Bob said. He ended the call.

At his feet, Booker began to stir. The back wall of the house was engulfed, flames licking the roof. The wind was blowing south, but barely. There was little chance of it jumping to the next house, but if it did, it was the bikers' other property at risk.

Down the street, a car alarm went off. A door slammed.

Bob kicked Booker hard in the side of the jaw, knocking him cold again.

He returned his attention to the phone screen as he made his way out the back gate and down the alley.

There was one number that had been called multiple times that day. That would be the boss, the guy they'd called Deacon.

He dialed it.

The voice that answered sounded gruff. "What!?"

"This Deacon?"

The line was silent for a moment. "And who might this be? Says it's Booker's phone. But you ain't Booker."

"Nah."

"Friend, you are looking for a world of hurt..."

"Your idiot friend Booker just torched your drug house. Not the trap house next door; the one y'all party at. *Y'all.* That's how y'all like to say 'you all,' right? As in y'all need to find another part of the city to live in."

Bob rounded the corner of the alley and approached the street. The line had gone silent.

"I suspect I know who this is," Riggs eventually said. "You said your name was Bob, if I do recall correctly."

"You do."

"You think it's smart to start a war with The Damned, friend? You think your buddies across the street aren't going to pay the price for that?"

"I think if you go after their house, you should know this neighborhood is going to be crawling with cops within about twenty minutes, and I don't expect they'll be going anywhere anytime soon."

He looked across the road, the home engulfed. The wind

had died, flames staying largely vertical. He could hear the distant klaxons of fire trucks.

"You and me, we're going to have ourselves a time," Riggs said. "This ain't over, not by a long shot."

"Well, I'll tell you what, pod'na... you'd better pray it is," Bob said. He ended the call. He checked the street both ways. People were out on their porches checking out the fire. He stooped and dropped the phone down the adjacent sewer grate.

The Greens' front door opened, and Don ran out.

"What in all heck is going on!?" the pastor demanded.

"It's your lucky night," Bob said. "Seems like your friends have had an accident."

Pastor Green jogged down the steps and joined him on the sidewalk. He stared at the flames. "Dang... I hope nobody's hurt..."

"I heard one of the neighbors say it looks like they were out," Bob said.

The pastor stood, hands in both bathrobe pockets, and watched the fire again. "Huh." He looked sideways at Bob. "You wouldn't know anything about this, now, would you?"

"Well now, I won't say I don't. But I didn't start the fire, if that's what you're asking. That was more on karma."

"Uh-huh. I'm guessing 'karma' ain't the given name of one of our local working girls. Are those bikers going to blame karma? Or are they going to come after you, friend Bob?"

Bob nodded. "Yep, probably that."

"And we can't be here when that happens?"

"Exactly that."

Pastor Green sighed once, deeply. "I'll go tell Wanda we need to pack."

The drive to the motel was silent for the first ten minutes. Bob took the wheel of the pastor's ten-year-old Honda Civic. Traffic was light as midnight approached.

Eventually, Wanda said, "Well... I do kind of wish you'd talked to us before you burned their house down, Bob."

Which was more patience than he deserved, Bob knew. "It was a fluid situation. One of them was walking out of the house with Molotov cocktails in hand and seemed likely they were heading over your way already. But... he tripped, and the wrong house went up. From his perspective, anyway."

"And why did you go over there in the first place?"

"I thought I'd have a little chat with one of them while he was alone, maybe convince the police to stop around."

Pastor Green scoffed a little from the passenger seat. "Yeah... like I said already, they don't come to our neighborhood a whole lot."

"They would if they had an active drug house."

The pastor turned to look his way. "Seriously? They were slinging out of there? I didn't see no traffic."

"They were using the back alley and storing it next door. Customers were forced to use the alley to come and go, but yeah. Cocaine or heroin would be my guess, maybe meth."

"Then they're going to be twice as angry," Wanda said. Her voice sounded plaintive, anxious. "What are we going to do? That's our home."

"Give me a few days," Bob said. "That's all I should need. Whatever they're doing there..."

"I thought you said it was a drug house," the pastor said. "Isn't that enough?"

Bob kept his eyes on traffic throughout, the streets still busy at close to midnight. "It's enough to get the cops to start paying attention. It's not enough reason for a motorcycle gang to move up here, buy four or five homes and then make a spectacle of themselves. That's not normal for these types. Their business is wherever poverty, crime and mental health are teaming up to produce desperate, emotionally discon-nected people."

"That sure don't sound like Lakeview," suggested Wanda. "Most folks here are retired or doing pretty good for them-selves. It's not ritzy, but it sure ain't poor."

"They're up to something else," Bob explained, "and I need to figure it out. If I have that, maybe it's enough to dissuade them from continuing."

The pastor's head sank. "But in the meantime, we have to run? That doesn't sit right with me, Bob. These are my people, my congregation. More than that, they're my friends. I can't abandon them."

"If you stay, those guys will figure out a way and they'll kill you. As things are, I have to make sure the cops know the bikers will try to burn your house down without incriminating myself. But let's face it, Don – they were already on their way over. Nothing's technically changed, except that you guys need to lie low, and they've lost at least one – and probably two – of their houses."

Wanda let that slide for a few seconds of silence. The car was stuck at a light. But once it began to roll again, she leaned through the gap in the front seats. "May I just note, Bob, that while that's probably technically true – technically, as you say – it sure don't feel too comforting from the back seat. But..."

"But?"

"But I'm still glad you got involved. If they'd firebombed our house with us sleeping... I mean... dang. So, thank you. You've done right by us."

Bob wasn't so sure. He'd been trying to overcompensate because his addiction had been battering him; lighting the fuses had been unnecessary. He'd let the beast out, let adrenaline take over. *Like those kids in the store back in Chicago. You could've killed them. Idiot.*

Any irritation they felt towards the Greens was probably now full-fledged hatred.

You may have made the situation worse. Now, you have to fix it. Was that the point? Are you just lighting fires to put them out, hoping you get recognition for it? Status?

It felt difficult, not belonging. He didn't have the brotherhood of booze to crawl into; his careers as a fighting man and covert operative were both dead and tarnished. He'd only known Dawn and Marcus for a few weeks before leaving.

Maybe that was why he'd gotten involved in their lives to begin with; maybe it wasn't just a sense of responsibility for the danger they'd faced. Maybe it was the need to have something resembling a family.

Or maybe you're just a gratitude junkie, Bobby. Maybe your subconscious figures that, in order to regain that sense of order, you need to start from a position of chaos.

As if reading his mind, Pastor Green put a hand on his shoulder. "You've got the look of a man who thinks he's his own worst enemy. But Wanda's right, Bob. That was fate tonight, the Lord bringing you around just when we needed you."

"Fate? Right."

"No, I'm serious. If you weren't here, I'd have still knocked that big goon down, and he'd have still decided to come get revenge, and we'd be dead or, at best, burned out of our home. I started this mess by losing my cool, not you. You just came to visit. This situation, running... it ain't great, I'll grant you. But it dang sure beats the alternative."

Maybe he was right, Bob thought. He turned the wheel, the car entering the motel parking lot. It was on the other side of the city, just off Crowder Boulevard, in the Ninth Ward. It was no one's idea of a tourist trap. In fact, it occurred to Bob that the Greens were the closest to righteous patrons the motel had seen in a long, long time.

Maybe they were right, and maybe there was something to be said for acting on impulse. But figuring out fault and learning lessons could wait. First, he had to defuse The Damned MC.

He'd called ahead to rent them a room. Bob parked the car and headed into the office to retrieve the key, then rejoined them. He drove the car to the motel's back side, away from the road, and parked it in front of unit 9.

They got out and took the bags into the room. Wanda

had packed three despite Bob's protestations that they wouldn't need more than a few days. Life seemed uncertain now, she'd argued. It was better to be prepared.

She laid the cases down on the long, flat shelf designed for such, by the closet. Don checked the table drawer beside the twin beds. "A Good Book makes a good room," he said, sounding vaguely satisfied.

Bob drew the .357 from his waistband speed holster. "I'm leaving this with you, Don. You were in 'Nam, so I know I don't have to tell you—"

"Keep an empty round on the hammer, trigger clear, safety on. But..." He was standing two feet from Bob's outstretched hand. He'd begun to reach out for the gun, but hesitated. "I genuinely don't know if I could shoot another man. I'm not that young man anymore. Heck, that young man is *why* I'm not that young man anymore."

"There's little-to-no chance of them finding you here. I paid in cash; it's miles from your community. As long as you lie low..."

The pastor took the gun. "I don't know..." he said.

Wanda walked over and put an arm around him. She was tiny next to her husband, but her expression was steely, as if he could've leaned his full weight on her without her budging.

"You don't worry about that, hon. You don't want to use a gun, you darn well don't need to. You don't fret about that at all. We'll be strong for each other."

Pastor Green kissed her on top of the head. He handed the gun back to Bob. "It's not my way, Bob, not no more. But I thank you. Besides, I figure you could use it more than us."

Wanda frowned. "That does not sound a whole lot better."

Bob gave her a little wink. "You don't worry either, ma'am. The best solutions don't involve Molotovs or guns, just an agreement in everyone's best interests."

"So," Wanda continued the thought, "you plan to..."

Bob smiled. "I plan to be very, very persuasive."

ichael "Dirty Carl" Napier was feeling pretty good. He had a meal in his stomach and a couple of shots of bourbon to boot. His bike's engine chugged throatily as he headed towards north New Orleans.

He was ten blocks north, downshifting to second on his way to the Colbert drug house, when he spotted the glow of flames and the column of smoke.

What the hell?

His phone rang. He tapped his headset earpiece. "Go for Carl."

"Where you at?" It was Deacon Riggs. It had taken three words for Carl to be certain his boss was not happy.

"I'm almost back to the crash pad. You still want me scoping out that dude, right?"

"How close are you, and what are you seeing?"

Eh? What the hell was he talking about?

"What am I... I'm on the road still. I mean, there's some smoke up ahead..."

"God-damn it!" Riggs bellowed down the line. "Goddamn. I can't believe the crazy bastard was telling the truth." His tone shifted to an angry snarl. "What the hell d'you get up to that took an hour to get there?"

"I ate dinner. Deacon, what the hell are you jabbering about..."

"That smoke, idiot! That's the crash pad! The freak who manned up on me this morning torched it!"

"You're kidding."

"Do I fucking sound like I'm kidding!? Get over there! Find Booker and find out what the hell happened."

"Booker?"

"We told him to stay back tonight because he got his clock cleaned by that old man. The old man's friend called me on Booker's phone, claimed Booker set the fire. Sounds like some bullshit to me. I want to know where that guy is, who he talks to, where he goes. If you'd done that when I asked, you dumb son of a bitch, this might not be happening! Am I clear?"

"Yeah. Yes! Of course, Deacon. I'm all over it, I swear." He took his left hand off the clutch for a minute and tugged nervously on his braided soul-patch.

"You'd better be. He'll have gotten the pastor and his wife out of there first thing, I'm guessing. I sent Diesel over, too; should join you shortly. Once you know where they're all staying, you call me toot fucking suite, you feel me?"

"I got it boss."

"And one more thing: tell Booker I'm going to kick his mountainous ass when I see him. Tell him he'll be gol' darn lucky if that's all I do."

Riggs hung up on him. Dirty Carl swallowed hard. His night was going from bad to worse.

. . .

FIREFIGHTERS WERE PUTTING out hot spots when Bob got back to the street. They waded among the charred remains of the home, jets of steam mushrooming skyward each time their hose water hit glowing embers.

At least it looked routine, nothing that required the fire crew to face imminent risk. That was a positive, he supposed. He still hadn't come to terms with how quickly it had escalated.

He parked a block north and walked the rest of the way. The street was still busy just after midnight, residents watching them work from front stoops.

A pair of police cruisers blocked the street to either side of the home, giving crews space to work, two fire trucks between them, noses pushed right up to the home's fence.

He slowed to a stop and scanned both sides of the street until he spotted them. Three bikes were parked fifty yards south, on the Greens' side of the street, their owners lolling around watching.

He recognized Booker right away. He had bandages wrapped around both hands, probably from trying to beat out the fire.

The two guys next to him were new arrivals. The balding guy with the soul patch was seated on one bike, his arms crossed.

Is he staring at me?

That made sense, Bob supposed. His conversation with Deacon was supposed to rattle the man. Whether it worked or not, his first move would be to send the cavalry, try to find out what they could from the scene.

The third man he remembered from the morning. The smaller of the two he'd fought, Diesel.

Their attention was split between him and the burning house and the building next door. Two unmarked police cars were parked outside it, yellow tape surrounding its perimeter.

A pair of detectives in cheap suits had brought out three or four bags of evidence already. They'd been handed to a crime scene technician whose van was parked across the road.

Chain of evidence, Bob thought. *I wonder if they've noticed the bikers yet...*

As if on cue, a detective handed a sealed bag to the technician, then took off south, walking briskly towards the three men.

They looked momentarily panicked. He was too close for them to all mount up and take off immediately, not without looking incredibly suspicious and exposing their tags for him to copy down.

The moment of indecision cost them. The detective was around Bob's age, he figured, maybe a little older: a weary mid-forties veteran cop, judging by the furrowed brow and receding hairline.

He nodded at the men from about eight feet away, one hand straying near his belt and his holster. He said something – they were too far away to be heard – and Booker nodded. The detective said something else, then nodded towards one of the unmarked cars.

Booker's head hung slightly. Bob couldn't help a small smile. Eventually, the biker – or his lawyer – would convince the police to compare his voice to the one on the tape, and they'd let him go. But until then, he was likely material suspect number one in their drug bust; he wasn't going anywhere anytime soon.

One down. A dozen more jagoffs to go.

Bob frowned. The bikers were a relatively toothless threat. They'd have little to no chance at isolating him, which meant with patience, he could pick them off one at a time, even set up a few more with weeks of police headaches.

But it wouldn't solve anything.

Someone was putting money behind their little real estate venture. Until that person was identified, nothing would change. They'd just find someone else to come in and scare folks.

Someone was "blockbusting" the neighborhood, trying to force as many people out as cheaply as possible.

He needed to figure out who and why.

Bob crossed the street and walked up as far as the barricade. He waited until one of the detectives reappeared from the house and was a few feet away.

"Sir!" Bob called out. "Detective!"

The detective nodded his way and approached. "If you could stay back, sir, we're just securing the scene, okay?"

"Do you have a business card?" Bob asked. "There might be some folks who saw something, but aren't around the neighborhood anymore, or who work nights."

The detective walked over and handed him one. "You see anything here tonight, sir?"

Bob looked at the card. It read "Det. Richard Armitage, Homicide, Criminal Investigations Division" and featured his phone number and email address.

"Me? Oh, no. Like I said, some of us work nights. Just got back."

"You live on the block?" the detective asked.

Bob shook his head. "No, but close, just two blocks south of here, off Catina Street. So... I have a right to be here. I'm not just... you know... being nosy."

The detective looked skeptical. "Uh-huh. Stay back from the barrier, okay, sir? You have a good night now."

He headed off towards the unmarked cars.

Bob pocketed the card and headed back to the Greens' Honda.

The car pulled away from the curb.

It was a few blocks away, the street still quiet, when he noticed the reflection of the two motorcycles in his wing mirror.

11

They were trying to stay back, out of view. But the mode of transport wasn't exactly deep cover.

It was only a short trip from their section of Colbert Street to Interstate 630. It ran east-northeast, bending north to the city of Slidell, following the curve of Lake Pontchartrain's southern shore.

Bob kept within the speed limit. The bikers weren't accustomed to running tails, and were remaining the exact same five or six car lengths back.

Instead of turning off to head south, towards the Ninth Ward, Bob stayed on the interstate. It looked down on more neighborhoods of single-family homes; it rolled past the Almonaster Avenue rail yards, across the navigation channel via the unflattering, single-deck Highrise Bridge.

He checked his mirrors again. The bikers were sloppy, having closed the distance slightly. Maybe they were nervous about him taking off, flooring it and cutting in and out of the steady traffic.

They passed another handful of neighborhoods flanking

Lake Pontchartrain, the homes laid out in perfect symmet-
rical rows, identically sized lots. Eventually, the road reached
the edge of the city.

The I-10 Twin Span Bridge took them across the lake;
brackish, foamy water lapped at its concrete piers. It led into
the suburban city of Slidell. Housing developments dominated the view left, marshes to the right.

He flicked on the turn signal at Exit 261. Three turns on
local roads led the Honda to the marina, a vast parking area
surrounding a tin barn that served as boat storage and
contained administration offices. Past it, he could faintly see
the rows of white yacht masts that occupied most of the
berths.

It made sense to keep them away from people and away
from their friends, deal with them quietly. The marina
allowed access to both the lake and the surrounding
swamps.

He checked his mirrors again. They were barely visible,
having backed off after the exit. It was nearly one fifteen in
the morning, no one else around.

The parking spaces in front of the marina building were
otherwise empty. He got out quickly and locked the doors.
Hopefully it would dissuade them from rifling the pastor's
car. Bob had scoped out a handful of isolated locations in the
city earlier in the evening; as he'd expected, no one was
using the parking lot at the late hour.

He walked around the airport-hangar-sized building to
the lake side. A former shipping container had been painted
green and converted into public washrooms. It sat just ahead
of the massive hangar-style doors. Would his pursuers stick
together? Probably. He hid behind the south wall of the
washrooms building and waited.

The crunch of wheels on gravel announced their arrival. He waited another two minutes before their voices drifted into earshot, getting louder as they neared.

"... somewhere back here. If it's... yeah, it's open. So maybe he's inside the boathouse."

"I don't like this," the second voice admitted. "There's only two of us, and you saw that dude move this morning. He had training or some shit. We should report in. Deacon just wanted us to follow the man—"

"Don't be a pussy!" his friend commanded. "Think about how much he's going to owe us if we smoke this guy and dump him in the lake."

"Just, like... you know, with weights and such?"

The voices drew nearer, just a few feet away. "There's probably more dead fuckers at the bottom than fish." They stopped walking. "Shh... hold up..."

"What?" the other man whispered.

"Stay quiet. He's here somewhere."

"Why here? Why did he stop here at this time of night? Don't make no sense," the other guy said.

One of them has a brain.

"Who gives a fuck? Maybe he likes boats."

And the other one doesn't.

"Well... I'm not taking any chances."

The pistol's slide was long, the click of its hammer cocking slightly metal on metal.

Sig Sauer P320? Possibly. Nice gun.

The pair walked by his spot, oblivious. *Roughly parallel, side by side, so they can't cover nine and three. Stupid. Gunman on the inside.*

He had enough information to act.

Bob stepped out of cover. He threw a short, hard right

hand, catching the inside man on the side of the chin, knocking him out. The pistol clattered to the ground between him and the remaining biker.

It stunned his friend, but only for a moment. He dove towards the gun. Bob didn't try to match him, instead stepping into a half-volley kick, catching the second man hard in the side of the head.

The blow was hard, the man stumbling sideways, falling over onto his back. Before he could rise, Bob dropped down on top of him, driving both knees into the man's arms, pinning his target as he threw a flurry of short crosses. It left the biker's chin unguarded, Bob's right hand catching him flush.

Bob got up and retrieved the pistol. The first man was stirring, shaking off the blurred vision, trying to right himself. Bob waited the minute it took for both men to come around completely. They pulled themselves up to seated positions.

"Well... you two sure fucked up."

"You going to kill us?" the gun owner asked.

"Diesel, right?" Bob asked. "I figured after the throw-down this afternoon, you'd be wiser."

His friend began to rise to his feet.

"Ah! Ah, ah, ah... gently, now," Bob advised.

"You fucking shoot us, this shit never ends. They will never stop until they kill your ass," he said. "Deacon's got powerful friends."

"Shut up, Diesel!" Dirty Carl warned.

"Sure he does," Bob goaded. "Real money guys, with power and influence. You could tell by the fact that he hadn't washed his shirt in two months."

"The dude he works for, they make assholes like you

disappear," Dirty Carl spat. "You let us go, get out of Lakeview, maybe they figure you're not worth the trouble. Maybe you walk out of this."

Bob gestured his way with the Sig Sauer. "Your idiot friend has a sense of the dramatic to him, Diesel. How about you? Do you get the sense I'm going to cut and run any time soon?"

Diesel looked crestfallen. "Nope."

"The guy he's talking about – the lawyer. The guy fronting the money for the houses," Bob said, taking an educated guess. Real heavyweights always worked through a lawyer, particularly when financing someone else's illicit activity. "What's his name?"

Diesel chuckled, but it was unconvincing, false bravado at the barrel of a gun. "We tell you that, maybe they come after us."

"If you don't, I'll shoot you in the head and dump your body in Lake Pontchartrain, just like you were planning to do to me. So, if I'm in your spot, my options are limited."

Diesel thought about it.

Before he could answer, his partner, Dirty Carl, said, "How do we know if we tell you, you don't shoot us anyhow?"

Bob shrugged. "No percentages in it. I already have the fact that you snitched to hold over you, keep you out of the game for now. You go back to The Damned, and I call your buddy Deacon, tell him you let me know all about the lawyer. Besides... why risk a murder charge if I don't have to?"

Diesel looked over at Dirty Carl. "What do you think?"

Carl shrugged. "Man... I love the brothers, you know that. But I don't owe Deacon sweet diddly fuck. The only money coming back to us is what we make. We ain't getting shit from him we didn't earn."

Diesel looked Bob over. "You sure don't look like a gangster, and you ain't no cop. But you got all sorts of moves. You a fed? DEA maybe?"

"Something like that," Bob said. "I'm from the Department of Another Stupid Question Wins a Bullet." He flicked the pistol their way. "Turn around, gentlemen."

They did as asked.

"Phones out and on the ground, please. Wallets, too. Let me see empty pockets."

They emptied their pockets.

"Okay," Bob said. "We're going for a stroll."

He marched them back behind the building and along Valley Island Drive. It was decrepit, cracked and pitted with potholes, an old road that led to the edge of the lake, perhaps a relic of a time when the slips weren't all owned and guaranteed to big-paying monthly customers.

A fishing pier dominated the shoreline. Water lapped gently at its footings.

There would be security cameras on the building, but it was a five-minute walk behind them, far enough away to make any video poor at best. And it couldn't be helped. If they were like most commercial operations, the digital recordings would be erased over in short order, particularly if there was no reason to keep them. He had no intention of shooting either of the idiots in front of him, after all.

The late-night wind was whipping the surface of the lake into whitecaps and ripples.

"Walk to the end of the pier," Bob ordered. He kept at least six feet away from both men, not offering them a chance to overwhelm him. When they were about fifteen feet from the end of the pier, he told them to stop.

"One more chance," he said. "See that little tin rowboat?" A skiff had been tied up illegally at a mooring to their left. "Go kneel on the edge, in front of it."

They did as ordered.

"I don't get it," Diesel said, hands clamped to his greasy scalp.

"Yeah... yeah, that tracks. I'm going to ask you for the name again. Then, if you don't immediately provide it, I'm going to shoot you in the head, Diesel. I'm going to shoot you first, and let your body drop into that rowboat, for easy disposal in the middle of the lake. The reason I'm going to shoot you first is that it'll show Carl here that I'm not bluffing in the least. As he's already about 90 percent of the way to blabbing his mouth off, I figure he won't need *any* more motivation."

"Man, I can't..." Diesel complained.

Bob flicked off the safety. "Safety's off. Last chance."

"Dude... I swear, I don't know how, but someone's going to..."

"Bye-bye, Diesel. It's been interesting." Bob gently pressed the tip of the barrel to the back of the man's head.

"*Roulette!*" Diesel barked.

"Eh?" Bob glanced at his prone friend. "Is he having a stroke or something? Because I'm about to resolve that for him."

"No! That's his name," Diesel whined. "Denny Roulette. He's got an office in the French Quarter..."

"What's he up to on Colbert Street?" Bob demanded. "Why buy the houses there?"

"He wants the old folks out. Some construction project some client has a stake in. They want the land cheap."

The bypass? It seemed likely. "Who's the client?"

"We don't know. Deacon... he's a real careful dude. He doesn't say shit unless necessary."

They weren't going to be able to tell him much more. "Why was he having me followed?"

"He figures you're not going away. So... dude... please don't kill me. I'm only twenty-three. My old lady wants kids."

Dirty Carl sneered at his friend. "Y'all want to exhibit some dignity, please? Damn, son."

Bob pushed Diesel's head forward slightly with the barrel of his pistol, to remind him it was there. "When the gang's on downtime, just hanging out, having a meeting... where's the clubhouse, or whatever you call it?"

"Mostly at The Purple Bird. It's a pool hall we own downtown. It's in some dude's name for legal reasons, but people know it's Damned turf."

Bob took two steps back to avoid any last-second heroics. "Okay... both of you, down into the boat."

Diesel took his hands off his head slowly and looked back. "Down...?"

"Yeah. Relax. I said I wouldn't kill you if you helped me."

The two men climbed down the ladder attached to the pier. The skiff wasn't much more than fifteen feet of aluminum shell; it bobbed dangerously as their weight settled into it.

"Throw the oars overboard," Bob said, gesturing with a wave of the pistol.

They complied, the oars splashing gently.

"I don't get it," Diesel said.

"Shocker," Bob replied. He reached down and looked

over the side of the pier. A twelve-foot barge pole was suspended from three hooks. He removed it. Leaning over the edge of the pier, he used its tip to shove the skiff away and towards the middle of the lake.

"Hey! Hey, man, wait! I can't swim!" Diesel said.

"Me too!" his friend implored.

Bob jogged down to the very end of the pier. As the skiff floated past, he gave it another firm shove with the pole. "Oh, relax. I'm guessing by this time tomorrow, someone'll find you and help you to shore. Assuming you don't sink, of course."

"Man... we done what you said!" Diesel called out, the boat now fifteen or twenty feet from the pier and drifting farther out.

Given the prevailing northeast wind, Bob figured they were in for a ride.

"This ain't right!" the biker whined.

"I said I wouldn't kill you," Bob called out. "If I were in your boat – I mean, quite literally – I'd get out of town, avoid questions from your friends about how I know what I know."

"Man, fuck you, man!" Carl called out.

"Pleasure doing business with you, gentlemen," Bob said.

He followed the pier back to the wooden boardwalk and the hangar beyond. He stopped halfway and picked up the men's wallets. Diesel's included a key card of unknown origin. Both were carrying cash. He counted it out quickly.

Six hundred and twenty bucks. That'll come in handy.

He looked back towards the lake. The tiny waves had helped his cause, the boat about thirty feet from the dock. He checked his old Omega watch. It was just before two in the morning.

By the time people were up and around, heading out for a day of fishing on the lake, the bikers would have figured out they could paddle their way back to shore with their hands. He doubted either was stupid enough to run back to The Damned. Snitches got stitches, after all.

And they'd given Bob a name.

12

WASHINGTON, DC

Nick Velasco should have been working. He had a genuine corporate security contract to fulfill under a new alias. It was a pathway to legitimacy, to coming out of hiding as a reinvented solid citizen. A square.

Instead, he was huddled over his laptop in the clubhouse of Silver Spring Golf and Country Club, dark sunglasses obscuring his face and a hoodie pulled up.

He had a corner booth. His back was to the room for the privacy factor, even though not being able to see the door made him uncomfortable.

But it was a point of principle.

Two days earlier, he'd tried to buy a membership in the club.

It wasn't that he loved golf, although he enjoyed the odd round. It was just that the club was the preferred course of several top tech executives, and when they were drinking and relaxed, they were careless. Good packet capture software and a poorly protected app on one of their phones or laptops could equal a windfall of saleable information.

But the general manager had turned him down. Now, the man was a few doors away from the wide, open café/bar area in his office. Nick wanted to know what the man had seen in him to prompt such immediate rejection. His money was as good as anyone's, and he'd offered to pay the three grand for a six-month membership in cash.

Maybe that was it. Maybe the cash spooked him.

It made sense. Everyone else he'd seen there used cards, usually of the gold, platinum or onyx varieties. They were the kind of men with enough money and power that a round of golf at ten in the morning was par for the course.

If the GM was like most management types, Nick knew, he would keep notes on his computer, personal information, close-held opinions on projects, customers.

He wanted to know what made the man tick.

It beat doing what he was supposed to be doing: serving federal time for wire fraud, among other hacking-related charges. His anonymity was more valuable than a curiosity.

He justified the fishing trip on the basis that the man might have spotted something, some flag that, in more dangerous circumstances, could cost him his freedom. It didn't seem likely; far more common would be typical biases: about his dress, his cash, his stature.

He was using the path of least resistance, mailing the man occasional emails bearing the letterhead of companies that supplied the golf course clubhouse and shop: equipment suppliers, clothiers, a coffee service, a local bakery. Eventually one of them would...

An alert box popped up in the lower right corner of the laptop screen.

Bingo.

The mark had clicked a link from his coffee supplier demanding payment for last month's supply.

The numbers were as fictitious as the borrowed letterhead, prices averaged from a handful of companies found online.

When the GM clicked the link in the invoice, it would send him to a message saying:

> *Thank you! This invoice has been paid in full! If you received it after payment has been made, our apologies for any inconvenience!*

It was a closed-loop hack, the target leaving satisfied and unaware they'd even clicked a bad link.

But in doing so, he'd downloaded a trojan, a virus that would not activate until his security software went down for an update. It would then release a worm, infecting multiple files in a series of operating system folders that users rarely visited, if ever, as well as creating a new operating account with administrator privileges.

Within a few days, Nick would have complete access, in real time, to the club manager's every move.

His phone buzzed in his pocket. He checked the screen. *Ah... hell.*

He let it ring twice more. The screen was displaying an eighteen-character string of numbers and letters, which meant it was being filtered through his encrypted unit at home.

You know who it is. Only one person has that number.

He hit the green button. "Alpha."

"Nicky."

"Where are you?" Before Bob could answer, he added, "Just kidding, of course."

"Hilarious. And where are you?"

"I'm at my office, working like a dog on legitimate corporate security," Nick lied.

"Sure. I need your help with something. And... please, stop calling me Alpha. I know it's habit for you, but that was a long time ago, and not a period of great pride."

Nick's stomach grumbled. "Fine. So why are you calling? I thought you said I was free and clear, that we were even after the DC thing."

"I did. I'm not telling you, I'm asking. For advice, mostly."

That was new. The great Bob Singleton looking for advice. So much for his invulnerability. "Okay, I'm curious," Nick said. "Shoot."

"I need to keep ears on a guy, but he's not going to be using landlines a whole lot. So I need to tap his cell phone. After that last trouble, I figured who better to ask..."

"Okay, okay... well, ideally – and I tell you this safe in the knowledge you'll owe me a substantial favor – you put spyware on his phone, a little piece of nightmarish tech made by our Israeli friends in the Mossad. But even getting that code to you without setting off national security alarms could be tough."

"Very helpful. What do you have in the realm of realism?"

"If you can get hold of the phone and clone the SIM card, you can listen in on his calls. You can buy a SIM cloner illegally at select security stores who also advertise on the Dark Web. I'll email you a few in your area, smooth the path."

"But... that means I need his phone."

"Yeah. I figure in a few years they'll have commercially available cloners that you can just pass near the source, like with RFIDs. But not yet."

Bob didn't sound impressed. "I'm not sure that falls into the realm of owing a 'big' favor, Nick. That sounds like something I could've figured out for myself."

"Coulda, woulda, shoulda. Get hold of his phone and your problem is solved."

"You've been of mediocre and incomplete help, Nicky."

"You're welcome. Watch your mail."

"I haven't told you where I am. How are you going to—?"

"Looks like New Orleans."

"I have location sharing turned off. That's a neat trick."

"Indeed. I know how to defeat it, too, which means it's only really useful to me."

"So you're managing to stay hidden from the prison authorities?"

"For now. They still haven't figured the wrong guy is behind bars, for one. If they ever do, things will change in a hurry."

"Ah... you know I'll always look out for you."

"Being charming isn't getting you that phone."

"Goodbye, Nick."

"Don't be a stranger, Alpha."

The line went dead.

Nicky pondered what to make of it. On the one hand, he had to figure there were heavy players who'd pay handsomely to know Bob Singleton's location.

On the other, he enjoyed breathing.

Discretion, Nicky my boy, discretion. He turned his attention back to the golf course manager's email.

13

NEW ORLEANS

After finishing up with Nick, Bob took a shower. The motel's water pressure was poor, but it didn't matter; he stayed in just long enough to scrub up. He let the water run fully cold, letting himself be shocked slightly by the frigid sensation when he stepped out of the tub.

It was a trick from a colleague at sniper school. The cold water shocked the brain into heightened activity before it would normally be ready, improving focus and motivation.

He needed as much focus as possible. Riggs and his men would panic on waking to find two men missing and Booker in jail. He'd know about the drug house already. They'd be making calls, telling contacts who to look for, sending around whatever images they'd managed to snap of Bob and the pastor.

Bob dressed in the same simple style as a day earlier; he was traveling with minimal gear, just three changes of clothes, all golf shirts and slacks. He looked anonymous, a name badge short of being any retail big-box store employee.

It was just after nine in the morning. He'd noticed a Mexican restaurant down the block and walked down to it, buying a trio of breakfast burritos and coffee, carting it all back in a brown paper bag.

He knocked on the door to the Greens' room.

The pastor was still in his bathrobe when he answered. "Hmmph. I figured you'd step out and get us some food," he said. "I'm grateful for that... although we do tend to rise closer to seven or eight on a Saturday."

He showed Bob in. Wanda was already dressed. "I keep telling him everything normal has gone out the window," she said. "But he's stubborn."

Bob put the bag down on the small round breakfast table under the front window. The three sat down together to eat. The pastor immediately reached out for Wanda's hand, who reached for Bob's.

"Bless this for our nourishment and in our service to you, O Lord," the pastor invoked.

"Amen," Wanda said.

Bob bit his tongue. His beliefs had been flexible for years and fell firmly into the camp of not really knowing.

Wanda began handing out the burritos. "I ain't had Mexican for breakfast in... ooh doggie, I'm going to say twenty-five years? Not since I lived in Tucson."

The pastor nodded Bob's way. "So what did you get up to last night, exactly? Heard you go out a couple of times, didn't hear you come back in. And I'm a light sleeper."

"It's true. Pin drop could wake him up," Wanda said.

"Business," Bob said. "First, I went back to the street."

"I suspect your newfound friends are none too happy this morning," Pastor Green said.

"You'd be correct. But I managed to glean a little information from a pair of them."

The pastor looked up, his face a map of concern. "You didn't... you know, do anything untoward or nothing?"

"Assuming the weather held and the boat didn't sink, I inconvenienced a pair of them and ensured they won't talk about it."

Wanda chewed on some egg and tortilla, swallowed it, then said, "And what did they tell you, these two inconvenienced gentlemen?"

"That your problem isn't just random thugs. Someone is trying to 'blockbust' your neighborhood."

"You're kidding me," Pastor Green said. "Like back in the '50s and '60s?"

"Exactly."

Wanda raised a hand sheepishly. "I might have missed that one. I mean, I'm no spring chicken, but I wasn't born for most of that."

"In the South, in particular," her husband said, "there was a practice called 'blockbusting.' What they'd do is use integration laws to scare white folks into selling their home cheap. They'd get one African American family to buy a home – preferably one that might actually cause some noise – and then they'd tell all the white neighbors that the whole community was going to be taken over by colored folk."

"It was an ugly period," Bob said.

"Or, in integrated communities, they'd import trouble: former inmates, sex convicts, mentally ill folk – whoever they figured would scare people off."

"Like bikers?" Wanda suggested.

"Exactly. Then their business partners would swoop in and buy the homes or lots up real cheap."

"That's awful!" Wanda said. "So the bikers are just hired annoyances, basically?"

"Basically," Bob said. "Being enterprising types, they also realized Lakeview is one of the few neighborhoods in the city with rear alleyways. That lets drug customers come and go to the houses unseen on the street, which makes a police presence less likely, but their original goal twice as effective: they're bringing crime and bad elements into the neighborhood, they're profiting directly from methamphetamine sales, and they're scaring off buyers and owners on behalf of whoever's funding them."

Pastor Green finished his burrito in two more bites. "Dang, son... I have to admit, salsa and eggs ain't bad together, not bad at all. Who woulda thunk?"

"Hmmph," Wanda groused. "I've been telling you that since we got together back in Bisbee."

He screwed up the wax paper wrapper and tossed it into the brown bag. "I take it when you say 'whoever' is behind it that you don't have any ideas on that front yet."

"I have a name to start with. He's probably just a legal front—"

"A 'front'?" Wanda asked.

"People set up numbered companies and then appoint their legal counsel as a director and spokesman," Bob explained. "Under the law, the lawyer's name can then be used as the public 'face' of the company, but under 'attorney-client privilege,' that legal face is restrained from giving up any more information."

"Dang," Wanda said. "That sounds like a difficult loophole to get around. That sounds real tricky."

"It can be. But I've got a few ideas up my sleeve."

The pastor studied him for a moment. "You know, you're going to awful great lengths to protect us, Bob... and you don't even know us. I need you to know how grateful we are. If you start feeling like maybe taking on someone else's problems is too great a burden, we'll understand if you want to..."

Bob felt a swell of embarrassment and held up both palms. He wasn't used to compliments, a human touch. His friends Dawn and Marcus in Chicago had been the only people to treat him like a human being in over a decade. "Please... I'm just paying forward favors done me, okay? It's not building a bridge or running into enemy fire. Taking care of this kind of stuff is what I do."

"Well... it's appreciated, is all," the pastor said. "Now, what about tomorrow?"

"Excuse me?" Bob said. "You don't think... Don, I can't resolve this in a day. You guys are going to be stuck here for a little while yet."

"Oh, I figured that," Pastor Green said. "We both did. No, I mean what are we going to do about the service?"

"The..." Bob felt like an idiot. Tomorrow would be Sunday. "You're asking about church?"

The pastor looked a little sheepish. "Well, I hate to raise it and all... but taking care of that kind of stuff is what *I* do."

"You don't have anyone else who can handle it for this week?" Bob asked. "It's a major risk." He didn't want to tell them how major. A church would feature crowds, blocked sightlines. He highly doubted the bikers would worry about offending God.

"He does," Wanda suggested as she screwed up her

paper wrapper and disposed of it. "He just doesn't want to admit it, is all."

The pastor looked mildly irritated. "She's talking about Derek. He's an enthusiastic young man and keen to have his own ministry one day. But he's not ready to lead. He's only twenty-four, for Pete's sake. I've got sneakers older than that."

"But for one week...?" Bob said. "Surely he can handle that. If you guide him through it all by phone in advance?"

"Don..." Wanda counseled.

The pastor did not look happy. "I suppose, given the circumstances, we could give the boy a chance. But won't they cause problems anyhow? They ain't going to know I'm not ministering..."

"I'll head over tomorrow before the service starts," Bob said, "ensure everyone knows you're away for a while. It'll give me and Deacon Riggs a chance to have another little chat if he's around, this time with lots of people in view to discourage any... unnecessary confrontation."

"And today?"

"Today? Today I've got to see a lawyer about a few things. I need to figure out who he's representing, who's paying the bikers..."

"Who the real threat is," Pastor Green said.

"Exactly."

"When I was in prison, there was always folks being shivved or beat up, usually on someone else's command. I know the score, son. What you're saying is the bikers are the tip of the spear. That means this could all get a whole lot worse before it gets better."

Bob smiled confidently and gave the sentiment a curt nod. There was no point elaborating on how much danger they were all in. Whoever was funding The Damned had serious disposable income, probably in the millions of dollars. It was adjacent to a city construction project proposal worth hundreds of millions more.

The wrong kind of people would have no hesitation in killing them to obtain it.

14

Bob parked the Honda at the curb outside the camera store. Given how many people had high-definition camera phones, he was surprised it still existed.

The door chimed as he entered. The left wall of the store was fronted by a long glass counter and register. The counter bore display cases full of camera bodies and lenses.

The man behind the counter had a bushy light-brown beard. He wore a tan golf shirt and slacks and had a tag on his shirt that read, "My name is John. How can I help you?" The red lettering had almost faded to illegibility.

John was expecting him. "You Bob?"

"The one and only. My DC contact let you know what I need?"

"He did. Not a cheap item. Well... cheap in China and Hong Kong. Not so cheap in North America because it's illegal here."

Bob looked around. It was like being in a time warp. Posters on the walls featured happy, smiling vacation-goers enjoying their gear from Fuji and Canon and Pentax. "How...?"

John sighed. "Everyone asks that. Professionals, mostly. Real photographers don't use cell phones except when necessary. They use proper SLR cameras, long lenses, tele-photos, wide-angles... it's just all digital now, is all."

"Must be tough supporting a business with just pros, given... Oh," Bob caught himself, the implication obvious.

"Hey, I don't knock it," John said. "If I didn't have side-lines helping gents like yourself, I'd be working retail some-where." Then he realized he was working retail. "I mean, for some other guy."

He reached under the counter and brought out a rectangular package in plain brown paper, about the size of a shoebox. "You know what this is, right?"

"I get the general idea."

"There's a brief instruction sheet just in case, but it's pretty self-explanatory."

"How much do I owe you?"

"That'll be six hundred."

Bob stifled an urge to argue. "Yeah... so that would be how you handle the high cost of retail leasing."

The store owner shrugged his shoulder quickly. "Eh. It's a seller's market for some items, my friend. But without the store as a front, life is a lot riskier, you feel me? So you pay a big markup. But even if you got it from the manufacturer in China, you're paying two hundred plus, wholesale. That's before shipping, markup, bribes and profit. So... I'm not burning you too bad, pal, believe me."

"Fine. What about my other request?"

"That was easier and cheaper." The store owner reached under the counter and retrieved a second package, this time a box not much bigger than a thumb. "You know how this stuff works, right?"

"I do. No more than a few drops..."

"That'll do it. That's another two hundred. So, all in, eight hundred."

That was most of the cash he'd found on the bikers and some of his own besides. But he didn't have other options.

He took out his money clip and peeled off the eight hundred dollars. The store owner accepted it, then appeared curious. The man nodded towards Bob's forearm. "Your tat...?" He was trying to crane his head around enough to read it upside down. "Looks mighty familiar..."

"Third Battalion, 3rd Marines."

"Ooh... star power." The clerk grinned and nodded slowly in appreciation. "Rifles?"

"Lima. You served?"

The man held up a closed fist. "Semper fi, brother. Lava Dogs, Afghanistan, oh-six to oh-eight." He held out a hand to shake, which Bob accepted. "John Butcher."

"Glad to meet you, man," Bob said.

The clerk looked a little embarrassed. "Hey... sorry about the prices, dude. It's the business. When most of the stuff you're selling is being bought by people who could bite the biscuit at any time, you don't get enough repeat business."

"I get it."

"But if you do need something, you'd be surprised what I can lay my hands on. I only sell to the righteously recom- mended, and if I can do a fellow Marine a solid – something that doesn't eat into my business – I'm always open to suggestions, brother."

He offered a fist to bump, and Bob answered in kind. "I'll keep it in mind."

Bob took the packages back to the car. He set them on the passenger seat. He made a mental note to thank Nicky again for his contacts.

Roulette's office was closed on Saturday. It had taken a court database search to turn up a home address, used to serve him in a lawsuit three years earlier.

Bob knew he might have to stake the place out for a while before getting a view of the man; lawyers of his stature tended to be on-call twenty-four seven.

He covered the miles to the 11th Ward in twenty minutes, traffic and lights keeping movement to a crawl. The house on Prytania Street was ostentatiously large, the sort of five-thousand-square-foot of old money that usually ended up as an interpretive historical site.

It was concrete, a French manor-style home over two levels. Bob counted sixteen double windows on the front. The oak double doors looked close to six feet wide. A quintet of increasingly wide stone steps ran down from it, past a pair of concrete lions.

An expansive lawn dotted with willow and ash trees surrounded it. The home was set back from the road by about thirty feet, a driveway starting at wrought-iron gates. Above them, in black capital letters, an archway sign read "Bonne Chance."

He parked the Honda on the curb opposite, about fifteen feet from the entrance. He rolled the driver's side window halfway down and retrieved the fold-up pocket binoculars from his jacket.

Bob watched the house patiently for about ten minutes. There was no sign of exterior movement, no guards or dogs, nothing to indicate heightened security. Outside the front doors, a silver later-model Jaguar was parked, along with a stretched jet-black Lincoln Continental limo.

A library newspaper clippings search had turned up plenty on Mr. Denny Roulette, much of it unpleasant. He was a perennial winner in court, a hired gun handling everything from civil libel and slander suits to high-profile criminal murder trials. His clients ranged from wife-murdering businessmen and associate-murdering gangsters to corporations playing damage control after polluting the Gulf of Mexico.

They had one thing in common: they were all rich enough to pay fees that, according to a New Orleans *Picayune* gossip columnist, ran more than a thousand dollars an hour. Said a professional colleague, "Police could find the head of your business partner in your freezer, and by the time Denny was done with them, a jury would be convinced police planted the head and stole your ice cream."

As far as Bob could tell, Roulette had never run afoul of the law himself and wasn't known to associate with criminals, although a local gossip columnist did refer to his golf club's membership as a "rogue's gallery of international corporate excesses, from pollution to addiction to political corruption."

Given that the lieutenant governor was a member of the same club, it obviously wasn't hurting the lawyer's reputation.

He watched the house for two hours. Just after noon, he took a short break, eating the sandwich he'd brought along and checking the news. There was nothing local on the house fire, which wasn't surprising, given no one had died. There was also nothing about empty boats washing up on the shores of Lake Pontchartrain.

Just before one o'clock, Roulette left the house, flanked by a tall, broad-chested chauffeur in a driver's suit and peaked hat. He had at least six inches on his boss. Roulette had mirrored aviator glasses on and wore what looked to Bob like golf wear.

The driver opened the limo's back door. He got in, and the driver closed the door, then rounded the car to the other side before following suit.

The limo drove off the property, and a moment later turned onto Napoleon Avenue, heading north. It stayed under the limit, allowing other cars to move around it, traffic busy on Saturday.

After five minutes, it turned off from South Claiborne and onto the Pontchartrain Expressway. A few minutes of traffic took them back onto the streets bordering the Mississippi and the Blue Crab Restaurant, and the driver let Roulette out before driving off, possibly to find parking, Bob figured.

Roulette jogged up the front steps, another patron anticipating him and holding the door.

Bob parked a half-block north and got out, returning on foot. Halfway back, he saw the limo parked across the street. The shape of the driver's head was just visible through the tinted glass.

He walked up the steps.

Inside, the maître d' stood at a small black lectern next to the cash register. She was a smiling, twenty-something blonde woman in a copper waistcoat and black tie. "Do you have a reservation?" she asked.

"Hoping I could just drop in for a bite of lunch," Bob offered.

She grimaced slightly and looked into the vast, wide-open restaurant surrounded by windows and overlooking the river. "I'm afraid we're pretty full; we're looking at thirty minutes' wait. But we can seat you at the bar if you're alone... and between you and me, it's the same kitchen, so it's *really* good."

She was accustomed to the pitch and delivered it smoothly. Bob gestured towards the raised bar area at the back of the room. "I'll just camp myself there, then."

"Greaaaat," she enthused, her attention and gaze already returned to the bookings computer screen on her lectern.

It was a stroke of luck, the raised area offering great sightlines.

Roulette was eating alone on the far side of the room, near the patio doors. His server replaced an empty martini glass. *He's been here for five minutes and he's already one in.* Maybe he was careless during his downtime; that could help.

The lawyer withdrew his phone from his pocket to answer a call. He said a few words, then ended it. Bob watched in anticipation, hoping he'd leave the phone out on the table.

Instead, Roulette pocketed it.

Damn it. That'll be habit, then. Plenty of people were careless with their phones, leaving them on bars or tables on the assumption no one can steal them from under their noses, or would bother. It would've made life much easier, Bob knew.

Now Bob would have to wait for an opportunity or, worse, get inside Roulette's home. Kidnapping and interrogating the man would be easier, but had a longer list of potential complications. For one, he was no longer in the business of silencing witnesses, so shooting Roulette was out of the question. He could spend days following the man without determining which of the people he met, if any, was his paymaster on the blockbusting job.

But there would be one. Roulette was well-paid insulation, likely nothing more.

He waited patiently, nursing the same mineral water while Roulette ate his meal.

15

WASHINGTON, DC

E ddie Stone needed an escape plan.

The septuagenarian spymaster had plans to spend Saturday watching tapes of college football games, including half the Bowl games from the prior season. It was now or never, a rare day without anything scheduled.

And then his in-laws called.

Stone's wife, Sophie, had committed suicide twenty-five years prior, a victim of chronic depression.

His in-laws had, inexplicably, insisted on staying in touch with him for years. It was like they thought him the touchy-feely type and not a hardened former Vietnam vet with multiple CIA overseas tours under his belt.

He'd never understand citizens, people living outside the game, he'd decided. They lacked the advantages he'd always had: intelligence, stoicism, dispassionate perspectives. They were awash in sentiment and empathy for the weak or troubled.

They lacked focus on goals.

Such was it with Jack and Helen Gross. He sat across the restaurant table from them as Jack droned on. They were sprightly seniors and went to the same "family" restaurant for the 4 p.m. senior discount buffet every Saturday. Window-shopping mall denizens strolled past their table, occasionally glancing inside to see what was for dinner.

"... and then he backs the car directly into the garage door, which has not moved an inch. Ed? Ed, you still with us?"

Stone's daydream was broken. "Hmmm? Sorry. The garage door. Rough."

"You ain't kidding! Try twenty-five hundred bucks rough! That's some serious scratch." Jack was a little older than Stone, but not by much.

Sophie had been twenty years his junior when they'd married. His years on the road, he knew, had contributed to her mental health issues. He refused to blame himself, however; she'd made her own choices. He hadn't forced her to marry a spook. He hadn't hidden who or what he was.

His phone began to buzz in his pocket. He practically snatched at it. "Sorry, I need to take this," he said, cutting Jack off mid-story.

He hit the green receive button. "Stone."

"Sir, it's Dan Simmonds over here at Fort Meade. My team is tracking your wayward asset."

Fort Meade was home to the National Security Agency. Its ability to access camera networks and even override and command private equipment in some cases gave it an unprecedented ability to find people, particularly when coupled with facial-recognition software.

But they knew better than to bother him on a Saturday unless it was pressing. "What's up?"

"We *may* have a hit on Bob Singleton," Simmonds said. "Strong stress on the word 'may,' as the intel doesn't make a whole lot of sense. But you wanted a heads-up if anything sprang loose."

"Skip the dramatics and bottom-line it." The two agencies had a grudging working relationship much of the time.

"A traffic camera on the city network in Slidell, Louisiana, picked up a side image from a car turning at an intersection. The image is poor and pixelated, taken through the window glass, and the driver's wearing a ball cap—"

"But?"

"But our software says the facial and earlobe shapes are a probable match."

"Have we rounded up any other—"

"Yeah, a camera from a nearby marina," Simmonds said, getting ahead of him. "That one's even farther away and less clear, but things get weirder from there."

"Weirder than a rogue asset going to a small city in Louisiana that has no ties that I can think of to either his personal life or the Special Operations Group?" Stone pondered. "I hesitate to even ask."

"If it's him, there's an image of him marching two men down a pier and into a boat, which he then set adrift. They looked like outlaw bikers, with rocker vests and everything."

For a rare moment, Stone found himself unsure of what to do next. Singleton was always unpredictable, but he'd been certain the former Alpha would head directly to Texas, where Tehran mission victim Tyler Gaines's stepfather lived, or to Arizona, where Jon Rice's mother lived. Texas made the most sense purely geographically.

"Keep me updated," Stone said. "Appreciated as always."

He ended the call.

Singleton's Samaritan complex was probably at work once again. He needed to touch base with a few freelancers in New Orleans. Singleton's futile attempts at washing the blood off his hands would cost him.

ORLEANS COUNTY, Louisiana

THE BOAT DRIFTED for six hours before Dirty Carl had the bright idea of using their hands to paddle.

At first, they'd argued about it, because Diesel wasn't sure it was worth the effort. Someone's boat would pass eventually and get them help, he'd offered.

The night had been cold, the men sleeping in turns. Eventually, as daybreak arrived, he'd agree that, as cold and hungry as they were, paddling beat doing nothing at all.

Two feet from an unfamiliar shoreline, they ran out of lake, the boat's bottom grounding out on silt and sludge. The two men climbed out and began to walk, sloshing through the brackish water and muck.

Diesel knew they were in trouble; he had no idea where they were, how far from a road, a home, any kind of help. His sprained wrist ached.

But Dirty Carl was leading the way, pushing trees and branches aside as they waded slowly through the foot-deep swamp. The mud threatened to suck his shoes right off his feet, but Diesel had other concerns. The bayou was full of gators and snakes.

"Just go slow," he intoned as they muddled along. "We probably ain't going to see the one what jumps out at us afore it happens..."

"You know, our present situation is shit enough without bringing that up," Dirty Carl groused back. "If we run into something bad, we run into something bad. But we sure as shit can't stay here, can we?"

"So... where the fuck are we going?" Diesel questioned.

"If we can find a road, we can get back to New Orleans, get the rest of the guys together..."

"Wait a second." Diesel stopped walking, his feet sloshing as they ground to a halt. "Are you suggesting we just go back to The Damned like nothing happened?"

Dirty Carl shrugged. "What else are we supposed to do?"

"We can't. You heard what—" He paused to wave away the mosquitoes buzzing around his head, then slapped one on his neck, a smear of blood left behind. "You heard what that dude said: he'll rat us out to Deacon. Then we're dead men."

"Sooo... so maybe we say the dude is full of shit. Who is Deacon going to believe: us or some stranger?" Dirty Carl resumed walking, slapping another mosquito dead.

"Uhhh... he ain't going to take any chances, is what," Diesel insisted. "He'll cap both of us just to be sure."

"Better to risk that than to cut and run on my brothers," Dirty Carl said.

He began walking again.

Diesel followed silently. It seemed an admirable, even noble sentiment from the other man.

It also seemed incredibly stupid.

But once Dirty Carl had made up his mind what to do, he didn't usually deviate.

He's going to get us both killed just because he's afraid of Deacon. Diesel felt morose. Becoming a member of The

Damned had been about partying, easy money, having a good time. Now this guy was going to...

He stopped walking again. They'd pushed through thickets of mangroves and past mossy vines hanging from the cypress trees that clustered, sometimes just inches apart. He was unsure if they were trudging back to civilization or deeper into the bayou.

But the tree to their right had a small X carved in the trunk. "Hold on a sec..." Diesel said. He sloshed through the mud to the tree, then oriented himself. "Holy shit! I know where we are!"

Dirty Carl leaned his head back and let out a sigh of relief. "Thank fuck for that. Where's the road?"

Diesel nodded to his right. "Head due east, and we should hit I-90. We're on St. Catherine's Island – the Bayou de Lesaire. There's a big fishing camp not four miles east of us. There's just a whole lot of swamp between here and there."

"Can we walk it?"

"Sure. Like I said, won't be easy. But there's solid ground in there, every so often. It ain't going to be nice, though."

Dirty Carl turned that way. "Then we'd better get moving."

"Well, now, wait a second," Diesel suggested. "Let's have a little think about this."

"What?"

"The cookhouse is less than two miles from here. They'll still be working on the next shipment, or just about finished."

"So?"

"So... we hide out there for now. There's food, propane, somewhere to sleep and a whole shitload of methamphetamine. We hide out there until this shit all blows over, and whoever comes out of it ahead, we blow town with as much of that meth as possible."

Dirty Carl turned and shot him a disgusted look. "Man, you don't have no shame, do you? You think we should evade our own brothers just so's we don't have to admit to snitching. Then you want to steal the meth and... what? Start over on our own?"

Diesel shrugged. It seemed sensible even when repeated back to him sarcastically.

"Not a fucking chance," Dirty Carl said. "You need to grow a pair, and we need to find that road."

He turned and began to walk east.

He was signing their death warrant, Diesel figured. Dirty Carl needed the others, needed them to like him or something. Or maybe just to feel someone had his back. Whatever it was, it was the kind of cloying sympathy Diesel had always hated, a weakness.

He's going to get us both killed. We're going to walk out of the bayou, and Deacon's going to march us right back in and put bullets in both our heads.

They continued the slow march. It was over ninety degrees; the mosquitoes chewed on them like they were a walking buffet. Their feet slogged through water, mire and muck. They were thankful for occasional breaks, strips of dry land for a few dozen yards.

Dirty Carl came to a halt. He held up his hand. "Shhh," he whispered. "Heard something."

To their left, through the thick vines and thin tree boughs, they heard something slowly swishing through the water.

Diesel risked turning his head. He could see surface

ripples ten feet to their left. "Don't fucking move," he whispered. "Gator, nine o'clock."

"Oh Jesus Christ...!"

"Shh! Don't fucking move, I said! If we move, he sees our feet disturb the water."

Dirty Carl did as instructed. Both men stood motionless, the water gently lapping against their shins as the creature swam by. It was big, Diesel thought, at least twelve feet long from nose to tail. It was just a foot or so away now, gliding by them.

A droplet of sweat ran down his nose and threatened to drip from the end of it. Would that be enough, if it hit the water, that momentary break in surface tension?

The droplet fell.

He moved a cupped hand under his nose, praying...

The sweat splashed against his palm.

The alligator's tail swished to and fro as the giant predator used it to move him along. Diesel's heart pounded as he watched the tip swish once more as it passed them. "Stay still," he murmured.

A mosquito lit upon Dirty Carl's neck. Then another. Then a third. "Oh damn..." he muttered, beginning to hyperventilate. "I have to swat them. I have to..."

The alligator swished its tail a few more times, disappearing under a thicket of mangroves.

Dirty Carl slapped his own neck, hard, squashing all three simultaneously. "Fuuuuck... We have to get out of this swamp, dude..."

He began to push east again. Diesel followed. But he knew the problem remained. Dirty Carl wasn't going to cut and run, and that was stupid.

He had to make a decision.

The small log presented itself with ideal timing. It was wedged between two larger pieces of deadfall, a perfectly round, three-foot-long club, one end at his hand height as he walked by. His right hand grasped it as he passed.

"Hey, Carl," he said.

Dirty Carl began to turn, meeting the full force of the club as Diesel swung it at the other man's temple. It smacked off Carl's skull like a spade slapping wet cement.

The older man collapsed in a heap and a splash, elbows sinking into the mud as he tried immediately to shake it off and right himself. But Diesel was on him before he could react, pounding his head, hard shots once, twice, three times.

Then a fourth, to make sure he was down for good, blood flowing from the wound at Dirty Carl's temple, mixing with the mud and sludge of the bayou.

Diesel stood up and threw the log to one side. He didn't admire his work, didn't want to see his former friend in that state.

But the man had brought it on himself, Diesel figured. He'd offered him a reasonable way out, and Dirty Carl wouldn't take it.

What else was he supposed to do?

He began walking again, this time alone.

The cookhouse was less than two miles north by his reckoning. He spotted another X on a nearby tree. He was close.

If he was right, he could hide out at the cookhouse for a few days. If the cookers weren't done yet, he could wait until they were at full inventory. The latest batch was supposed to be completed soon. It would be stored in the underground chamber they'd developed for that purpose, hidden from overhead cameras and heat sensors.

And Diesel had a key.

16

Denny Roulette's solitary lunch had been followed by a round of eighteen at New Orleans Country Club.

Bob had managed to spot him twice from the parking lot, when Roulette reached the two holes adjacent to City Park Avenue. Bob sat patiently in the Honda, listening to the sound of tennis balls recoiling back and forth at the nearby courts.

He used binoculars to make sure he knew when the lawyer's first nine holes were done, then waited in the clubhouse to catch Roulette's mid-round drink.

Bob sat at the bar, one eye on the room and his target's foursome. They sat around one of the cheap steel and laminate tables, talking cases, probably all lawyers. Bob wondered in the moment how much happiness he'd preserve in the world by killing all four of them. A lot, probably.

But that was no longer the way. It wasn't the evildoers he mourned, the targets he'd rightfully put down before many others were hurt. It was those hit by the fallout: from failed missions, from politicians' decisions, from greed and lies. It was his own blindness in paying fealty to bad men.

He glanced at the bathroom door. He'd momentarily considered waiting until Roulette hit the head, then following him in, beating him until he coughed up a name.

But that had consequences too, the potential for unexpected fallout. What if Roulette was more scared of his paymasters than the immediate risk? What if Roulette called his bluff? Bob had no intention of killing the man, so physical threats were out.

It was going to take guile to get that phone, patience.

He left before they'd finished their midway break, heading back to the Honda. He got in and dialed the pastor.

"Bob, what's the good word?" Pastor Green answered.

"Yeah... this is going to take me the rest of the day. Have you had a chance to talk to your associate pastor about tomorrow?"

"He's here now," Green said.

Bob winced internally. "I thought I was clear, no visitors. You used the phone I left?"

"I did, sure. But you don't have to worry about Derek. He's a godly young man, full of the Lord's energy. He's up for the task."

"Good. I'm going to be keeping tabs on that lawyer I mentioned until after you're asleep. But I'll head over in the morning and keep an eye on the service, make sure your neighbors play it straight."

"You don't think they'd cause trouble at the church, do you?"

"No," Bob said. "Too high profile, and someone is still

paying them. But they'll know everyone is away from their homes for a couple of hours."

"Dang. Jon helped us, sure, but I worked dang hard to help pay off that house, Bob. I do not want anything to happen to it, or any of my neighbors' homes, for that matter."

"I'll do what I can."

"I expect there'll still be some police about. You watch yourself, now, okay?"

"I intend to. I'll talk to you later." He ended the call.

There was no point heading back inside. According to the course map, most of the back-nine holes were far away from prying eyes.

Instead, he waited for another two hours, until Roulette appeared with his bag at the exit to the clubhouse. His driver quickly got out of the limo, made his way over and retrieved the clubs. He stashed them in the trunk while Roulette climbed back in.

The surveillance continued for four more hours. Roulette met yet more colleagues for dinner, heading home just before seven o'clock.

Bob parked across the road from the man's house again. Roulette was cautious about his personal space, focused. There was a potentially easier route than waiting for the man to be sloppy, however.

After about an hour, just before eight o'clock, the driver left the house. Bob watched him lock the front door behind him.

The driver walked down the front steps and across the gravel parking area to the adjacent three-car garage. He clicked a fob on his key ring, and the left-side door rolled up. He went inside.

A few moments later, a crimson hard-top Jeep pulled out of the bay and headed towards the road. Bob waited until it pulled out and into traffic before following. He kept the Honda at least four cars back.

Whatever Roulette was paying, it wasn't enough to afford a place downtown. The driver followed South Clairborne Avenue and drove for another ten minutes, turning occasionally.

Bob checked the road signs; they were in Metairie, a nice suburb, rows of single-family homes, some with pools.

The red Jeep pulled into the driveway of a modest single-story house. It looked about a thousand square feet, Bob figured, a leftover from the construction boom of the 1950s. He watched as the driver climbed the short staircase to the front door and opened it, waiting for him to pause in the entrance, suggesting he was announcing his presence. Instead, he swung it closed immediately behind him.

Probably alone, but that's not definitive. Need to take a closer look.

He sat and waited for an hour, until the sun was no longer dappling the horizon with orange. The streetlights began to glow a pale yellow, barely cutting through the darkness, the sky cloudy and the moon hidden.

He waited yet longer, until traffic on the street was reduced to the occasional car drifting by. The home didn't appear to have central air or window AC units. It was another hot night, over ninety degrees. That meant windows would be left open.

Just before eleven, he got out of the car and checked both ways for anyone paying attention, before crossing the street. He hopped the short front fence and followed the side of the house, ducking under a window. At the back deck, he glanced around the corner and through the back patio doors.

The driver was on his couch, watching basketball, back to the sliding doors.

Bob followed the back wall to the next window. It was open, a vertical frame that cranked wider via a handle inside. He tugged on it, the loose, older mechanism allowing him to pull it yet wider.

He kept wary glances on the two neighboring homes. With no cover, anyone stepping out would see him immediately. But the late hour suggested he had a few minutes to work.

Bob took out his pocketknife and slashed the sides and bottom edge of the bug screen covering the window, creating a flap. He pulled himself up and inside.

Halfway through the window, he heard footsteps. They were close. He froze. If he tried to pull himself through quickly or drop back outside, the noise would betray him.

Six feet away, the driver walked through the kitchen door, an empty glass in one hand.

Bob didn't move a muscle.

The refrigerator was against the opposite wall, near the door. The driver had changed into jeans and a T-shirt. He turned Bob's way without looking directly toward him and opened the fridge. He took out a bottle of ginger ale, leaving the fridge ajar. He moved a half-step sideways, to the counter by the stove, and retrieved a half-empty bottle of Black Velvet whiskey.

The man poured a couple of fingers of booze into the ginger ale. He put the bottle back on the counter and screwed its top back on. He didn't bother with ice. He slammed the fridge door and sauntered back out of the room.

Bob let out a hard breath. He waited a few more moments for the man to get back to his TV. He pulled himself through the window, then quickly removed the vial from his pocket.

Nick's contact had stressed not to use too much. He opened the refrigerator. It was eleven fifteen, so it was possible the guy wouldn't have any more to drink; but the basketball game he was watching appeared to have almost a half to play.

He opened the whiskey bottle. The thumb-sized vial had an eyedropper attached to its lid. He used it to deposit four healthy droplets into the bottle, then sealed it.

A few moments later, he slipped back outside the house. He pushed the window back to an ajar position, then moved back to the tiny deck by the patio doors.

It took another thirty minutes before the driver returned for a top-up. Fifteen minutes later, Bob watched as his target's head nodded sideways in his chair, one hand dropping from the arm and hanging beside it.

He checked the patio door, but it was locked.

The dose of flunitrazepam would last for hours and wipe the driver's memory from just prior to taking it, as well as most of the few hours immediately after. The drug was dependable in that regard, which was why it had been an illegal "date rape" drug for decades. He headed back to the kitchen window and pried it open once more, then crawled inside.

He headed directly for the living room and made sure the driver would remain unconscious, lifting his hand and letting it fall. His key fob was on the coffee table ahead of him. Bob retrieved it.

He let himself out the front door and locked it behind him. The man would be out for at least eight hours, possibly more.

He made his way back to the car.

The drive from Metairie back to the Garden District took less than fifteen minutes. This time, he parked the car several blocks away and proceeded on foot.

At Bonne Chance, he followed the wrought-iron fence around the half-block it occupied. The thirty-foot setback was true on all sides, but he found what he was looking for: directly behind the house, a small gate led to a right-of-way between Roulette's back fence and the home behind him, likely a utility corridor.

The gate was padlocked. He examined the driver's key ring until he found a match for a Master lock. Bob unlatched the gate and moved inside the backyard quickly, closing it behind him.

Instead of trying to cross the wide-open backyard, he hugged the fence line, keeping himself difficult to spot from a rear window. At the back corner of the house, he climbed the steps up onto a wide covered porch.

If Roulette was like most people, he disabled the alarm system while still up and moving around, then likely set it again before going to bed.

Bob checked the patio door.

It was locked. He searched the driver's key ring for something that appeared to fit the keyhole and tried again. The door swung open.

He let himself in quietly.

The impromptu entrance led to a dining room, a long

rectangular table central to it. He set the small box he was carrying down on it.

Bob checked the doorway, peeking around it quickly. Outside the dining room, a skinny hallway led to other rooms.

He stepped into the hall, closing the door quietly behind him.

At the end of the hall, Denny Roulette walked around the corner.

17

B ob knew he had to act quickly.

Roulette's eyes widened at the sight of an intruder, and for a moment, he froze in place.

Bob charged at him.

Roulette turned in panic and sprinted the way he'd come. Bob rounded the corner of the hall. It led into a long, expansive living room. At the far end was a teak desk; Roulette ran towards it. He reached into his pocket and fumbled for his keys, then tried to open one of two hutches.

Bob threw the punch while still running, leaning into it. He caught Roulette square on the side of the jaw.

The lawyer's legs buckled, and his eyes swam as he collapsed, unconscious, to the parquet hardwood floor.

Bob didn't waste time, crouching beside the man and withdrawing the vial from his pocket. He didn't have time to rely on the eye dropper. Roulette would be awake in less than a minute, in all likelihood, two at most.

He rummaged in his pocket until he felt the long, thin form of the hypodermic.

The syringe was the length of a cigarette. Its needle tip pierced the rubber membrane on the vial. He inverted both to avoid air bubbles and drew in twenty units' worth of the solution. He turned over Roulette's arm, pressing his index and forefinger to either side of the blue vein that showed in the crook of his elbow. He injected the solution with slow, cautious pressure.

With the drug working its way into his system, if Roulette woke, it wouldn't be for long.

He stripped off Roulette's necktie and cut it in half with his pocketknife. He used one half to bind the man's hands behind him, the other to tie his feet. Then he rolled him onto his stomach.

He reached down and retrieved the man's keys, then checked inside the hutch. A 9 mm Smith & Wesson M&P sat on top of some papers. He withdrew the magazine and emptied it, storing the shells in his side pocket. Then he put the gun back in its storage spot and locked it.

Bob returned the keys to Roulette's pocket just as the man began to stir. He walked over to the sofa, sat down and waited.

"What... what the heck happened..." Roulette mumbled as he stirred back to consciousness. "What the... Hey! *Hey!*"

The lawyer yelled a few more times, then began to wriggle around. Bob was fifteen feet away, at the other end of the room. It would take some wriggling to even get off his stomach, let alone realize he wasn't alone.

After two minutes of struggling, Roulette slumped, unconscious. If Bob had applied the drug orally, it could've taken twenty minutes. But it was a powerful intravenous dose of a strong sedative. He'd be out until morning.

Bob returned to the lawyer's side and found the man's phone in his pocket.

He took the phone next door, to the dining room, and opened the box. Inside, a rectangular plastic device about the size of an old tape recorder sat waiting. He turned it on. It whirred to life, a blue light coming on next to the one of two slots on its top side already filled by a SIM card.

After prying loose the back of the phone, he took out the SIM card and placed it in the slot, then hit the "copy" button. It took less than a minute for another tiny light, this time green, to appear next to it.

Bob removed the SIM card and returned it to the phone. He returned the phone to Roulette's pocket. Then he crouched to drag the man, by his underarms, slowly across the room. He lifted him up in two stages onto the couch.

A few feet away, on the glass coffee table, a tumbler of dark liquor sat two fingers from empty. He slid it into a spot nearer the sleeping man's head, within reach.

If the drug worked its typical malevolent charm, Roulette would wake up in front of a near-empty glass of booze. The last thing he would recall would be sitting there drinking it.

Bob checked the time as he exited the house. It was just after midnight. He yawned, realizing he was about to go a second straight night with less than six hours' sleep.

He still needed to drive back and return the keys to the unconscious driver. Then it would be time to get back to the motel, grab some shut-eye and prepare for Sunday.

The service was a predictable, tactically sound time to act. Deacon Riggs did not seem like a foolish man. He'd see the window of opportunity and take it.

18

It was nearly one o'clock in the morning. That the pool hall was still busy wasn't surprising; Deacon knew Sunday would be difficult. He avoided drinking, made sure the boys kept it under control.

Instead, he sat alone at a back table and watched them knock pool balls around.

Soon, he figured, they'd turn the tables on this "Bob" character. It didn't matter what martial arts bullshit he knew or how confident he was. He couldn't take out a dozen guys on his own.

But first, they had to resolve the problem of their missing brethren. Booker was awaiting a first appearance, charged with trafficking. They'd need a lawyer to get bail for him on Monday. Dirty Carl and Diesel hadn't checked in since the night prior, when they'd been ordered to follow the pastor's new friend.

He doubted the pastor was in the business of associating with hard men. Whoever Bob was, he was probably ex-military or police. Someone like that wasn't running around capping bikers, which meant Dirty Carl and Diesel were being held, or had cut and run, or a third explanation he hadn't come up with yet.

At the far end of the hall, he saw the front door being opened by the server. She'd locked it at his request, to prevent drunk average-joe patrons from stumbling inside. But she'd evidently recognized the new arrival, as she unlatched it temporarily to allow access.

It was Booker's younger brother, Paul Harris. The rotund biker made his way past the tables without stopping to greet anyone, heading directly to Deacon's table. He looked nervous.

"Deacon... hey," he said, barely raising his eyes from the floor.

"Spit it out, Paulie... Jesus H, you look like a kid caught in the cookie jar."

"We found their bikes."

That didn't sound good. "What do you mean, you found their bikes? Their bikes... but not them?"

The younger biker looked like he was worried about being cuffed, fidgeting in place. "Yeah... see, they were parked down at the marina in Slidell. We asked the guy at the shop there to check his security tapes, and he said some guy from the feds took it already."

"The *feds*? What the fuck...?"

"He did say he talked to a government guy who told him they'd gone out on the lake in a rowboat or some shit. So we spent all afternoon driving around the shoreline as best we could, trying to find people who might've seen them. No signs of either of them."

Deacon tried to hide his confusion. What the hell were they doing in Slidell? What the hell were the feds doing grabbing the marina's security video? It didn't make any sense.

Unless...

He'd wondered about Bob's training, where he'd learned to move like that. But maybe it made sense; maybe he worked for the feds. Maybe he was the guy who stopped by the Marina and had a quiet word.

Had he tracked down the two men and taken them in? Had he been trying to follow them to the ranch?

Or worse, had he left them dead in the swamp?

Including Booker, it meant they were three down. But it wouldn't matter. No matter how clever the pastor's friend was, church was only nine hours away.

If Deacon had his do-gooder credentials sussed out correctly, Bob would make sure those churchgoers weren't being hassled.

And that meant the street four blocks away would be practically empty.

19

The Fellowship in Christ St. Christopher's Church looked right out of the old South, Bob figured. It was whitewashed, with white siding and a tall steeple. The arched windows were wood-framed, filled with old leaded glass, warped by the decades.

The crowd outside could've come from any time in the prior century, too. Everyone was in their Sunday best, ladies in floral-print dresses and matching hats, white gloves and dainty purses clasped ahead of them. The men wore dark suits. It wasn't the biggest church Bob had ever seen, but there had to be forty or fifty congregants milling around outside.

"A penny for your thoughts, friend Bob. You look concerned." Associate Pastor Derek Bevan had sidled up to him. He had his clerical collar on, under a black, short-sleeve shirt.

He wagged a knowing forefinger to accentuate his point. "A penny for someone's thoughts is always a good investment, because when we learn, we earn. That's what my daddy used to say."

Bob noticed the man's fine manicure job. For all his protestations about the cost of that suit two days prior, he certainly paid attention to his appearance. His skin was immaculate, his shaved stubble skintight; Bob didn't see a hair out of place.

"Sounds like a sensible man," Bob offered. "I told Pastor Don I'd keep an eye out today just in case the neighbors decide to drop in."

"The service? You think..."

"I think that until everyone goes inside, I'll be here."

"And then?"

"And then I'll head back down to the Greens' block. I suspect the bikers will think it's a brilliant move to trash a few homes or yards or cars while everyone's gone."

"Intimidation?" Derek asked.

"It sounds stupid, I know. But people can only take so much; they probably figure that every time someone has a window smashed, or their car busted into, or their mail stolen, they get one more foot out the door, one step closer to putting their place up for sale and getting out."

The pastor crossed his arms and frowned. "I just don't understand how anyone benefits. This isn't a rich neighbor-hood, Bob. These aren't ritzy places. Half the homes have some sort of flood damage or other caveats on them. The rest are just new, middle-class homes."

"It's a matter of timing." Bob scanned the crowd, watched the parking lot. It was still quiet, people chatting in small groups. The organist was already playing; the music could be faintly heard outside through the open front door.

"Timing?"

"First, any construction project involving the neighborhood could lead to lawsuits from the homeowners if enough are determined to stay. Lawsuits are expensive. A multimillion-dollar settlement could wipe out any profit margin a developer might make."

"A developer? You mean... the bypass proposal?"

"Even if the neighborhood is chosen for one, civil suits could prevent it. And if word comes down that the homes are to be subject to eminent domain, it stands to reason any cheaper homes that can be 'upgraded' – or at the very least listed at inflated prices – will go up in value—"

"Because they're about to have a guaranteed buyer in the form of the city," Bevan said, finishing the thought.

"Those increased values will cost the city more money if they seize the properties. The city, in turn, will try to extract that value from whoever builds the project."

The young pastor crossed his arms, the ramifications dawning on him. "A lawsuit could cost millions, a massive shift in property values hundreds of thousands more."

"It's easier just to get them all out if possible," Bob said. "There's no legitimate grounds to demand they go or drive them away, so..."

"Insidious," the pastor muttered. "Terrible, terrible behavior." He checked his wristwatch. "We're five minutes away."

Bob nodded south. "I'm going to head down the street, see what I can see."

"Be careful."

"Oh, I plan to," Bob said as he ambled down the steps to the sidewalk. That was one great thing about Lakeview; all those private alleyways helped avoid prying eyes.

20

P aul Harris scratched his beefy left forearm with his right hand absentmindedly. The biker had been standing behind the Greens' house for fifteen minutes, staring at the back door.

It was almost ten, almost time for the church service to start. They had less than an hour, to be safe, to get everything done.

He was kicking himself for letting Danny D run up the road for smokes. Chances were that no one would come home until after the service, and the Greens probably wouldn't come at all. But they were under strict instructions to stay as briefly as possible. Police still had tape up across the door of the stash house across the road.

Harris's colleagues, Animal and Terry, had broken in through the Greens' back door to make sure the place was properly doused; they wanted to make sure it would burn to the ground before the firefighters could get there.

"Would you guys hurry the fuck up, please?" Harris muttered, trying to keep his voice to a loud hiss.

Terry stuck his head out the back door. "Pretty much ready to roll." Then he disappeared back inside.

"God damn," Harris whined. "Sweating my ass off here for no good reason, just so Deacon can save face from some asshole."

A finger tapped him on the shoulder. Harris turned reflexively. By the time he realized he should be thinking defensively, the fist was already whistling in on him. It caught him on the chin.

He felt his legs turn to rubber, and he went down. He was conscious but had a strange lucidity to his thoughts, the strength of the punch rocking him. "Wha... himmee..." he muttered as he tried to stand.

He barely recognized the blurry image of the man in front of him as the fist came crashing in again, the lights going out.

THE BIKER HAD MADE the mistake of standing in the Greens' backyard, near the door, rather than in the alley proper.

Bob crept up behind him, cleared the four-foot chain-link fence and got within a foot, all without the man even turning his head.

Special Forces they're not, he thought as the biker crumpled to the ground. *Keep your head in the game; that means heightened focus, not less.*

He crouched and disarmed the man, taking a pistol from his belt and a knife from a boot sheath. He pocketed both.

He removed the man's phone and tossed it to one side. He found a money clip in his back pocket. Bob riffed the cash quickly. It was sizable, maybe more than a grand.

He stuffed the money clip into his boot, old street habits dying hard.

From his position, the outdoor man was a guard.

He scoped out the rest of the backyard. A small shed sat, door open, against the south fence. He leaned in through its door to ensure no one was inside, then moved back to the house.

The guard meant more men inside. He stepped quietly to the back door and peeked into the kitchen.

Bob ducked back out of view just as quickly, two men almost within arm's reach. They were spilling liquid over everything.

The smell suggested gasoline.

His anger surged, but he held it in, burying it, unwilling to brook distraction. They were brazen; police were still watching the remains of the house across the street.

Fighting two big men in such an enclosed space was asking for trouble. He also needed to keep an eye on the man behind the house, who would be conscious soon.

He leaned against the outside of the doorjamb and muttered, "Take a look at this," loudly enough to be heard. His hand slipped into his side pocket, and he withdrew the guard's pistol, gripping it by the barrel.

A pair of cowboy boots stepped through the door, their owner's head pivoting as he looked for his friend. Bob smacked him firmly at the base of the skull with the gun butt. The man dropped to his knees, then pitched face-first in the dirt.

"Terry... what's going..." the second man uttered. He was two steps out the door when Bob swung the makeshift cosh.

The biker caught a glimpse from the corner of his eye

and turned at the last second, the gun butt barely grazing him.

He stumbled sideways, his hand going for his gun. Bob tossed the pistol, sidearm. It smacked the biker nicknamed "Animal" in the face, his hands flying up reflexively to protect it.

Bob dropped low and shot out a side kick, the ball of his foot finding the side of the biker's knee joint. Animal yelped in pain, hopping onto one leg, then falling flat on his back. Before he could recover, Bob threw a hard elbow that caught the man square in his face, nose bones shattering.

Animal bellowed as the skin split, blood streaking down his face. Bob threw the elbow again, just as hard, catching the man on the mental nerve of the chin, knocking him out.

Good timing. The other two were beginning to stir, limbs shaking involuntarily for a split second as their consciousness returned. Harris rubbed the side of his chin and blinked repeatedly, trying to clear fog.

Bob kept an eye on him as he retrieved the other two men's guns. He tossed them into the house and out of reach. "Terry" was beginning to stir, rolling over onto his stomach, then pushing up until he was on his knees. He looked as dazed as his friend.

"What hit me?" Harris mumbled.

"I did. Now we're going to sit here while I call the police, who have a car in the area already, given what's been going on," Bob said.

He took out his phone. Harris was sitting up, knees bent, like a kid on a field trip. He began to grin wildly.

"What's so funny?" Bob asked.

"Nothing. Just... you done fucked up, son," the biker said.

Bob heard a slight shuffle on the grass behind him.

Instinct kicked in, and he began to pivot on his left heel, raising his elbow to strike...

The blow came down hard, smashing him in the temple, knocking him to the ground. Before he could rise, a boot came from nowhere, hammering him in the jaw.

Everything went black.

21

T erry Beauchesne didn't usually ask questions.

He'd ridden with The Damned MC for two years, since getting out of high school. He'd learned the mouthy guys were the ones who got a smack most often.

But in that moment, he felt the need for answers. He had one of the unconscious Samaritan's feet, while Danny D – who'd returned from the store with cigarettes just in time to ambush their guest – had the other. Animal and Paul Harris had a firm hold under each arm.

They were carrying him towards the house.

"Why don't we just shoot him?" Terry said.

The other men stopped walking for a moment. Danny D threw him an annoyed look. "Well, maybe you should call Deacon back and ask him," he said. "It's his idea."

"He wants to pin the fire on this guy," Paul explained more gently. He knew Terry wasn't exactly gifted in the brains department. "So we dump him inside, tied up and doused with gas."

"But... he's tied up." The first thing Danny D had done after knocking "Bob" out was to retrieve a small section of rope from the back garden shed.

"When he burns up with the house, it burns the rope on his wrists and ankles," Danny D said, "and all they find is a body, with matches in his pocket and the remains of a gas can within reach."

They resumed walking.

Terry nodded. It still seemed risky. "Still... I mean, I get it and all, but... isn't this, like, the part in the movie where the dude escapes because the other guy didn't just shoot him when he got a chance? I mean, we should just be sure, right?"

Danny D stopped walking again, the others stumbling a little from the sudden weight imbalance. "I don't remember Deacon saying 'oh, and by the way, ask that idiot Terry about it.' Last I checked, when he gives an order, the brothers follow it, or this shit don't work."

They were halfway through the door in the kitchen when the man began to stir. He must have realized he was suspended in the air, Terry thought, because he began to wriggle and kick.

They dropped him, hard, on the kitchen floor. Danny D went down on one knee, leaned in, and hammered the man with another short, sharp punch, knocking him out again.

He rose and turned to Paul Harris. "You have that little bottle I gave you earlier?"

Harris fumbled in the pocket of his leather jacket. "Here."

Danny D walked over to the kitchen counter and grabbed a tea towel from the rack. He unscrewed the bottle and poured most of its contents into the towel. Bending at the knees, he leaned in and held the rag over Bob's face for about ten seconds.

"That should keep him out for a while." Danny D noticed his friends' quizzical stares. "Chloroform, like in the movies."

"Does that actually work?" Terry asked. Getting answers to his questions without a cuff to the head had emboldened him.

Danny D shot him another hard look. "Of course it fucking works! They wouldn't keep doing it in movies if it didn't work, you idiot."

It occurred to the younger man in the moment that they did lots of things in movies over and over again that could never happen in real life. But he preferred not being hit.

"Come on," Danny D said. "Let's get out of here. Paul, you and Terry head around to the front, keep an eye on the door, make sure he doesn't try to get out. We'll watch the back."

The bikers filed out. Terry was sure Deacon knew what he was doing. As they passed through the door, Danny D turned around, leaned down, and flicked the flint on his lighter as he held it to a puddle of gas.

The puddle lit quickly, the flickering flame beginning to creep along its liquid trail into the kitchen.

22

The dream had been jumbled and chaotic, images of Nurse Dawn running, blood spraying out like fine red mist from Gerry Dahlen's chest at a bullet's impact...

Bob's leg started to kick. His brain clued in that he was dreaming just as he began to regain consciousness.

Something smelled bad.

It was a sharp, sour smell, something old but familiar.

Chloroform.

He wondered how long he'd been out. His head was a little foggy, but nowhere near as bad as it should've been. Most operatives didn't bother with the chemical, as it would take several minutes of high-dose exposure to knock someone out.

They dosed me, but they messed it up.

The room was hot. It took him a couple of seconds to reconstruct what had taken place. He opened his eyes and looked around. The kitchen was burning, flames licking the bottoms of the wall. He felt heat on his ankle. He looked down to see a flame the size of a saltshaker creeping up the outside of his jeans.

Shit, shit, shit!

Bob shook his legs frantically, the ankle binding not tight enough to prevent all movement. He leaned back on his tail-bone and lifted his feet, shaking them furiously, then rolled over, trying to avoid twisting his right shoulder out of joint as he smothered the burning denim.

He knew he had to act quickly. Gas had been spread randomly, the floor around him on fire in spots, vinyl tile bubbling and melting. On the opposite wall, the flame jumped, suddenly moving higher, licking the corner of the ceiling.

He yanked at the rope around his wrists. It wouldn't give, the knot tightening. Bob frantically scanned the room for something in reach that could cut through it.

Wait a second. You're in a kitchen, Bob. Think.

He pulled his feet in close so that he could hop to his feet. He hopped a few steps to the right. Then he crouched again, falling onto his backside. He leaned backwards, using his toes to pry the kitchen drawer open.

If the Greens were like most people, it would be a cutlery drawer, Bob figured.

The room was getting hotter, flames on the floor licking his elbows, scalding him. He tried to rub them back and forth to smother them. He reached up again with his feet and jammed his toes as far under the drawer handle as he could. Then he pulled his knees back, the momentum yanking the drawer clear of its sliders.

It crashed to the ground, cutlery and kitchen knives spilling out. He turned onto his side and shuffled as quickly as he could to the nearest large knife. He grabbed it with his bound hands by the blade, maneuvering it to between his knees, using them to grasp the handle. They immobilized the knife and held it steady so that he could move his hands back and forth, sawing the rope against its sharpened edge.

The room was smoky, and he coughed. Even low to the ground, there would soon be too much to inhale without choking to death on it.

Flames roared up the front and back walls. His pant leg caught ablaze again. Bob ignored it, sawing against the rope.

"Come on, come on, you little..." The rope parted with a snap, his hands free. He grabbed the knife and sliced through the loop around his ankles.

Bob frantically beat on the flaming pant leg, extinguishing it. He rose to a low crouch and moved to the door, trying to avoid burning vinyl. The smoke was stinging his eyes, and he coughed twice, spitting out loose phlegm.

He opened the door a sliver and looked through the gap. He could just make out a man standing near the back fence.

They're watching the exits. If he had a few minutes to wait, firefighters would probably arrive on scene, preventing the bikers from trapping him inside.

But you don't have a few minutes to wait, Bob. Think.

The kitchen sink had a spray hose attachment. It wasn't enough water or pressure to help with the fire, but...

He reached over and grabbed the spray head, then dropped it again. It was already burning hot. He grabbed a tea towel from the adjacent rack, its edges beginning to smolder. He used it to hold the spray head, then turned on the tap full force. He angled it towards himself, soaking himself down in a matter of seconds.

Bob headed for the kitchen door to the central hallway.

He held his arms up to shield his face from the heat, flames billowing up the walls.

He stayed crouched slightly, to remain as much below the smoke as possible. But it was still hard, lungs beginning to burn and feel tight.

He pushed along the hallway. Behind him, he heard glass shattering, the heat having cracked the kitchen windows beyond stability, glass tumbling to the counters and ground outside.

The Greens' downstairs bathroom was along the north side of the house. He barreled through the door. His head was beginning to feel woozy, disjointed from breathing in carbon monoxide. He stepped up onto the toilet, not worrying about weight, feeling the cover begin to bend under his bulk. Light streamed through the smoked-glass window above it.

He threw himself forward, full force, the wooden window frame buckling. He crashed through the pane of glass and fell hard, to the firm ground below.

23

Bob breathed in clearer air, his eyes and nose streaming. He rolled away from the spot where he'd landed, towards the side fence.

He shook his head, trying to clear cobwebs, then coughed twice, three times, each harder than the one before, last traces of smoke exhaled from his lungs.

If he was lucky, the breaking window would've just sounded like more cracking from heat. The front of his shirt made a perfunctory towel as he wiped off his face, clearing away the tears, grime and snot.

The home was engulfed, heat beginning to emanate off it in waves. He staggered to his feet.

The fence was a little over five feet tall. He clambered over it to the neighbors' yard. It was wooden, made of slats. If he stayed low and followed the fence line, it would offer cover until he was clear.

He followed it around the back of the property, to the far side. He climbed yet another fence, putting another property between him and his captors.

He crept up to the back gate and looked past it to the alley beyond.

Two of them were there, arms crossed, watching the house burn. Not far past them, another neighbor to the east was leaning over her back fence, watching them, suspicious but oblivious to their role.

Bob stayed inside the garden, following the far fence line until he was in the front yard. He looked around the corner of the house. The other two were on the other side of the road, watching their handiwork. A handful of residents who evidently hadn't gone to church were standing nearby. Several were on phones, suggesting the fire department had already been called. A uniformed cop was corralling the onlookers into a group to keep them watchable.

He checked his pockets. They'd taken the burner phone and the guard's pistol and knife, but they'd missed the car keys, or not bothered with them. He had no way to even contact the Greens except to drive back to the motel.

Just as well. They wouldn't want to see this.

He looked down at his charred trouser leg. The skin underneath was scalded, but other than that, he'd been lucky, he knew.

He retreated ten steps and climbed the fence to the next neighbor. Once he was four more houses clear, he used the gate to exit into the back alley and headed back toward the church and the waiting Honda.

At the church, parishioners were gathered outside, the service just ending. They stood and chatted amiably, but most were facing toward the plume of smoke from six blocks south.

Pastor Bevan was on the top step, a Bible in one hand, his phone in the other.

"Yes. Yes, sir, that's fine. Thank you for keeping us informed. Lord bless. Uh-huh. Okay, bye now." He ended the call as Bob approached.

"Bob, My Lord... you look terrible," the young preacher acknowledged with a grim nod. "What happened?"

Bob shook his head. "It wasn't good." He'd seen his face in the rearview mirror, soot stained, cut.

The pastor's face fell. "Was anyone hurt?"

"No, but the Greens' house is going up as we speak."

They both turned toward the road, drawn by the sound of sirens approaching. A moment later, the chatter outside the church was drowned out by their klaxons. The fire trucks zoomed by, one after the other.

The pastor waited until they were out of sight. "We have to call them," he said. He looked down at his phone.

"No." Bob held up a palm. "No, I'll tell them in person. If they come down here... well, chances are the bikers won't act, with cops and firefighters around. But it's dangerous exposure. Getting them out again without being followed or threatened could be tough."

"I understand." Pastor Bevan sighed. "I do wonder when this will all end."

"Soon," Bob said. "I promise."

ob's anger was building, but he tried to concentrate on the road, on other traffic. His hand gripped the wheel with white-knuckle tension.

He wanted to step on the gas, to zip in and out of the congestion. The sooner he got back to the motel, the sooner he could tear off the bandage and break the news to the Greens that their home was gone.

But he had to be careful, he knew. He had ensured he wasn't being tailed from Colbert Street. Instead, he took a long route, turning left every few blocks, then right, then heading back south and east. The sidewalks seemed quiet, but Bob didn't notice. His focus was split between the road and controlling his temper.

The old you would've shot those three jackasses through the forehead before they had time to think.

Three bullets, three fewer problems for society.

Go on.

Have a drink, Bob.

You just survived a house fire. You let a guy get the drop on you because you were so damn tense you weren't operationally ready. You have to be relaxed to do the job.

Relax.

Have a drink.

His inner voice wouldn't shut up. He turned on the car radio and hit the first "preset" button. It was a talk show on 99.5 FM, WRNO. They were discussing the benefits of federal electoral debates. He didn't care about the content; he just needed background white noise. He turned it up slightly and turned his concentration back to the road.

He was coasting in idle, the Honda rolling through the motel parking lot, when he heard the gunshots.

Bob put it back into drive and floored the gas. He threw the wheel right, back end sliding out in a squeal of tires and smoke, as the car swung behind the main building.

Two men in brown suits and tan shirts were trying to force their way into the couple's room. One had a pistol in hand.

Bob slammed on the brakes, threw the car into park and got out, not bothering to slam the door. His hand went to his waist – and he realized the bikers had disarmed him.

It didn't matter. In the moment, all that mattered was protecting that couple. He screamed at the men as he sprinted towards them, still thirty yards away. *"Hey! Stop! You! Stop!"*

The two men heard the commotion. The man with the gun raised it in Bob's direction.

Bob dove sideways, behind a rusting Oldsmobile parked by the first unit door. The crack was loud even from a distance. He heard the slugs tear through the car's sheet-metal body and out the other side.

If they decided to pin him down, eventually they'd wing

him, Bob knew. The car lowered his target profile, but it wouldn't stop bullets.

He needed an exit strategy, a way to get—

His thoughts were interrupted by the roar of a big engine. He stayed low and looked around the corner of the car's back end. A Cadillac SUV backed out of a space near the room, tires squealing, body leaning. Its driver hit the gas, and it shot past him, clipping the curb before coming down hard on Crowder Boulevard.

A moment later, it was out of sight.

Bob sprinted back to the room. The door was ajar. He tried to push it open, but something obstructed it two-thirds of the way. He squeezed through the gap.

Pastor Green was lying on his back, clutching his side, a bloodstain on his shirt growing, a second nearer his shoulder. Wanda was crying, holding him.

Bob ran over to the room phone and dialed 911.

"New Orleans Emergency."

"A man's been shot. Twice, once in the shoulder, another in the right midsection. Please hurry!"

"Hold for just a moment." The line went momentarily silent. "An ambulance is on its way, sir. I'm going to give you some instructions now, and I need you to follow them, okay? We need to prevent bleeding."

Bob listened as the dispatcher finished up, half paying attention. He already knew how to staunch a wound. Pastor Green's life relied on the ambulance getting there as quickly as possible.

25

W anda Green stirred to consciousness.

She was sitting up, in New Orleans East Hospital's Emergency waiting area, near her husband's room, clutching her purse ahead of her. She had a black eye, a result of Don's elbow catching her by mistake as he'd held back the pair at the door.

They'd seemed like nice men, and he'd been in the bathroom. She'd been careful and put the chain on, but they'd immediately tried to barge past it. The chain had snapped just as Don got there.

He was so strong, a bull of a man even at sixty-nine years old. He'd leaned into that door, muscles straining against the efforts of two adults. After what seemed a scant few seconds, one had managed to get a gun barrel around the corner of the door.

Don had taken two shots, but he'd kept fighting, refusing to go down even as his blood spilled out onto the seashell pink motel carpet.

Now, he was lying helplessly on his back, tubes coming

out of his nose, barrel chest under sheet and blanket, an EKG machine a few feet away pinging a steady tune.

The thought of losing him was terrifying.

She'd buried her first husband, Mike Rice, twenty-five years earlier, a victim of a pack-a-day smoking habit and his own stubbornness about seeing doctors.

She'd gotten past it, moved on to raise her son, Jon, up to be a strong, proud man, a US Marine and then, apparently, a government agent.

And then she'd lost him, too. She'd never even really gotten past it. She still thought about her beautiful, brave boy every day.

He was essential to her, precious.

But he was gone forever, always would be, no matter how much she wished it weren't true.

Not Don, too. Please, Lord. I beg you. Please don't take him away. He loves life too much, people too much, to be taken from us now. Please. He's too good.

She gazed momentarily at the empty seat next to her. It had been so long, so many years, since she'd sat anywhere alone.

Bob had gone to get them coffee. He'd looked shattered as the paramedics had worked on Don. They'd leaned over her husband on the motel floor, trying CPR and then using the small white paddles, placing them on his chest. They'd jolted him with electricity to get his big heart started again.

Bob had to leave when the police arrived, with just enough time to grab his overnight bag and head out the interior corridor door. He'd met her at the hospital thirty minutes later, then disappeared again for two hours when the detectives had shown up to ask them questions.

She'd told them about the bikers, the fire the other night,

the news about their house. But she'd had to be honest and tell them these men did not match any of that; they'd been Mexican or maybe Arab, in tan suits, sunglasses. She had no idea who they were.

The detectives had tried to steer her back to the possibility that they were working with the bikers, but Wanda knew better than to hedge about something so important, so likely to have more consequences down the road.

Consequences.

She wondered if Don had considered consequences when he'd walked across the street the other morning to confront those men. He felt protected by his faith, she knew, even as he preached to others that the Lord lets us guide our own path.

It was a singularly foolish decision, she supposed, but a brave one. He cared about other people far more than he cared about himself.

She didn't notice the set of plain brown dress shoes until they were almost under her nose. She looked up as Bob proffered a paper cup of coffee.

"Thank you, dear," she said, trying to smile, but unable to find the strength. "I feel pretty tired, I must say."

He sat down next to her. "Wanda... Nothing I can say is going to be enough to make this up to you, to make this right."

She turned and studied him in profile. He looked forlorn but focused. He really was blaming himself, the poor man, just like he did with Jon. *He didn't start their dispute with the bikers, Don did. He didn't sign Jon up for foreign service, Jon did.*

But in both cases, he wore his failure to save them as badges of shame.

He needed to hear it wasn't so. She needed to be brave, at least for a few minutes.

"It ain't on you to fix this, Bob. Never was," she said. "Folk being good does not make them wards of Bob Singleton. You are not their guardian angel. Nobody has to bear that kind of responsibility over other men, not really."

He didn't look convinced at all. "My decisions left both of them vulnerable. I miscalculated on them finding you at the motel. I miscalculated on the risk in Tehran of a betrayal."

She took a deep breath. "Now, I've had just about enough of that hooey!" Wanda insisted. "You ever consider that by taking all the blame, you're disempowering them, Bob? You're saying they weren't men at all, just puppets you pushed down the wrong alley at the wrong time of night. That's insulting, to Don, to Jon, to what my son stood for. To what Don still stands for, and will again once he gets out of here."

She could see him taken aback by the forcefulness of the statement, but he'd needed to hear it.

"Leadership matters," Bob said defensively. "I'm not trying to insult either of them. But they listened to me—"

"Which was their choice." As bad as the circumstances were, there seemed to be something deeper eating at the young man. "We still love you for doing what you did, but you are not their guardian angel."

He nodded twice, curtly, but didn't say anything.

"What happened to you?" she said directly. "I mean, if you don't mind my asking. What set you to thinking every time someone you know is hurt, you bear the responsibility?"

"I... ah... I mean... I don't know. It's not that, it's just..."

"You lose someone, son? Someone close?"

He nodded. "But that was a long time ago. I just... can't let it happen again, not if there's any chance..."

She leaned over and touched his cheek. He looked weary, slumped forward like the energy had been sapped from him. He looked like a man who wanted to cry, but could no longer summon the tears.

"It's enough to be good, Bob. It's enough to try your hardest. None of us gets to do more than that, not all the time. Sometimes, life's beyond us. Sometimes life is beyond control."

"I know. I know that, but..."

"No buts! That's how it should be. If it wasn't, men like Don – men who are also strong and proud and brave – wouldn't fulfill their purpose. If we didn't have free will, self-determination, what would the point of any of it be? They'd just be following your perfect lead. Now, does that make any sense to you?"

She thought she detected the barest hint of a smile. On one level, it irritated her slightly to have to be strong right then for this broken man. But she tried to think about the compassion Don would show.

"I have a friend in Chicago; she'd get along with you just great," he said. "She... touched on some of this before, the last time someone I knew got into deep trouble."

"Sounds like a bright woman," Wanda said.

There, that was definitely a smile. That was something.

"You don't worry about Don," she said. "I ain't lying, this stuff scares the heck out of me. But I know that man. I know he'd walk through concrete to do right, and he ain't going nowhere. Not yet."

Bob was silent for a few seconds, staring off into space.

"You okay?" Wanda asked.

He nodded. "Yeah. Yeah... I just can't help wondering how I miscalculated so badly with respect to The Damned MC. I figured they'd head back to the street, and sure enough, there were a bunch there. I didn't see Deacon Riggs, but... it was enough to make me think that was their focus, not looking for you two."

She realized his error. "No, Bob, that's not... you weren't wrong, son. The two men at the door, they weren't with the bikers, I'm sure of that. Those men, they had accents. They knocked and said they were with the government, and I was going to open the door, figuring you must have sent them. But at the last moment, I remembered what you said about being extra cautious, so I put the chain on."

"You probably saved both your lives," Bob said. "Accents? Like..."

"I thought maybe Mexican, at first. But that wasn't right. I mean, I was a Zonie for a long time, so I know my Mexican. Then I thought maybe it was more like Omar Sharif. He was Egyptian, I believe. So maybe it was an Arabian accent, something like that?"

He didn't show much reaction to that, Wanda figured, but his eyes betrayed his confusion. "That doesn't make no sense, does it?" she asked.

"Not really, no. Jon died on a mission in Tehran, so that's technically Persians. The language might sound the same to a western ear. But there's no reason to think they had any personal beef with Jon. And that was fifteen years ago."

"So who were they?" Wanda wondered aloud.

"No idea. But I'm going to find out." He looked over at the room. "Starting tomorrow."

She shook her head. "Nope, you can't stay here. You said you couldn't be dealing with the police, am I right?"

"That's right. People in Washington are looking for me, and they have a long reach."

"Then you'd better hightail it out of here soon. They've got a policeman coming to keep watch at eight o'clock. Detectives are worried the men who did this might come try here. Said they might want to ask more questions, too."

Bob looked up at the waiting room clock. It was 7:38. "Okay. I'll get a new phone and call you as soon as I can with the number. I'll have to find a motel well away from here, though."

"I understand."

He got up to leave.

"Bob..." she said, giving his pant leg a brief tug. "You be strong, now. Whatever you've got bundled up inside, don't give it the satisfaction of taking over."

"You're a strong woman, Wanda."

"Lost a husband, a son and now our home. But you know what? I'm still here. Don's still here. As long as that's so, we keep on fighting."

"I understand."

"I know you do, son, I know you do. Oh... before I forget..." Wanda leaned over and reached into her purse, by the chair leg. "I've been holding onto this for a long time. Jon said if anything was ever to happen to him, I should make sure it got to his friend Tyler from work."

She withdrew her hand from the purse, holding a white napkin. Inside it was a two-inch-by-four-inch photo of the two men.

Bob felt a swell of sadness as she handed it over, followed by confusion. Jon and Tyler had hardly talked while in the group. With the exception of Tyler trying to save the younger man, they barely seemed connected. "I don't know how to tell you this, but..."

"Tyler's dead. Yes, dear. When he didn't try to contact Jon for years, we sort of figured the government had some story about his passing, too. I just figured it's better off with one of the people he most trusted and respected."

Bob held the photo between his thumb and forefinger. Fifteen years had passed surprisingly quickly. Then he realized she probably wanted it back. "Unless you'd like to..."

She waved him off. "No, that's fine. I didn't really know this Tyler fella. He visited a few times, is all, and we've got a thousand pictures of Jon. You keep it, for old times' sake."

Bob nodded, trying not to seem grim in the moment.

"I'll get going," Bob said. "I'll find us a new place to stay, and call you from my new phone as soon as able. Okay?"

"You do what you have to," Wanda said, with a curt nod. "Let me know what's what. I'll take care of Don."

26

A t a corner store, Bob bought a disposable cell phone with a data package. From the Honda, he called Nick Velasco.

He hung up after two rings, then called again. He repeated the action, a signal the pair had set up in case Bob needed to contact him from a new number.

Velasco answered on ring six. "What's up, Alpha? A new number already? You just picked that up in Miami."

Bob could never be sure if Velasco was mocking him, using his old title, or if old habits just died hard. There was no percentage in correcting him. He'd come to realize he would need the convicted hacker's help more often than he'd hoped.

"I ran into complications. The people I came to see have run into some trouble."

"Yikes. I know you, dude. If you say 'some trouble,' you mean serious fucking trouble."

"Yeah, well... something of the sort, you betcha. Local criminals working on some sort of blockbusting scheme."

After years of working with, for and against the best interests of the CIA's partner, the National Security Agency, Bob had learned about monitoring software and to avoid specifics, even on a clean line. Depending on how well-heeled Denny Roulette's employers were, it was possible they'd engaged proper pros by now and were monitoring local cell phone traffic for keywords.

Nicky cut to the chase. He had his own business to tend to, Bob supposed. He always did. "So... what's up? If you need me, then you have something – I mean, keeping in mind the running 'favor' tab I have going."

"As long as the same rules apply," Bob said. "I won't kill anyone for you. I won't rob anyone of their legal possessions. I won't intimidate anyone."

"Hey, that's all still cool with me, boss man," Nicky said. "So what's the deal?"

"I need an app that will automatically record calls on the cloned SIM, whether I'm listening in or not."

"Done. It'll be winging its way to you in a compressed file in a few minutes. That's not enough for me to get another favor, is it?"

"Not really. Let's call it one-third of one. You can earn another if you find me a new safe house, preferably in the far southwest of the city, or just beyond... That would make life infinitely easier."

"Will do. Upscale, downscale, public, private..."

"As private as possible, sleeping for three... sorry, make that two." Bob winced even as he said it. Wanda's gratitude aside, his typical sense of having contributed more problems than he'd solved was coming to the fore. "Just... do it quickly, okay? Things here are unraveling a bit, and I need a bolt-hole. Make it cheap, too. I'm running light on cash."

"Hah! Don't worry about that part, I'll pick it up. You know I have fairly... *fluid* access to other people's credit."

"Just make it someone lousy, okay? Don't leave me thinking Joe Citizen is paying my bills."

"Okay, done and done. Man!" Nicky let the exclamation hang there.

"What?"

"Oh. Nothing. Just thinking about the list of nefarious shit I'm going to ask you to pull is making me gleeful."

"Stay cool, Nicky."

"Later, boss man."

Bob ended the call as he arrived at the car. He opened the driver's side door and climbed in. It was another hot one, the clouds high and thin, the sky a deep blue sheet, humidity rising off the parking lot asphalt.

He pointed the car towards the western suburbs. Whatever Nicky found, it wasn't going to be much worse than the motel they'd been chased out of. As long as Wanda was okay with it, he figured.

THE DOCTOR'S expression was unreadable, absolutely neutral. His heels clipped the tile floor as he walked down the corridor towards Wanda's waiting room chair, an associate and a nurse trailing him.

She could see from his pointed stare he was heading right over to her, so she rose, her joints aching and creaking a little. She was only fifty-nine, but arthritis was already an issue. She tried to stay active, to ward it off, but the few days prior had eliminated any chance of getting out and about.

"Doctor," she greeted him. "They said you'd be around

eventually. Didn't know it was going to be four hours after we got here, mind..."

He looked uncomfortable. "My sincere apologies, Mrs. Green. It's been a busy day for shootings in the city, and emergency has been swamped. I thought you'd like to know your husband has undergone his preliminary prep. We were quite fortunate that both slugs went right through him without hitting major organs. However, he lost a lot of blood, and we have some serious repairs to do, okay?"

"Bottom-line it, Doc. I ain't getting any younger."

"The prognosis is pretty positive, given that he was shot twice," the surgeon said. "We've got some repair work to do that we'll be ready to begin in about ten minutes. The serious bleeding has already been stemmed, and his vitals are all holding positive. We never promise anything, particularly as surgical risks rise with age, but we'll do the best we can."

Was that supposed to be optimistic? Wanda wondered. He might as well have said he was going to flip a coin.

"When will I know something? When can I see Don again?"

"It'll be a few hours. If you have somewhere else that would be more comfortable, we do recommend people try to take their mind off things."

"I'll be staying right here; never you mind that," she insisted.

"Okay then, I'll make sure to have someone stop by and make sure you're doing all right."

"Never mind that," she said, crossing her arms. "You just set to fixing him up."

The surgeon and his associates headed down the hall.

Wanda was about to sit down again when she felt a tap on her right shoulder.

The man behind her was smiling warmly. He was middle-aged, short, bald, with a goatee and dark, beady eyes. He looked sort of like TV host Montel Williams, was her first impression, right down to the green-brownish plaid three-piece suit, which seemed pretty fancy for a hospital visit.

He extended his hand to shake, and she did so. "Mrs. Green? I'm Detective Pullman Lewis, New Orleans homicide."

"Well, I'm pleased to meet you, sir, but there haven't been any homicides today, that I know of, no sir. My husband's going to make it."

"I'm rooting for him, ma'am; you can bank on that," he said genially. "My division handles cases of 'attempted' homicides, too, when a determination can be made that that was the case."

She wasn't sure how to deal with him. Don worked with the police whenever possible, but they made plenty of her friends nervous. They didn't have the best reputation in the Big Easy. The one thing she was sure of was that she couldn't mention Bob. If he and Jon had been involved in sensitive government work, there was a reason for his anonymity and constant movement.

"Okay," she eventually offered. "I'll help however I can, of course."

"You told the uniformed officer who asked the initial questions that you figured the two men were Arabic. Is there a reason for that in particular, ma'am?"

"Are you asking me if I'm racist against Arabic people, Detective? I sure hope not."

"Nothing of the sort, Mrs. Green. I didn't mean to imply..."

"Uh-huh. I lived in Arizona for years, so I know what Mexican Spanish sounds like. This wasn't that. This was more, you know... in-the-throat sort of speech."

"When they approached the door, what did they say?"

"Well, as I recall, they knocked real hard, sort of bang-bang-bang, three times in a row, like they were angry or urgent or something. Don and I were being real cautious on account of—"

"The fire at the biker place across from your house. I read the file on that incident," Lewis said. "That's why I asked about the description. It doesn't sound like there's any obvious connections there, but at the same time..."

"It does seem a heck of a coincidence, doesn't it?" she offered. "Can't say as I ever saw any Arabic gentlemen in our neck of the woods, excepting Mr. Choudhry, who's one of the East Indian Muslims, so not Arab per se."

"The bikers. They started moving in when?"

"Oh, I believe the first house they moved into was a little over a year ago now, about four blocks north and two east of us. Don did a little sniffing around and got a copy of the title from public records. It seems the same company has bought up at least five homes now, and that's just those we've noticed change hands, so..."

The detective appeared fascinated by that, deep in thought, looking beyond her for a moment. He broke away from the trance and fixed her with a stare. "You had a friend staying with you, according to some folk."

Dang it. There was always someone among the biddies on the street who couldn't keep to her own business. Wanda wasn't going to lie to a police officer. But she'd been around a year or two and knew a few things about tact.

"We did, for just one night before he moved on, an old friend of my son. I think he was intending to head west."

"Uh-huh. And what was your son's friend's name?"

"Tyler," she said. "Tyler Gaines." Again, not technically a lie, given the question asked. "My son passed some fifteen years ago now, serving his country."

The detective looked slightly solemn. "You have my condolences, and thank you for his service, ma'am," he said. "Did he leave any kind of number, this Tyler fella?"

"He did not."

"And where out west was Mr. Gaines headed?"

"He didn't say," she said – also technically true. Bob was headed to Texas and eventually San Diego, he'd mentioned. But Tyler Gaines hadn't told her a dang thing.

He thought on that some. Then he changed the subject. "Do you have somewhere to stay tonight, Mrs. Green? Can we offer you some help to find something?"

"I'll be just fine, officer, thank you," she said, deliberately downgrading his rank. She wanted the man to feel at least a little awkward, questioning an elderly woman outside her husband's recovery room. "I believe someone has made arrangements for us already, but if I need you... well, do you have a business card or some such thing?"

Get his card and he should read the cues, she thought. *Time to leave the victim's wife be.*

As if stage-managed, Lewis sighed a little and reached into his pocket for his wallet. He produced a card and handed it to her. "If I were in your shoes, Mrs. Green, I would try to think real hard on anything that might make it easier for us to catch whoever did this."

"I'll be sure to do that, thank you," she said, taking the card. She backed up a half-pace and sat down on the vinyl waiting room chair. "Good evening, Detective. It was nice meeting you."

Lewis snapped the wallet shut and held it aloft for a split second, as if about to wag it authoritatively. Instead, his expression shifted, an understanding that now was not the time. He nodded politely once before heading back down the corridor.

27

Nick Velasco had done himself proud, Bob figured. The new safe house was an online vacation rental unit, a two-bedroom condo apartment in Harahan with a view of the Mississippi River Trail.

It was a busy place, but it appeared the vast majority of residents were also there temporarily, flocks of out-of-state license plates dotting the condo unit's parking lot.

It also had a Breaux Mart within walking distance. After getting the keys and securing his extra cash and IDs under the oven grease drop tray, he'd paid the store a visit.

He'd picked up some basic groceries: eggs, milk, cream, Greek yogurt, bacon, ham, chicken thighs, and a handful of frozen veggies.

He'd paused outside the milk cooler, staring at his own reflection in the tinted glass, the store laid out behind him. The image staring back seemed like a different person. Certainly, it wasn't the long-haired, disheveled bum who would have been there just two months earlier.

Everything had changed that fateful day in Chicago.

He'd stopped three punks from terrorizing a clerk and wound up with a chest-load of rock salt, and then in Nurse Dawn's world, helping a kid named Marcus rebuild his life.

He walked back to the condo, taking the elevator to the fourth floor.

Inside, he'd set the brown paper bags down on the open-plan kitchen's marble breakfast bar and taken a deep breath, drinking in the normalcy of it. He felt strangely civilized, as if a moment of ordinary life had made its way past the noise and confusion, the fog of war.

He began to put the food away, storing the eggs and ham in the fridge.

He opened the freezer to put the chicken away.

The freezer was not empty.

The bottle sat on its side next to the freezer's only other occupant, a half-full bag of ice. The bottle's "Ron Bacardi" label was partially obscured by frost.

The brown liquor didn't quite make it to the neck, suggesting it was less than half full of rum.

Bob stared at it.

Sometimes, life just had a way of throwing up tests.

It was probably a good six or eight ounces.

Enough to get drunk, anyway.

But that was the old you.

This is the New Bob, Bob 2.0.

He reached in and withdrew the bottle. The glass was freezing. He turned and set it down on the breakfast bar.

It was the good stuff, too, Bacardi Dark. He'd had a forty-ounce bottle a few years earlier, a Christmas gift left behind on the rear step of a business, still there on Boxing Day. It had been theft, sure, but not one that would be missed.

But theft, nonetheless. The dark liquid had burned his

throat pleasingly, drunk straight from the bottle, cold after being left outside in a Chicago winter. He'd been oblivious for more than a day, warm and safe in his flop behind the dumpster.

Safe. Strange use of the word, Bob.

He studied the booze. There were pieces of ice floating in it, the water content freezing even as the alcohol separated.

Don't you even think about it.

What would Nurse Dawn say? That there was nothing good to be gained from it. Even when he'd been a drunk, it had been to become oblivious, disconnected, insensible. It hadn't been about feeling good. That was just the lie he'd told himself for years.

He picked up the bottle, then stepped on the pedal to the adjacent trash can. The lid opened. He dropped the bottle in.

After making an omelet, he sat down at the small writing desk and computer plugin along one wall of the living room and took out the phone. He followed Nick's instructions to set up the recording app. He set it down on the desktop and plugged it into its wall charger, to ensure it wouldn't die before gathering the intel he needed.

He checked the wall clock. It was 8:35 p.m. He'd called Wanda with the address already, but she was adamant about not coming until they kicked her out of the hospital.

He leaned back in the desk chair and closed his eyes for a moment.

BOB WOKE SUDDENLY, dreams instantly forgotten. He felt an immediate sense of panic at not recognizing his surroundings.

Then he remembered.

The new rental.

He checked his watch. It was just after six in the morning. He'd slept, motionless, in the chair for nearly ten hours.

He looked over at the burner phone. There were no new calls.

Bob took a shower and changed into fresh clothes, an innocuous black T-shirt and jeans to go with his summer jacket.

He checked his other phone on the way to the kitchen, but there were no calls from Wanda. Eventually, they would tell her she had to get some rest, probably give her a police escort. But a day after her husband was shot, leniency was to be expected.

That meant she probably wouldn't show up at the condo until that afternoon or the following day if the police were being compassionate. He'd left the spare key with the building's resident manager in case he wasn't there.

He went through his morning exercises. Despite no longer being recommended, due to punishing the joints, he followed the Canadian Air Force 5BX calisthenics program from the 1970s, a grueling half-hour regimen of stretches, push-ups and jogging in place.

Another half-hour passed as he cooled down. He cooked an egg-white omelet and watched the news on the small flat-screen provided for guests.

The shooting investigation was offering nothing new, but the story did say police were aware of the biker harassment and equally stumped by the connection to two men at the motel.

He glanced over at the cloned phone.

How long before Denny Roulette says something incriminat-

ing? He had no way of knowing. But given the troubles of the two prior days, he expected it wouldn't take—

The cloned phone began to vibrate.

MONDAY MORNING CITY planning meetings were never easy.

Denny Roulette's head ached slightly. He'd had too much brandy the night before, falling asleep in front of the TV, which he practically never did. He felt foggy; he remembered making dinner, then sitting down to knock back a few brandies.

And that was it.

He was irritated as he paced the waiting area outside city council chambers at just after eight, hands jammed into the side pockets of his suit jacket, shiny black dress shoes sinking into the pile carpet.

Alderman Ron Leavy had asked him to wait at his office, but Roulette knew that would give him reasons to slough him off, such as the intercession of an assistant in "urgent need" of help.

If he intercepted him outside chambers, he could hold Leavy to his promise of a coffee at Mammoth Espresso. The chairman of the city planning appeals committee held considerable sway over development in New Orleans. He was an important man to have as a friend, albeit one with broad and sometimes expensive tastes.

His phone rang. He checked the number.

Damn it. Can't skip this one.

"Denny Roulette."

"Hold for Mr. Habsi."

The line went silent for a few seconds. Roulette's heart raced a little. Sammy Habsi rarely called. His casino kept him busy, along with God only knew what else. Roulette didn't ask his clients those kinds of questions.

But lately, the calls had become frequent, terse. Habsi wanted progress, and Roulette had little to report.

"Denny. Sammy."

"Sammy! Good to hear from you."

"Is it?"

"Of course, Sammy, always..."

"Because I thought I made it clear that I expected at least six listings by now, at fire-sale prices. The clock is ticking, Denny. If we do not hit my target price for the cumulative purchase... well, I will be most displeased."

"I heard your men found the pastor—"

"Pttth! Please, Denny, no specifics, even on my private line. The matter appears to have been dealt with, for the most part..."

"The friend?"

"He was not present. They encountered surprising resistance, and a man showed up towards the end who forced them to retreat without finishing things. But I do not expect problems in that area."

Roulette figured that was optimistic. As tough as the old man was, his new friend had caused Riggs's boys more trouble. The bikers thought he'd gone up with the old man's house, but firefighters at the scene had claimed there was no one inside.

Still, Habsi didn't need to know that. The Saudi-American did not react well to failure.

"We'll get back on it this week, get things going again. Don't worry, Sammy. I'm all over it."

"This best be the case, Denny. You have one more week

to get at least three homes listed. I have people to answer to, which means you have people to answer to."

"Of course, Sammy, of course."

"In two days, I am hosting a party for members of city council at my home. I expect by the end of that meal to have several of them agreeable, enough to carry the bypass vote when it comes up. I want this mystery man dealt with by then, I want that pastor out of the way, and I want those people terrified."

"It'll get done, Sammy, you have my word. The pastor... do we have to...?"

"Of course. He may even have figured out what is going on, and he clearly has no trouble hiring muscle of his own. That's got to be who this mystery man is. If that guy doesn't show, none of this happens. Your hoodlum friends beat up the old man, people sell their homes, but nobody gets hurt, other than money out of pocket. Now... now we've got to deal with him, make sure he does not come back to cause more problems."

Roulette fairly sighed, but he didn't try to contradict the man. "Okay, so they can take care of that too, then. But, I mean, with this fire and all, it's not going to be easy. Police are watching the neighborhood."

"Have your boys make a statement. Something really bad that will scare the rest."

"Really bad? You mean like..."

"I don't know. They are scum; have them behave like scum. They can have some fun with one of the old ladies. Or perhaps help them part with a few pets. Just don't tell me about it. I swear, man, you cannot cost so much and be so careless."

"Okay, Sammy." Roulette's voice had taken on a fatigued edge.

"Get it done, Denny. I would hate for you to have to take up a new line of work, say, feeding the bayou alligators."

Habsi ended the call. Roulette stood in the council atrium, staring at his phone.

He needed to get hold of Riggs. The biker boss was worried about cops paying the neighborhood attention now, but that wasn't Roulette's problem. He'd been promised effective muscle, and the bill was coming due.

BOB LISTENED in as the call ended, the man they'd identified as Sammy Habsi hanging up on Roulette abruptly.

Habsi had not been pleased.

He stared at the phone for a few seconds, although he was so lost in thought, so mired in sudden depression, it might as well have been a week, for all he'd have noticed.

What had Habsi said? That if he hadn't gotten involved, they had no plans to hurt anyone. Pastor Don would've been beaten up, but he'd be home and safe now, not lying in an Intensive Care Unit with two bullet holes in him. His home with Wanda wouldn't be gutted by fire.

If I hadn't gotten involved...

That sinking feeling had returned, the sense that the world was better off when he wasn't taking part in it.

Pastor Green had opened his home to a complete stranger, a friend of a stepson he never knew, and his reward for that was to be clinging to life, his home gone.

You feel like a piece of total shit again, don't you, Bob?

Yup. Piece of shit. That was about the sum of it.

You know, there's no reason to be wallowing in self-pity. You need to put that shit behind you.

He knew he did. The inner voice wasn't lying to him, for a change, making excuses. The inner voice was right. The inner voice—

You need a drink.

Goddamn it. Why is this so hard?

Ah! Hear me out, now! You don't have to become a drunk again. You don't have to drop out and stop helping folks or anything like that. That's the old Bob.

The new Bob can handle one drink.

He wanted to call Dawn Ellis in Chicago. She'd know exactly what to say, he knew. She'd remind him of that devil on his shoulder, the one promising a path to happiness, then leading him back down the road to misery.

But he couldn't call the nurse. The risk her line was being monitored was just too great. She had a burner she'd bought to call him in emergencies, but he didn't have the number, and it wasn't supposed to be a two-way street.

He was the one who needed redemption. He was the one who was supposed to do the saving.

Besides, maybe the voice was right this time, telling it true. There was a bottle in the trash can just twenty feet away.

One drink wasn't going to kill him.

Would Dawn agree?

No. She'd probably say he couldn't do anything stupid without first convincing himself it was smart, or something like that. She'd probably tell him to find a twelve-step program, or some such thing, because that would suit her religious bent.

But Bob knew anything like that would just mean

involving more people in his problems, more exposure, more risks to others who didn't deserve it. Good people.

People like Don.

Then quit, you coward, the voice suggested snidely. *If you're not part of the solution, you're part of the problem. Get out of the way and let the big dogs hunt.*

Or, you know, at the very least, you can just... you know...

Have a drink.

He got up and wandered back to the kitchen. He stared at the trash can, as if it might make his mind up for him, or offer solace that what he was about to do wasn't pathetic.

But it stood silent.

Bob stepped on the pedal, and the trash can lid flipped open. He reached in and retrieved the bottle, his hand suddenly slick from the melting frost.

He pulled it out. Some coffee grounds already in the can came along for the ride, smearing the side of his palm.

Go on. Crack it open. Who's it going to hurt? Don and Wanda don't need you. Not while he's laid up. He ain't going nowhere any time soon, Bobby boy...

The thought of them in Intensive Care – Wanda's face puffy from crying, Don with tubes coming out of him – stopped him short.

He stared at the bottle's label again as it sat in the palm of his right hand. *So many bad memories, masquerading as freedom...*

He dropped the bottle back into the trash can. Then he walked over to the counter, found a paper towel and cleaned off the coffee grounds. He threw away the paper towel and went back to the desk.

There was no time for that shit. No time for self-pity or worry or wallowing. He needed to focus.

At least now he had some sort of timeline. He had to deal with Habsi and the bikers before the week was up, or things were bound to escalate beyond one man's ability to fix them.

In the meantime, he would keep recording Roulette's conversations. He didn't need to gather legitimate evidence on the man that would hold up in court; he just needed enough discussion to link him to Habsi's project. Once it fell apart, Roulette's reputation would be so tarnished he wouldn't be able to lay down a bet in the city, let alone hurt anyone else.

Habsi and the bikers were another matter. They came bearing deadly gifts, which meant an answer with reciprocal force. That was how the game worked, the only rule anyone played by.

He felt a surge of adrenaline, followed by a slight tremor in his hands, a sense of building anxiety. That was how it had been ever since he left the team, ever since Maggie's death. The same electric sense of drive and motivation that used to push him to his goals now produced trepidation, even some fear. Uncustomary doubts were always just around a bend.

You've got a job to do. If you drink at all, you'll just drink more. If you drink at all, you can't do the job. If you don't do the job, more innocent people will be hurt. That's on you, Bob. There's only one priority now, and that's getting it done.

He regulated his breathing using the techniques he'd learned in martial arts, steady inhalations through the nose, exhaling as a normal breath through the mouth, until the slight tremor had almost subsided.

One more day without booze. One more day without the troubles it causes. One more day of getting better.

Works for me.

His hands were calm, the tremor gone.

He picked up the phone and dialed Nick Velasco once more, waiting as it rang. He needed intel on Habsi and Deacon Riggs, at least enough to make some judgments about how they would behave in the coming days.

He needed to make their lives very, very difficult.

28

Clayton Thibodeaux leaned his beefy six-foot frame against the raised shelf by the front window of the small barber shop on Perdido Street. An elderly man was trimming a customer's hair, Thibodeaux just out of his line of sight.

Thibodeaux stroked his broad mustache and studied the old man. He'd always been the most dependable gossip in the city. Maybe times had changed, however.

He'd been patient, waiting ten minutes while the barber dealt with his client. Given how much money he'd paid the informant over the decade prior, it rankled somewhat. Plus, Thibodeaux's luxuriant head of chestnut hair, nearly to his shoulders, made it feel a little like enemy territory.

"This ain't like you, Freddie," Thibodeaux told the man, his Cajun accent as thick as gumbo. "Normally, someone drop a dollar bill in the Quarter, y'all hear before it hits the sidewalk. Heck, y'all could make change before they've retrieved it. But... it's been *two days, bon ami.*"

The barber continued clipping. "You have some friends

you need to keep happy, young Mr. Thibodeaux? You sound more worried than a typical skip trace might warrant."

"Uh-huh."

Freddie stopped clipping for a moment and looked his way again. "That did not sound optimistic. This some kind of criminal thing, young man?"

"Naw! Naw, nothing like that, old man."

"Government? You two done some mercenary work after the military, I know that from your father before he passed." The lack of a prompt answer told the barber all he needed to know. "Uh-huh," he grunted gently before turning back to his client.

"Big money, Freddie. You help me out with this, I'll be real generous. Drop a lagniappe on there for ya." It came out as *lan-yap* to an American-English ear and meant *a little extra something.*

"Never complained about taking your money before now, Mr. Thibodeaux, no, sir."

"But speed's important. The man I'm looking for isn't going to be around long. And like I said... it's been two days."

The barber didn't change his posture, but swiveled his head just enough to glance the younger man's way. "Young Mr. Thibodeaux, as your father no doubt taught you, patience is a virtue. I've got feelers out all over New Orleans. If he's here..." He walked past his client and set the scissors in a jar of blue antiseptic liquid before retrieving a shaving mug and brush. "Eventually, he'll tip one of my people that he's your boy. Tall, thin, dark hair, physically gifted fighter, Good Samaritan complex, Midwestern accent..." He rounded the client again and fluffed the brush in shaving cream. "It narrows it down somewhat. Besides, I'm sure if I don't hear something, whoever Fletcher is paying will."

Thibodeaux scowled at his brother's mention. They were technically partners in the bounty hunting trade, but they'd been competing over everything since childhood. "This guy isn't the type to keep quiet. If he's here, chances are he's been in a dust-up already, another carpetbagging northerner causing trouble."

"Uh-huh, yes, sir. Should make it easier."

He reached around the customer's head with the brush, but the man turned abruptly in his chair. He was frowning, a chubby, pink face framed by ginger locks. "Hey, man... did you say Midwest accent?"

"Yeah... what's up, my man?" Freddie asked.

"My brother slings beer at a bar on the next block from here, The Purple Bird?"

"The biker joint," Freddie said.

"Uh-huh. Yeah... they were talking about some guy yesterday, some dude who sounded like he was out of the Ditka sketch on SNL. Burned down some drug house, kicked the shit out of a couple of the brothers. They figured he was crazy because he was sorta upbeat the whole time. You know, like he was enjoying brawling with a bunch of bikers."

Thibodeaux stood up straight. "Okay, you got my attention, *etoile*. Where they run into this *couyon*, anyhow?"

The man looked up at Freddie, then back at Clay Thibodeaux. "You said something about money?"

29

J ohn Butcher looked surprised when the store's front doorbell rang and Bob walked in. The store owner took a few steps closer to the cash register.

Probably a piece under the counter there, shotgun, something guaranteed to do damage at close range and in close quarters.

"Let me guess," he said, keeping his demeanor casual to avoid accidents, "your right hand is on the stock of a sawed-off pump. Or maybe a double barrel."

He stopped at the counter.

Butcher withdrew his hand. "The latter. That's kind of spooky, dude."

"People and their guns. I don't know if it's always true; I'm not saying that. But if you can read a person's character, you can usually figure out what kind of piece they'd choose."

"Yeah... like I said, that's a little spooky." Butcher crossed his beefy arms. "What next? You tell my future by reading shell casings?"

"Nah. In my experience, nobody gets that right."

"So, what can I do you for? You want to return the gizmo?"

"No, no. I don't imagine you're giving straight cash refunds, and I might need it again. It's not too bulky, and it's got prospects."

"Then?"

"You mentioned doing a fellow Marine a favor."

"I did. You caught that, huh? Smooth move, John! I got all nostalgic."

"Hey, don't feel bad about it," Bob suggested. "I already threw some business your way. I have other things I need that you can supply."

"I sense a 'but' coming."

"But I'm a little tight on cash for everything I need."

"How tight?"

"Depends. I need a piece – a twenty-shot FN 5.7, prefer-ably with the higher-velocity SS190 NATO-standard ammo – the blacktips; some C-4 and a trigger; a GPS tracker; a good listening device that supports battery power. What else...?"

"Okay, while you ponder that..." Butcher did a little mental math. "The piece, bug and C-4 are going to run you two thousand – that's because of the FN, which, as you know, is costly to begin with. I should warn you, too, the 5.7X28mm ammo is going to run you sixty a box... and a hundred and fifty if you want the SS190 armor-piercing variety, because that's some seriously illegal shit. The C-4 trigger will depend on which type you want. How much do you have?"

Bob retrieved the biker's money clip from his boot and counted it out. "I've got... fifteen hundred and twenty in cash, plus..." He retrieved his own clip. "Another three hundred and sixty there. So I'm going to be about four hundred short." He had another forty in his other boot, but that was emergency money, Bob figured.

Butcher leaned on the counter. He scratched at his beard thoughtfully. "Well, now... can we chop some of the cost by making the GPS and the bug loaners?"

Bob shook his head. "Unlikely. I mean, I'll keep an eye out for the possibility, but this one is probably going to end with me getting out of Dodge."

"Okay. Well, what else do you have to offer? I can't eat that much without getting something back."

"I can owe you the difference and a favor. I'm good for both. Ask Nicky. He'll fill you in."

Butcher shrugged. "He sort of did already. I mean, all he said was that I didn't want to know, but that you're, and I quote, 'on the side of the angels.'"

"He has a certain Jersey charm to him."

"I owe Nick big time, so... if he's sure you're good for it, so am I." He turned his attention to the security monitor on the wall by the office door. "Hang on a sec... Street's clear."

Butcher walked over to the counter wicket and opened it, leaving it up. He walked over to the front door and locked it, then flopped over the "open" sign. "The joy of having low foot traffic," he said as he walked back to the counter. "Follow me."

Bob followed Butcher behind the counter. He walked to the filing cabinet at the end of the room and removed a key ring on a stretch cord from his belt. He used a small key to open the first drawer in the middle. Once open, he turned its handle counterclockwise a half-turn. He pulled on it, the handle moving to one side on a small hinge. Behind it was a small red button.

He tapped it.

The cabinet and a section of the wall behind him slid forward, motors whirring gently. After about a quarter foot, it stopped. The motors whirred again, and it moved sideways to reveal an entrance to a stairwell.

"Now, being ex-military, your panties are about to get really wet," Butcher said as he led him down the stairs. "Just remember: this sort of business only works if we keep things to ourselves."

"Not an issue," Bob said. "My life requires working with others."

At the bottom of the stairs, a steel door was painted white. Next to it, on the wall, was a number pad. Butcher blocked Bob's view with his body and punched in a code.

The door lock clicked back with a "clunk." Butcher opened the door.

Bob's eyes widened.

It looked like something out of a trade show for mercenaries. The walls were covered by gun racks for an array of machine guns, long rifles and submachine guns. Racks of pistols sat in the middle of the room. Along the far wall, shelves held grenades, flashbangs, scopes and spyglasses, binoculars, detonators, charges.

Neon lights cast everything in a too-white glow.

"This is…"

"In reasonable demand," Butcher explained. "My client list isn't enormous, but it's global. Some don't last that long, for obvious reasons, but they pass me on to reliable new customers, typically."

Bob picked up a .44 Auto Mag resting in an upright holder on a glass display case. He held it up, the chrome glinting, and sighted along it towards the far wall. The barrel was the length of a small child's arm. "This thing could stop an elephant at twenty feet."

John looked mildly unnerved. "Now, that's an original run 1973 in mint condition. That's going to run a feller right around eight grand. So... maybe put that one back in its spot."

Bob put the gun back down and looked around. He knew he shouldn't have been enjoying himself quite so much, but...

"You mind if I tack a few items onto that list?" he asked as he picked up a blank from a row of cartridges in different calibers. "If you're worried about the tab escalating, you know..."

"I know you're good for it. But... I wouldn't grab too many of those blanks, neither. They're twenty dollars a pop."

"Uh-huh." Bob strolled towards a rack of assault rifles. "It's going to be that kind of shopping trip."

A few extras couldn't hurt, he reasoned, even with his budgetary constraints.

ORLEANS PARISH, Louisiana

THE COOKHOUSE HAD BEEN DESERTED when he'd arrived. It was an old fishing camp for kids, the main bunkhouse converted from housing rows of bunk beds to tables scattered with Bunsen burners.

Diesel had been in his element. He'd spent the first day away from the city drinking cold beer from the generator-powered cooler chest. He'd listened to the radio, gotten nothing new on the fire. He'd spent a few hours on the river nearby, catching catfish and crayfish for a boil.

He'd slept for two nights on one of the plush cots they provided for the workers, complete with half-inch mattress. Compared to the boat, it had been like silk.

Eventually, on Monday morning, he'd remembered to check the storage bunker. Uncovering the giant double doors had required moving aside two picnic tables, a layer of mulch and then a giant tarp.

Once open, he realized just how good his timing had been: the rectangular white packets filled the nook almost to the brim. They looked like soft, powdery sandbags, he figured, a sense of genuine affection coming over the biker for just a few moments.

There had to be twenty kilos, all told, enough that he wouldn't have to worry about money for a long time, even if he only skimmed a few packets off the top.

Now all he needed to do was to figure out how to get it back to civilization. That could require patience. He might have to wait until the situation with the pastor had blown over, or risk sneaking back into New Orleans or Slidell to steal a vehicle. The dirt road in from the subdivision off I-90 would be his route out.

As far as the club knew, he was dead, or at best, missing. If he stayed that way by playing things cautiously, he'd be out of town and rolling in product, and they'd be none the wiser. They'd show up imminently to load the dope, they'd discover some missing, and they'd blame the cooks.

If he jumped the gun, ran down the road and stole a car from the fishing camp, they could be loading it when he got back; he had no idea how soon they'd arrive. Or he could be spotted by one of the club's many tipsters.

It was safer to wait. He'd been able to get the propane turned back on and the stove working. The freezer chest was full of food; they kept the cooks well fed, given the risk and danger they were working under. He'd cooked a ham steak, with French fries, and an apple pie was defrosting in the oven.

It was too bad about Dirty Carl. Diesel sat at the picnic-bench-style table in the small kitchen area and plucked his gumline with a wooden toothpick, thinking about how Carl had looked getting his head smashed, the combination of distress and shock on the man's face.

That part had been pretty funny, and he chuckled at the memory.

But the gator had scared the shit out of him. It had probably come back, dragged Carl off. Not that he was going anywhere on his own.

It wasn't that he'd hated Dirty Carl or anything, he just had never felt much sympathy or warmth towards anyone, so even the guys he liked were pretty much disposable. It had always seemed sensible to him. People who got close to each other just ended out getting hurt, like his mom. She'd gone with man after man, each one more brutal than the last, until finally one of them had killed her.

But that was the city for you, Diesel figured. Eat a person up if they didn't handle their shit, if they got close to anybody or made the wrong move.

Just like that gator.

If he hadn't been so high and mighty, Dirty Carl would have approved of the plan, Diesel figured. He was going to unload the first two layers of bags, move them to a stash hole nearby – still on solid ground, but closer to the swamp.

And once they'd loaded the rest, he'd hightail it into the

woods. They'd blame the cooks, and gone, he'd take off. A new start. Texas, or maybe Tijuana. He knew good people down that way, people who kept their mouths shut and minded their business.

30

M onday's early afternoon traffic was busy downtown, which suited Bob fine. He found a free spot at a meter with a decent view of The Purple Bird and parked the car.

He got out and fed a dollar fifty into the meter, then headed back to the car. He had an herbal tea in a travel cup lodged in the center console. He removed it and took a few sips, enjoying it while it was still hot.

Experience told him that stakeouts weren't the time to down too much liquid. He had no idea how long he was going to sit there before Deacon Riggs showed or made a move.

He'd circled the club once that morning before heading to the camera store. He wanted to be sure people weren't regularly using the back door to come and go. In the process, he'd also spotted where the bikers parked their wheels. They had a small row of spaces set aside on the next street over.

Bob drew his folded-up binoculars from his jacket pocket and scoped out the front door. There was a steel main door that would be double-locked, at least. There was the telltale jutting-out handle to indicate a steel security shutter that would be pulled down ahead of it.

The binoculars sought out the upstairs window. Bob studied the edge of the glass. They were using reflective contact tape around the pane, which would sound an alarm if broken. But they'd applied it in amateur fashion, hugging the frame so tightly that a skilled glass cutter could easily work around it.

Reflective contact tape probably meant a proximity contact system. Each door and window would have a pair of sensors attached that held contact with another sensor on the frame. If the contact was broken, a signal would be sent to the central alarm system.

It would then, typically, remain silent for long enough to alert the police. After a minute or two, it would sound an audible alert if designed to do so. If they were hardcases, it would also lock the intruder in. But given that insurers railed against it, it seemed unlikely The Purple Bird was in that category.

It was an easy system to circumvent with enough fore-knowledge. The contact sensors were usually reflective, a signal bouncing between them. One could be removed if an alternative took its place – mirrored glass, chrome, even silver oven foil could be used in a pinch if careful.

But even that might not be necessary, he thought, as the sidewalk traffic flowed by, a constant mix of tourists with fanny packs, businessmen, students. It didn't look like the bikers worried too much about company. Likely everyone in the French Quarter knew who they were.

Time passed slowly with nothing to occupy him. But he avoided the temptation to turn the radio on or use his phone's data online. He needed to be on target from the moment Riggs appeared until the moment he left.

It took another forty minutes. The biker emerged from the narrow lane between The Purple Bird and a cigar shop next door. Riggs checked the street both ways, casually, then sauntered over to the front steps before heading inside.

Bob waited until he'd been inside for ten minutes, long enough to order a beer. He got out of the Honda and crossed the street, pausing outside the club to peer for a moment – just long enough to look curious, no more.

Riggs was seated alone at a two-person café table, in the rear middle of the front room. The bar was against the right wall, and pool tables occupied most of the rest.

He walked a block west before turning north until he reached the end of the rear laneway. He followed it to the back entrance to the building, on Gravier Street.

The door opened, and a kitchen staffer came out carrying a pair of plastic garbage bags. Bob hugged the wall of the building next door until the man had walked the fifteen feet to the dumpster and deposited the bag.

The worker walked back to the door, then leaned slightly, using a proximity card around his neck on a panel by the door handle, triggering the lock. He disappeared inside.

Okay, so the rear door is the kitchen.

Bob walked past the door. The bikers' rides were across the road, eight motorcycles, mostly Harleys, each with custom upholstery and paint job. He recognized Riggs's purple teardrop gas tank, a skull and roses logo spray-painted expertly across it.

Bob reached into his pocket. He turned in place once, to make sure no one was watching. He walked past Riggs's bike and dipped at the waist momentarily. His hand snaked under the tank. He attached the GPS tracker with its magnet to the bike's frame.

He stood up and walked around the end of the row of bikes until he was even with the chopper he'd seen parked next to Dirty Carl's the night they followed him to Slidell. It had a giant hairy eyeball spray-painted on the gas tank. He reached into his left pocket and withdrew the other item, about the size of a mouse trap.

Bob repeated the procedure, leaning back slightly as if using the bike's seat to support his weight, then reaching under it to attach the magnetized object to the frame.

A pedestrian on his phone walked by. He looked up at Bob for a split second as the older man straightened up. Bob gave him a smile. The man went back to his phone and moved on.

Bob got moving. He continued on down the street for another five buildings before circling back around the block to his car.

Once behind the wheel, he took the phone out again. Butcher had helped him install the tracking app. He checked to ensure it worked. The map gave him a correct real-time position.

Now all he could do was wait, for more intel, for Riggs to make a move.

IT WAS a solid two more hours, just before one in the afternoon, when the cloned burner began to vibrate in his pocket.

He took it out. Roulette was calling someone, but he didn't recognize the number right away.

"Yeah?" It was Deacon Riggs. "I thought you weren't associating with us low-life types anymore, counselor."

"I've spoken with our friend. He's unhappy."

Riggs didn't respond for a second or two. Then he said, "Way I hear it, your boss had a pretty good day yesterday. Took care of a problem. So did we."

Roulette wasn't getting any happier. "About that: I thought we'd agreed on subtlety, at least."

"Nobody got hurt," Riggs protested.

"You torched a shooting victim's house on the very day he was shot. That's your idea of subtle?"

"It was supposed to get blamed on the feller what's been helping them," Riggs tried to explain. "But it didn't go right."

"So he got away is what you're saying."

Riggs was getting sick of biting his tongue, worrying about the money. "You got a problem with how we do our business, counselor, you can always find someone else. Or, you know... you might try watching how you talk to me. I've only got so much patience for your bullshit."

"Maybe that's what I'll have to do," Roulette said, calling the biker's bluff. "Or maybe what I'll do is call up my client and tell him what you said. You think those two gents he had pay a call at that motel yesterday are the only muscle he's got?"

"Then how come they ain't on Colbert Street, trying to scare the bejesus out of people?"

"Because, as I've already told you, a bunch of Saudi guys in suits attracts important types of attention. You losers don't make waves with anybody."

"You want to watch yourself, counselor. Watch your step. Like I said, whether you tell him or not, we live in the same city, and The Damned ain't going nowhere."

"Yeah? Well, here's a suggestion: go to Colbert Street. Get back out there. Let the other old folks know that what happened to the Greens' house could easily happen to theirs – with them in it."

"The street is crawling with cops now," Riggs said. "How're we supposed to..."

"Don't show up dressed like a biker, maybe. Show some initiative. Dress up in civvies. Maybe wear a suit so y'all look like Bible salesmen. The fact is, it does not matter to me one whit how you do it; just get more homes listed. He wants five more purchased by the end of the month, which realistically means getting the ball rolling right now."

"Then... then I guess we'll head on back down there."

"You do that."

"You'd better remember though, counselor: you only get a pass on slagging the club because we need each other right now. Don't push your luck."

Riggs ended the call.

They were headed back to blockbust Colbert Street, Bob realized. All the increased attention hadn't been enough to scare Habsi off.

He kept the tracking app active and his eyes on the door. After fifteen more minutes, it swung open. Riggs stepped out along with Paul Harris and a third biker Bob hadn't seen before. They walked down the front stairs and turned left before turning again down the narrow lane to the side of the building.

A few moments later, the tracking app showed them moving. He set the phone down in the car's first cupholder, although he already knew where they were going.

31

B ob kept three car lengths back, at least, as the bike wound its way north towards Lakeville. At the corner of Colbert and Porteous Streets, he sat at the stop sign for a few seconds longer than necessary until he was sure Riggs had parked his bike.

The biker headed south, towards the Greens' block, on foot. Bob wondered how they were going to accomplish their intimidation tactfully with police around. Surely Riggs wasn't telling them to door-knock residents in full biker garb?

Regardless, he needed a way to watch the street inconspicuously. Confident the GPS tracker was working, he turned the car around and navigated it through the light Monday afternoon traffic until he reached Savers, a used-clothing store on North Galvez Street.

Inside, he searched through the racks of castoff clothing until he'd found what he needed. He took the garments to the cash register, where a gum-chewing young woman in a red uniform rang them up.

"Do you have any sort of Halloween makeup?" he asked.

She kept chewing on her gum as she folded and bagged the clothes. She nodded to the far-right aisle. "Whole display case of the stuff down aisle one."

"Hold that thought," Bob asked. "I'm just going to add a couple of things."

After the thrift store, he stopped at a Dunkin Donuts for coffee, leaving it on the small square table by the store's front window while he headed for the bathroom with his store bags.

He was halfway back to the table when the clerk spotted him. "Hey! You can't be in here unless you're buying some-thing," the young man ordered.

Perfect, Bob thought. *Time to head back to Colbert Street.*

DENISE GREEN SEETHED, arms crossed, as she watched the street from Mrs. Summerlea's front porch, two doors down from the smoking ruin of her uncle's home.

"So they just moved on back in? Like nothing happened?"

A few feet away, Mrs. Summerlea rocked gently on her wicker porch swing chair, knitting. "Exactly that, child. Police said the house next door wasn't in the name of the feller they charged, and they can't just shut it down. I guess they moved in there instead. Or they went in about an hour ago, I should say, and haven't left yet. 'Moved in' is probably a mite too strong."

"That's not right, Mrs. Summerlea," the college student said. "They can't just let them come back into the neighbor-hood like this."

"Well," the elderly resident said, "I 'spect they argued it's a public street, and they got rights, like the rest of us. But I don't like it none, that's true enough."

Denise wondered what she could do to help. She was only home from college for another two weeks before the fall semester was set to start. Now she was worried the next time she visited, the street could be gone, torn up for a city project. Or worse, people just moved out, scared of gangsters moving in.

"Someone ought to do something," she said.

"Now, you just settle," Mrs. Summerlea warned. "You saw what happened to your uncle's place when he talked back to them. It ain't worth the trouble, so long as they're keeping to themselves."

Denise wondered how long that would remain the case. There had been police stationed right across the street, watching the burned-out gang house, when her uncle's home had gone up in flames. Everyone saw bikers in the area around the time it happened, but no one saw them enter the home itself.

If they were willing to set a pastor's house ablaze, there was no telling the lengths they might go to.

Across the road, the front door to the second home opened. A pair of burly men walked out, but dressed in dark suits, as if heading to a funeral. A moment later, two more joined them, similarly dressed.

They looked uncomfortable. *What are they up to?* She supposed even criminals had to dress up sometimes.

But instead of climbing on their bikes and roaring off, the men split up. Two followed the sidewalk north, the others south.

Whatever they're doing, it can't be good, she thought. That's what the neighborhood was going to become: more trouble.

If police didn't do something to crack down on the bad elements.

She looked the other way down the street. At the bus stop a half-block away, a wino had decided to sit down on the sidewalk and lean against the bench, a paper-bag-clad bottle sitting in front of him. He had a big coat on, despite the warm weather, and long black hair, a beard. Occasionally, he'd take a deep swig from the bottle. Then he'd lecture someone invisible standing just ahead of him, as if in deep debate with a colleague.

That's how it starts, she thought. *First the criminals come in, then they attract the addicts, then the bums figure there's enough money and vice around to make living here a little easier than somewhere else.*

This is how a neighborhood falls apart.

Two of the suit-clad bikers walked past the bum, ignoring him. They stopped at the next house and mounted the steps, then rang the bell.

THE ELDERLY WOMAN who answered the door was obviously nervous. She left the security chain on and spoke to them through the two-inch gap.

"Uh-huh. I ain't got any money to donate or nothing," she said.

They'd been told to expect some resistance, Paul Harris thought as he clasped his hands in front of him, trying his damnedest to look like a Bible salesman or other door-to-door do-gooder.

"Mrs. Jessup, we're just folks living in the neighborhood like yourself. We wanted to come over and give you some helpful advice."

"Well, like I said, I haven't any money to spare."

"We're not selling anything, ma'am," Harris said. "We're just advising folks that if they get an offer for their home, now is a real good time to think about selling." He nodded back down the block. "You saw what's been going on here, with the troubles and such."

He could see the anxiety etched into her gaze. She was trying to reconcile Harris's long frizzy hair and rings with the suit he was wearing.

"I don't want no trouble," Mrs. Jessup insisted.

"And we don't want you to get into any trouble; no, ma'am." Harris tried to sound reassuring. "And you can be sure nothing's going to happen to you or your home... so long as you let the nice man who comes to visit on Friday in and have a chat."

"I... I don't want to talk to nobody about selling. I lived here all my life," she said.

Harris smiled sweetly at her. "And you get to keep living." He dropped the smile and scowled at her. "If you're smart about it. Old place like this..." He stared up and around, as if assessing its brittle façade. "Old place like this ever catches fire, it'd go up real quick. Imagine if it happened at night while you was sleeping. You like that idea, Mrs. Jessup?"

"Please," she implored, a teardrop tracing its way south. "I don't have much..."

"We don't want your useless old junk," Harris said. "We just want you to be a smart old bat and think about your future." He smiled sweetly again. "Goodbye, now."

They made their way back down the steps to the sidewalk. Booker was in jail. Diesel and Dirty Carl had disappeared. But they still had eight guys and could cover a lot of homes by Friday, Harris figured. If they all looked as terrified as Mrs. Jessup, Riggs would be pleased.

"Next house?" Danny D asked.

"Sure."

They strolled past the bus stop. Harris was about to kick the bottle away from the wino slumped beside the bench, but thought better of it at the last moment.

There were still police routinely patrolling the street in a cruiser, rolling by every few hours. They weren't supposed to attract attention.

A BLOCK SOUTH, towards the very end of Colbert Street, Clay Thibodeaux sat behind the wheel of his Ford pickup and watched things unfold.

He'd gone home and changed before following up the barbershop client's tip. This was about as middle class as local neighborhoods got, and dirty jeans and a leather jacket was less of a fit than casual men's wear, slacks and a golf shirt, a fanny pack.

The neighborhood had life. People sat on porches, gathered in front yards, or just went about their business. Despite the two fires, their lives continued to unfold.

The crew in suits was strange, though. They'd piled out of a house about fifty yards away. He'd seen the motorcycles parked side by side outside the house and figured maybe it was the bikers mentioned in the newscast. But then two groups of four guys in dark suits had walked out, five minutes apart, like they'd been attending a wake together or something.

Four had crossed the street. Each small group had then

begun going door-to-door. A religious thing, maybe? They sure didn't look like Jehovahs.

They look like bikers in suits. What the hell is going on here?

Farther up the block, residents were gathered on porches, also watching the men. He considered whether he should stroll up, have a chat. *Find out what's what.*

He reached down and unzipped the fanny pack, dipping into it momentarily. He took out a stick of lip balm and applied it to his dried lips. His brother would be against him engaging the wayward spook on his own, he supposed. For the most part, Clay defined their partnership. He picked their targets; he ran the business side of things.

Dealing with a contract on his own was just good business; it reminded Fletcher not only that the elder brother was in charge, but why.

They'd never failed an assignment. After serving overseas, they'd spent five years working as mercenaries, making enough money to buy a small apartment building as a revenue source and home. Chasing bail jumpers kept the bills paid.

The real money was in murder for hire. Hitmen were less in demand than the movies seemed to suggest. But when a need arose in the Big Easy, they'd learned it was financially prudent to be first to target.

How would Fletcher handle talking to the locals? *Stick a gun in one of their mouths and they'll talk pretty quick.*

It wasn't that he was wrong; it was more a case of safer, less insane options being worth trying first. But then, that was probably why he sometimes opted to leave Fletcher behind. His hair trigger could come in handy in the right circumstances. But he was no leader.

Then again, neither am I. Not really. But you point at some-thing and say "kill that," and I'll get it done.

Time to chat with the residents of Colbert Street, he decided. Besides, it was a nice sunny day, and walking beat sitting in the car.

TACTICALLY, separating into four groups of two had been a mistake, Bob thought as he watched the bikers going door to door.

He sat on the cement at the bus stop, the long black wig and false beard disguising him enough, the wino coat and bottle completing the ensemble.

But they're not thinking tactically. They're just assuming no one's going to interfere. If the cops patrolling the neighborhood aren't stopping them, why would anyone else?

Two of the men from the fire had walked right by him without a second glance. He'd left the bottle in front of him, knowing one of them might swipe at it with a boot, that he might have to play-act outrage, that it was risking a confrontation. He knew that was what he really wanted, to cut loose on them, make the point stick this time.

But first, it paid to assess his options.

They likely wouldn't stay on Colbert. They had other houses in the neighborhood, other residents to intimidate. The distance between the four pairs would grow. When they were furthest apart and least able to help each other, he'd act.

Across the street, people were seated on the porches of three out of the four homes next to the Greens. It was as if they could sense something bad going down and had lined up a front-row view.

Confronting anyone on Colbert was out. Too much collateral risk. He needed to lure them into the back alleys, use cover to lower his profile, avoid danger to the public or the need to kill anybody.

You keep worrying about killing bad people, eventually one of them is going to kill you. Or someone you care about.

This time, he didn't ignore the inner voice. He knew it was true. He also knew it was important to resist the urge to solve problems permanently, to arrogantly assume he had that right. It had gone wrong too many times.

If he ended up killing Riggs or his men, it would be because they left him no choice, not because he had a license to play judge, jury and executioner.

Sammy Habsi and his men were another matter. According to the background file "obtained" by Nick Velasco, he ran a casino, and he claimed to be related to the Saudi royal family. But according to his visa applications and residency certificate, he was an Egyptian national.

His casino money was probably dirty, too. He had silent partners, investors who stayed in the shadows. But National Security Agency intel suggested they had similar investments in Las Vegas, with old, organized crime money behind them.

Habsi's men had come to the motel with a single objective. When they tangled, it was unlikely to end in anything but pain.

But the bikers needed to learn a lesson, first. Isolating them was job one.

Figuring out where Riggs was? That had become job two. His bike wasn't parked in front of the second house, rather a block farther south, towards the freeway. Bob figured the gang leader was up to something.

Maybe he's in the charred wreck across the road, with a scope? Something like that seemed likely. But Riggs would arrogantly assume Bob would go after him first. Whittling down his supporting cast made more sense.

On the opposite sidewalk, a guy was walking past the Greens' house. He was younger, in mirrored shades, perhaps in his thirties, a bushy, droopy mustache. He looked innocuous, just another dude in a golf shirt on a hot day.

The man tipped an imaginary cap towards Denise Green and Mrs. Summerlea, and the older woman gave a pleasant wave back.

The man returned his attention to the sidewalk ahead. He barely moved his head Bob's way at all.

But he moved it a little.

Bob clocked the small motion, a slight tick to the left. In a sense, it was worse than if the man had just looked over; anyone might take a quick look at a bum. Few would try to hide their visual objective unless they had a reason to.

Bob took another swig of "wine," making sure the cherry Kool-Aid in the bottle stained his lips a little, then belched.

The man kept walking, passing Bob's spot on the other sidewalk.

Earpiece. Could just be super busy, a businessman making sure he stays in touch...

Lump at his ankle. Backup piece? Probably.

The golf shirt looked less innocuous, all things considered. Its tail was untucked, which would let him conceal a speed holster on his belt.

It had been a minute movement. But Bob didn't doubt it; the guy had been checking him out. That, plus the backup piece, plus the earpiece?

There's a new player involved. Undercover cop?

It didn't seem likely. They were making their presence visible via drive-bys.

Plus, the dude just seemed... off. Maybe it was the way he walked, or his body type and movement, or the vacant smile behind mirrored shades.

He felt the hair on his neck stand up.

A solo operator made the most sense. Eddie Stone's boss, Andrew Kennedy, had apparently vowed to throw his considerable resources behind tracking Bob down and ending him.

The man stopped walking and backtracked to the prior home, raising a finger to denote a question, as if he had something he'd meant to ask them, but forgotten. Bob could see Denise's head move slightly, as if answering him.

He's assessing the situation, figuring out what's going on.

So he's not here for the bikers or the Greens.

He's here for me.

THE SMELL of wet charcoal stung Deacon Riggs's nostrils.

He'd been sitting on the half-melted kitchen chair for a half hour. It was pulled up in front of the remains of the living room window so that he could watch the front street and the former drug house beyond.

His anger had been building all day. Towards mystery man "Bob," who kept interfering. Towards Denny Roulette, an asshole in a suit who thought he was better than the men he paid. Towards the laid-up pastor, for challenging them in the first place.

Sooner or later, he figured, Bob would show up at the house. That wasn't a man who would give up easily. He'd turned the tables on The Damned three times already, suggesting he saw it as a fight worth having.

Which means eventually he'll try to bring it to us. When he does, I'll be waiting.

A 9 mm pistol sat on his lap. Paul Harris had suggested he find a rifle with a scope, but Riggs wasn't a hunter and hadn't fired long rifles in years.

He withdrew his phone from his pocket and dialed Harris.

"Yeah."

"Where are you? What's going on?"

"Not much," Harris said. "It's quiet. Folks are coming to their doors. Like you said, a suit fools anyone. They don't like what they're hearing, but that's what we want."

"The others... Animal and Dozer were doing the blocks south..."

"Yeah, they're all done. No one else home."

"Shift them a block over, have them go south to north. Once Colbert's done, split the other three groups up, each take a side of a street, and we'll move north, block by block."

"You got it."

"Keep your heads down. Let me know if you see anything strange."

"There's nothing so far," Harris insisted. "We've got a wino by the bus stop, a looky-loo talking to the old ladies. Cop cruiser's gone by twice."

"Yeah, yeah, but no sign of—"

"Bob? Not so far, boss."

"Okay, then. Y'all get back to it."

Riggs hoped he wasn't coming off as nervous. Nothing scared him, he told himself, not even the dude who'd already whipped his men multiple times. He felt the heft of the chrome-plated pistol on his thigh, saw the sun glint off its barrel as it poured through the gap where part of the roof had been.

Dude might be skilled, but he isn't going to outrun a bullet to the back.

He picked up the pistol and worked the slide, chambering a round. Then he put it back on his lap and reached over to the milk crate two feet to his left, retrieving the already burning cigarette from the faux-crystal ashtray he'd rescued from the backyard debris.

He inhaled deeply, the cherry tip glowing orange in the broken home's dim half-light. Deacon Riggs wanted his pound of flesh.

The glint from the corner of his eye caught Clay Thibodeaux's attention, even as Mrs. Summerlea continued to explain how quiet the neighborhood had always been.

He didn't turn his head. He kept smiling and nodding, playing the pleasant tourist. But it had definitely come from the burned-out shell of the house next door.

"... and by that time, my husband was ready to retire," Mrs. Summerlea was concluding. "Of course, he passed a few years ago, but we still talk on the regular. I know he's gone, but it still feels like he's with me."

"That right there's a lovely notion, ain't it?" Thibodeaux told her, turning his head casually towards two o'clock.

There it was again. Just the slightest glint through the front window of the burned-out house. But it jumped about an inch, which meant it was moving. He'd been taught to look for it in sniper school, light reflecting off the chrome of a weapon.

"I swear, Robert's right there with me some nights," Mrs. Summerlea was saying. "I can sit in my armchair and feel his hands on my shoulders, like he used to do, letting me know everything's going to be all right."

"Uh-huh. I guess that must be a comfort given..." He nodded towards the Greens' wrecked home. "I mean, if they're as bad as folks figure..."

The girl next to Mrs. Summerlea hadn't said anything throughout. But now she crossed her arms, her gaze suspicious. "You an insurance investigator or something?" she asked. "You got a lot of questions for a guy who's just passing through."

"Oh!" Thibodeaux exclaimed. "I did not mention... I used to live just a few blocks east of here, a decade ago. Yeah... just visiting family on this trip, but I hadn't been down here since, and we were in Lakeview a long time. But... it seems things changed a mite."

The house across the street was the other arson victim. The motorcycles were parked at the house directly south of it. Whoever was in the pastor's home was keeping an eye on the bikers' front door.

It was the kind of sneaky move a veteran would pull, he thought.

"... get worse before they get better," Mrs. Summerlea was saying. "That's not a nice thought."

"Ladies," he said, checking his watch, "it's been lovely chatting with you, but I do have to go. Y'all have a nice day now, you hear?"

They both smiled as he made his way north. He walked as far as the next corner and did a situational assessment. There were police around; a cruiser had passed twice in the last hour. There were the bikers in suits, or that was who they appeared to be. Across the road, a wino leaned, oblivious, against a bus bench.

He's here. You can feel it, he told himself. Singleton had stuck his nose into some fight, probably the pastor trying to ward off the bikers, and they'd retaliated by shooting the preacher. *There's no way Singleton lets that go, not based on what Stone said. It's not in his nature.*

That left him with the mystery light source in the burned-out house. He turned right, heading east, until he reached the entrance to the long alley that ran behind the homes. He followed it cautiously, keeping an eye out for people in their backyards, potential witnesses if things went south.

But it was quiet, his only company the weeds growing up through the cracked asphalt.

When he reached the remains of the Greens' home, it was obvious the fire had started near the back wall, which was gone, a charred hole consuming everything except the central beams and columns holding up a small chunk of roof. Through the hole, everything was black from fire damage, but it appeared to have been the kitchen.

The yard was a jumbled mess. Blackened remains of furniture sat a few feet from an overturned washing machine. A pile of charcoal he assumed had been shelving at one time sat precariously balanced. A small wooden chest was now just a charcoal briquette save for its oversized metal keyhole and strapping. Someone's keepsakes or memories, maybe.

Shit is tough, and then you die.

Thibodeaux had fought in the Sudan, Syria, Angola. He'd seen real suffering, and he hadn't worried about it then.

Nasty shit happened to poor folks in New Orleans all the time.

The Greens' plight didn't even register.

He checked the alley both ways one more time, then hopped the fence, not risking a loud squeak from the gate. He drew his Glock from the speed holster on the back of his belt.

If he was lucky, Thibodeaux figured, Singleton was sitting thirty feet ahead of him, unaware that his life was about to end.

32

The tourist with the earpiece turned east.

Bob watched him disappear down the alley behind the Greens' home.

Whoever he was, he was a pro. He checked his perimeter regularly; he'd carried on a conversation with a local without setting off alarms. And he was headed straight for a home burned out by bikers days earlier.

Maybe his first guess had been right. Maybe the dude was an undercover cop. Either way, he was screwing up Bob's plans. He'd intended on circling the surrounding blocks on foot, drawing each group of two away from the main thoroughfares, laying down some damage.

Take their money, their phones, their guns; wreck their bikes. Embarrass them, while leaving them with the realization they were only left alive because he chose to do so.

But the new arrival changed the equation. Bob needed to know if the man was a civilian stumbling into a problem, or a new problem altogether.

Change of plans.

He got up, making sure he stumbled to one side slightly, staggering to stay upright. The wine bottle was clutched in his left hand. Bob stumbled across the road, following the sidewalk until he reached the alley.

If he was still back there, the tourist had disappeared into someone's yard. Bob ambled south slowly, staying in character. He stopped two houses early and lifted the lid of a trash can, some theater for anyone looking out a back window.

At the Greens' back fence, he peeked quickly into the yard.

It was empty of people, full of debris.

He hopped over the fence quietly and approached the house.

THIBODEAUX CREPT down the home's main hall, his Glock at the ready, butt resting on his left palm to support it.

He barely lifted his feet, to avoid splashing. There was an inch of water on the floor, at least, lapping at his boots. The walls were charred black, the roof above destroyed all the way to the front room.

If the tipster at the barber shop was right and his Midwesterner was Singleton, it was puzzling. Why this couple, these bikers? Why get involved in problems that didn't involve him?

Thibodeaux figured people weren't complicated. They were slaves to their fears and obsessions. But Singleton's background defied explanation. From what little he'd been told, Singleton was an efficient and ruthless assassin. Then he'd disappeared. Then he'd reappeared, helping people, but living on the street.

That was despite owning a home in Chicago and having friends he'd known for decades. It was like he blamed himself for something, but Thibodeaux didn't have enough information to know what. He was lethal, a chameleon despite being on the taller side, locally knowledgeable wherever he was sent, fluent in multiple languages.

It seemed like a waste, taking himself out of the game. Why he might have changed was something Thibodeaux could not fathom, lacking as he was any sort of guilt, shame, remorse or fear of pretty much anything.

He reached the living room, peeking his head in from the hallway. A man was seated on the remains of a kitchen chair, its back gone and the frame charred. He had his back to Thibodeaux, his right hand on the butt of a pistol. It appeared as if he was watching the house across the road.

But it wasn't Bob Singleton. The man was, at most, five eight or five nine, stocky, with gray-black hair.

Well, now... who the fuck is this guy?

Stone's orders had been clear: no collateral damage. If they winged a civilian while going after Singleton, local law enforcement would be all over them.

So just capping the guy was out, although Thibodeaux was tempted. He was sitting in a prime spot to watch the road, but hadn't even worried about leaving his six exposed.

Amateur.

But they came with their own complications. *Better to just remove him from the board.*

The man reached to his left to stub out a cigarette.

Thibodeaux took two quick strides up behind him,

allowing his footsteps to alert the man. He needed him to turn his head slightly.

The biker obliged.

The pistol butt came crashing down against his chin, knocking Deacon Riggs unconscious. He slumped out of the chair and onto the dirty floor.

Thibodeaux removed a set of plastic cuffs from his fanny pack and knelt beside the man. He put his Glock down on the ground so that he could use both hands to pull the man's arms behind him. He tied the biker's hands behind his back.

He removed a ball gag from the fanny pack and slipped it over the man's head, ensuring he couldn't cry out, then tightened the elastic strap.

He heard a rustle behind him. Thibodeaux realized his gun was just behind and to his right. If he turned quickly—

"I wouldn't if I were you," a man's voice suggested. "This FN has a light pull on the trigger, and I imagine you'd like to keep your head attached to your neck."

Thibodeaux had been under the gun before, but he'd never let someone get the drop on him so thoroughly. A third party had been unexpected, after all.

The man had him dead to rights. He couldn't assume his opponent would shirk that advantage. If he didn't act, he was probably going to die.

But the gun was at a bad angle.

He knew he'd have to turn towards the man covering him, making it almost certain he'd be shot at least once before his hand found the pistol grip.

Or...

"Hands behind your head," the man ordered.

Thibodeaux complied.

"Huh. 475th Infantry. You were Army?"

Fuck this guy, Thibodeaux thought. He'd read Thibodeaux's tattoo. "Rangers lead the way," he spat. "What's it to you, eh?"

"I see you tied his wrists," the man said. "You got some more of those plastic cuffs on you, maybe in that fanny pack of yours, there?"

Thibodeaux dove sideways, praying his timing was right.

33

The guy on his knees was a pro, no doubt. Bob had heard the short struggle go down from what had been the kitchen. Riggs hadn't had a chance to put up a fight, and now he was hogtied and gagged, lying on his chest.

Next to the kneeling man beside the biker – and just slightly behind him, fortunately – was a Glock G23, a light .40-caliber pistol.

"Hands behind your head," Bob ordered.

The kneeling man complied. His biceps and triceps were large, defined. On his right forearm, he bore a tattoo.

"Huh." That was a surprise. "475th Infantry. You were Army?"

"Rangers lead the way." His captive half-spat the words out. He sounded pissed. "What's it to you, eh?"

What else was he carrying in that fanny pack? It paid to be careful, have him take it off, toss it to one side. Might even come in handy. "I see you tied his wrists," Bob said. "You got some more of those plastic cuffs on you, maybe in that fanny pack of yours, there?"

The man's hands began to drop... and then he dove sideways. Bob kept his aim on the moving figure; he didn't want to shoot an ex-serviceman if he didn't have to.

The ashtray came out of nowhere, flung backhanded, backwards. It was heavy, made of glass or something. Bob tried to duck it, but it caught him near the left side of his forehead.

He fired a shot, wild and high, as he staggered sideways, hoping to dissuade the man from trying anything else. His free hand flew up reflexively to his forehead, where a small cut was stinging and bleeding.

Bob had expected the man to roll back towards him and the Glock. Instead, he rolled the other way, a hand coming up, muzzle flashing a split second before the crack of the gunshots.

Bob threw himself left, into the cover of the corridor.

The piece in his sock... a .38 Special? Something small and cut down.

"Bad move, *mon ami*," the other man called out from around the corner. "You should've capped me before I knew you were there."

"It seemed a little ungentlemanly," Bob suggested. "I mean, certainly, the Geneva Convention would not approve."

"I don't think that applies to assholes in New Orleans," the tourist called out.

"Oh... no, I'm pretty sure it applies to you," Bob said. "But only in an official war. Whoever you work for—" He cut the sentence off midway, leaning around the corner, finger pulling the trigger three times in quick succession. His target leaned away, firing back twice, the gunshots echoing around the darkened, sooty room, forcing Bob back into cover.

"Whoever you work for doesn't want this on the books, or you'd be liaising with the cops, accepting their help. The middle-aged-dad getup, the Dockers-and-golf-shirt look..."

"Speak for yourself," Thibodeaux yelled back. "The wino, huh? Clever. I'm thinking you must be the fella we're looking for."

"I highly doubt we know each other," Bob lied. Whoever the dude was, he didn't want to encourage any of this.

"Oh, not personally, I guess. But a whole lot of important folk want the great Bob Singleton dead."

That answers that question.

It was a true standoff, Bob realized. Neither could get a clear look without offering one to the other guy. There was no cover in the room.

The gunshots would be freaking out the neighbors. Doubtless Denise or Mrs. Summerlea had already called the police. If that cruiser was nearby, they didn't have long to resolve things or get out of there.

"You Alpha?" Bob asked. "That G23 is a nice piece. Bit lighter than Eddie usually prefers."

"Yeah, don't know what that means, 'cept it being a nice gun. Give me even an inch of that head of yours to look at, and I'll show you."

Bob heard a slight creak. *He's trying to close the distance to the corner, trying to get the drop, surprise me.*

From a distance, they heard the wail of a police siren.

"If you're expecting a low drop around the corner to catch me, you're kidding yourself," Bob warned.

"Cops will be here soon. I've got people working on my side, excuses that can be made about my presence,"

Thibodeaux suggested. "What about you, Bob? You looking forward to meeting *les gendarmes?*"

"Don't kid a kidder. You don't want them involved any more than I do."

"We could solve this quick," Thibodeaux suggested. "You know the walls in this place were probably paper thin even before the fire, eh? We could just shoot each other through cover. One of us, we gonna hit something important."

"Or I could back down this hall to—" He didn't finish the sentence, a hand poking around the corner and tossing a small, cylindrical object towards him.

Grenade. Instinct kicked in, Bob turning and leaping, pushing off hard with both feet, aiming for the kitchen door. He turned in mid-flight, trying to slide backwards into the kitchen, gun at the ready.

But the inch of water stopped him dead, even as Thibodeaux leaned around the corner, barrel blazing, a bullet catching Bob in the shoulder. He pushed backwards with both feet, sliding on his backside past the doorway, rolling sideways into cover.

He heard the tinkle of spent shells hitting the floor as Thibodeaux reloaded. He leaned around the corner.

A stick of lip balm rolled slowly to a stop.

Bob cursed inwardly and clutched the wound with his free hand.

But the other man had a point, he decided. He lined up the wall about where he figured Thibodeaux would be standing and fired twice.

The bullets tore through the scorched walls.

"Aiieehh! *Putain!*" Thibodeaux screamed. He leaned around the corner and fired three shots in quick succession as Bob ducked back out of sight. "You fucking shot me!

Asshole! Two tours without a fucking scratch and you fucking shot me!"

There was no percentage in sticking around, Bob thought. He had the metaphorical high ground: the only safe exit was out the back, as the police would be out front momentarily. He was already in the kitchen. He rose and silently backed up to the huge gap where the back wall had once been, stepping over it.

Bob ran over to Mrs. Summerlea's fence and climbed into the backyard. He stripped off the wig and overcoat. The shooter would be stuck there for at least a couple of minutes, unable to be sure he could step out of cover and check if Bob was still there.

The siren blared from out front as the police cruiser squealed to a halt. A pair of doors opened and slammed. Bob hugged the side of the house so that he could peek around the corner of the wreck next door. He couldn't see the officers; they were likely headed for the still-standing front door.

He risked a step into the front yard. The street was empty aside from the police cruiser and the motorcycles parked a half block away. Denise Green and Mrs. Summerlea were sitting on the porch, watching the police action unfold. Denise spotted him.

"Mr. Singleton!"

"Denise, Mrs. Summerlea... I'd get inside right away if I were you."

They both rose nervously and headed towards the door.

Bob ducked back around the corner and headed for the alley. He waited until he was two more houses away before taking out his phone. It was important that the police didn't get into a shoot-out with the two men in the house; he didn't need innocent deaths on his conscience, not again.

And he needed a distraction for egress. The Honda was two minutes north.

He dialed a number.

The explosion was thunderous, the C-4 charge under Paul Harris's motorcycle gas tank enough on its own to shred the bike. The gas tank added to the explosion, the flames and heat setting off the tank of the bike next to it, and the next, and yet another.

It shook the asphalt under Bob's feet. Cars from blocks away shrieked a chorus of car alarms.

That would keep the police busy and send a message to the bikers. They'd be questioning Riggs's leadership, at the least.

He put his phone away and clutched his right shoulder. The blood splotch was growing, but slowly, suggesting no arteries were hit. It felt like the bullet had passed through cleanly.

He needed to get to the condo, patch it properly. He turned at the entrance to the alley and headed east, away from the unfolding chaos.

34

The shoulder wound proved painful but relatively easy to mend, a trough of torn tissue where the fat gathered, under and just ahead of his left armpit.

He stood before the bathroom mirror so that he could see properly as he sutured the wound, clearing away excess blood and cleaning it, using ethyl alcohol to sterilize it.

Bob used his teeth to tear open a small white packet. He set it down on the counter next to the sink and removed a new needle. He gritted his teeth against the pain so that he could hold the end of the thin black thread with his left hand, threading it through the needle's eye with his right.

He stitched up the wound slowly, the needle stinging each time he poked it through his skin. The finished job wasn't perfect, but it looked okay.

He tried to raise his arm and winced again. If he used the trapezius muscles on that side, he realized, he could tear the wound open again. That bore watching.

In the kitchen, Bob retrieved the carton of milk from the

fridge and poured a cold glass. He sat down at the island and let his muscles relax.

By now, the scene would be crawling with police, he supposed. Riggs wasn't going anywhere, hogtied as he'd been, and would have some explaining to do. He wondered about the gunman and whether the wound had taken him down.

Probably not. Err on the side of caution.

He needed to get some painkillers. There was still work to be done that night, while everyone was preoccupied with the shooting gallery and explosion on Colbert.

He didn't envy the poor soul trying to figure that mess out.

It had begun to rain, droplets coming down hard and steady, the dark skies rumbling that things might get worse.

On the curb across from the Greens' wrecked home, just ahead of the burned-out shell of the biker house, Det. Pullman Lewis stood in his tan raincoat, notepad in hand, and tried to figure out what the hell was going on.

The hogtied biker with the fetish gear in his mouth hadn't offered any clues. One of the first officers on scene had identified Deacon Riggs as soon as he saw the figure on the Greens' living room floor.

But the biker boss claimed to have been hit over the head while walking down the street. He didn't see who did it; he didn't hear anything. Of course, his attacker could've worn a neon T-shirt that said "Charge Me" and Riggs still wouldn't have helped them, Lewis realized. That was how the game worked. Snitches got stitches.

Neighbors had reported multiple gunshots, and there was evidence in the form of spent shell casings, also on the Greens' living room floor. Somehow, in his coma-like unconsciousness, Riggs had missed that happening, too.

It all smells like a lot of bullshit to me, he thought.

But if the biker boss had been incapacitated by someone, who was behind the shoot-out? The preacher was out of commission; his visiting friend "Tyler" had allegedly gone west. And how did it connect to the two allegedly Arabic men at the motel?

A dozen feet away, one of the uniformed officers was interviewing a biker named Paul Harris about his motorcycle. Or what was left of it.

"... kind of crap treatment we get from you guys. Someone burns down our house, and nothing. Now someone blows up my bike, and you're telling me—"

"Sir, if you'd just calm down and give me the information I need about the model and year number—"

"I told you already; it wasn't no single year or model. I built that bike from the ground up using the best parts from Harley Davidson. That there was a Harris 1.0, irreplaceable."

A few feet away, Lewis silently cursed himself for getting out of bed that morning.

The patrolman finished up with the biker and walked over. "Detective—"

Lewis scoped out his badge. "Officer Bell, my sympathies."

"Bad bunch. Look..." The young man looked sheepish, as if he had something awkward to share.

"Speak freely, Bell, please."

"I just wanted to say, if I get to be half the law-enforcement officer you are, sir..."

Lewis sucked on his tongue. Getting himself on television a few times had elevated his reputation. *How little they know.* "Aim higher, Officer."

He walked over to his car and opened the door, glaring at the young man once more before he left.

35

Sammy Habsi looked out from high above the casino floor, the afternoon customer traffic already steady, the stools in front of the slot machines full.

He kept his eyes on the last stool in the row. Mrs. Lafayette was in her usual spot. She was retired, about seventy. She got there early, usually around 6 a.m., which coincided with his first tour of the gaming floor. She would not leave until her bucket of quarters – worth about sixty-eight dollars, his people reliably informed him – was gone.

She did this every day, without fail, without exception for holidays. Every day, she played until her money was gone, her movements fluid from years of practice, her gaze never wavering from the spinning dials behind the glass screen. Sometimes, she would win a relatively handsome hundred or two hundred dollars. She would then sit down and play that money until it was gone.

When she left, usually around four o'clock, she never looked depressed or disconsolate. Her expression, Habsi had noticed, was best described as "blank." Each time he saw it, his heart filled with warmth, a glow that came from knowing that she would stay at that stool, day after day, until everything she had had been given to him. And then she would die, and another would replace her. It felt almost like owning her, as if her soul was being siphoned into him, making him more powerful.

He sighed at the thought of it, like the first taste of a favorite meal.

The casino was a license to print wealth, a steady flow of people giving him money for nothing but the faintest chance of getting more back in return. Given that even the most forgiving of games, roulette, favored the house, Habsi never lost.

The millions he'd made over the decade prior were sufficient to buy him professional protection of an international standard. The four bodyguards who followed his every move were all former Egyptian intelligence, recommended to him by a cousin still with the government in Cairo – at least until it was decided he should join Habsi and the rest of the family in exile.

He worried it was not enough. There was something strange about this mystery man who'd so derailed their plans, something abnormal.

He'd put in requests with his brother and cousin to tap their US government sources. The man clearly had superior combat training and thought through his actions tactically. He'd made fools of the bikers.

"You look pensive, my brother," his chief bodyguard, Molham, said in Arabic from across the room, where he was perched on the edge of Habsi's desk, reading off his phone. "You are stressing yourself too much over this man."

"He's coming for me, old friend; I can feel it. It is a curse, for hurting a man of God. Or perhaps for years of claiming to be someone I am not."

Molham shrugged. "It was a necessary subterfuge to get things done. Egyptians are continually discriminated against by the American government. Not so Saudis, despite everything."

"Hmm, yes. Oil money." Habsi fairly spat it out. As far as he was concerned, Saudis were a bunch of Bedouin savages. But his contempt wouldn't protect him from their justice if he was found out, he knew.

"This man 'Bob,'" Molham asked, "has he threatened your businesses in any way? Or to take information to the police?"

"He has not."

Molham took a box-top pack of Marlboros from his pocket and lit one. "Then you're worrying for nothing. He only wants to kill you, not expose you."

"Oh, is that all?" Habsi said sarcastically. "Just to end my life. No problem, then."

"It is no problem because you have me and my men. I don't care how well trained he is, he will be no match for four of us. We are not stupid bikers, my friend. We will be patient, wait for him to come to us."

"And?"

"And then we'll kill him and dump his body in the bayou, to feed the snakes. Good?"

"I damn well hope so."

"And when that's done," Molham suggested, blowing out a plume of blue-white smoke, "we'll clean up the rest of this mess. The pastor, the bikers, that idiot lawyer, God willing."

The idea of them all dying, screaming for mercy, gave

Habsi a warm feeling, a profound sense that everything could be all right again. He turned back to the window and watched the players giving him their money, receiving, on the whole, nothing in return.

It was how it should be.

36

At the Criminal Investigations Division of the New Orleans Metropolitan Police, Det. Pullman Lewis sat at his desk, as a lamp beat back the evening gloom, and stared at the forensic report.

He had his desk phone receiver cocked under his left ear.

"Tell me what I'm looking at here, Lydia, because it sure looks like a whole lot of nothing."

"What can I say, PT...? If there's nothing to tell you, it's because there's nothing there."

"They were casings from black-tip ammo, illegal in America except for a small number of approved federal agents."

"If I had to guess, they were made overseas, for a police force or government agency in a European nation. The FN is more popular there as a service weapon."

"And that doesn't strike you as weird, them showing up here?"

"I didn't say that. Sure, it's a little odd," she agreed. "If I had to guess, you're talking pros of some sort, guys who aren't worried about leaving people behind to testify."

"So that makes them..."

"Mercenaries or spooks, if I had to guess."

"Agency dogs," Lewis suggested. "Secret service, NSA, FBI?"

"Sure. Any of the above. I'd throw in CIA, assuming you don't buy that hokum about them not operating domestically."

"Well now, shit," Lewis muttered.

It was out of character for him to swear. "You okay, PT?" the analyst asked.

"Yeah. Look, I need you to keep quiet about all of this, okay?"

"Sure, of course. What's eating you? Where did this cartridge come from, anyhow?"

"A crime scene in Lakeview, one involving some local heavies, bikers."

"Yeahhh... weird place to find hi-spec, armor-piercing ammo."

"Indeed. We don't know who or what is at stake here. So..."

"My lips are sealed."

"I owe you one," Lewis suggested.

"You owe me a house by now," she retorted before hanging up.

Lewis dialed another number, beginning with the 202 area code for Washington, DC.

It was answered on the third ring. "Price."

"Heyyy... Kenny Price. How're you doing, man?"

"Pullman? Well, get out of town! How's my old partner doing at... what is it, seven o'clock New Orleans time?"

"Yep."

"You're working late, or is this the social call it should be?"

Lewis winced a little. "Yeah... Guilty as charged, old friend. I've got a weird one on the go."

"Yeah... well, I sure do miss chasing down wife killers and psychotic meth heads, but..."

"Don't rub it in, man, I know that NSA money is pretty sweet."

"Our beat is the nation," Price said. "So... what's up?"

"Had a shooting down here earlier today, related to an attempted murder earlier this week. Some biker thing with a local preacher, nothing super weird. But I landed a piece of evidence that looks like it would be more at home in your neck of the woods: some military-spec ammo. You feel like making a few calls for me?"

37

Bob slept until 3 a.m.

His phone alarm sounded, and he reached over to the bedside table and shut it off.

He got up and dressed in a black shirt and trousers. He added a light black coat, which had deep, wide lining pockets, from the thrift shop.

He packed a few items in them, then drove back downtown, the sidewalks alive with clubgoers and music fans well after midnight.

The first parking space available was blocks from The Purple Bird, the metered spaces jammed full of cars the closer he got to most of the nightclubs and restaurants. New Orleans didn't sleep, and a half-block walk could mean listening to three different bands or the strains of a piano bar.

That was fine. Speed was not of the essence.

The last visit had offered him an overview of the nightclub's security... and he'd noted that the Bird closed at three o'clock in the morning. The proximity security panels on the door were made by the same firm as the swipe card he'd taken from Diesel's wallet.

He knew exactly where Riggs normally sat, which gave him a chance to get in and out quickly. Contract-strip alarm systems usually had a delay of at least forty-five seconds before they began to blare, so that the business owner had time to enter their security code.

He didn't have the code. But for his needs, that was a lot of time on the clock.

First, however, he had to wait. Staff locked the doors at 3 a.m., but that meant at least an hour of cleanup before they left for the night.

Sure enough, at 4 a.m., a woman stepped out the front door, letting it lock closed behind her. Once down the two steps to the sidewalk, she reached up and pulled on the metal cage handle, sliding it down in front of the business, protecting its glass.

She made her way down the street on foot.

Bob waited five minutes to be sure she was the last person out. He got out of the car and headed south to the next corner, then turned east towards the next block. He took and followed the sidewalk until he was opposite the back door.

The street was busy even at four in the morning, cars going by, pedestrians talking, some just hustling by. He jogged up the steps, waved the security proximity card in front of the panel, and opened the door in time with the small green light.

If he was correct, to any observer, his comfort level and use of a security card would look casual, at home. Nothing worth noticing.

Inside the door, a small corridor featured an empty

cloakroom. Beyond it, a swinging galley door led into the kitchen. He ignored the chrome counters and cooktops, heading straight for the opposite door.

Beyond it was ten feet of empty space to Riggs's table. He clocked a security camera in the top-right corner of the ceiling, but it was stationary and pointed directly at the front door. He crouched by Riggs's table and reached underneath, securing the listening device to the top of the leg assembly.

He rose and jogged back the way he'd come, already down the back steps by the time the door swung closed.

He was another fifteen feet down the sidewalk when the alarm began to ring. He looked back casually, as if wondering where the sound was coming from. Once again, no one was paying any attention.

By the time the police responded, he would be back in the condo, making breakfast.

38

At the brothers' apartment building, Fletcher Thibodeaux waited on the balcony walkway, outside his brother's front door.

He was playing with his sheath knife, balancing the tip on the wood railing that overlooked the parking lot.

With his other hand, he raised a green, half-eaten apple to his lips and took a mighty crunching bite.

He chewed loudly, turning his head to acknowledge the figure coming up the concrete steps. "I wondered when you were getting back. I thought you were going out to 'clear your head.'"

"I had an idea to check out. Almost paid off, *mon frere*," Clay said. He had his left arm in a sling.

"You went to check out those bikers." Fletcher stared at the sling. "What happened?"

Fletcher was always riding him, challenging his decisions, keeping him sharp. "I found them."

"And?"

"I got there a few minutes after a gun battle and spooked

one of them," Clay lied. "Seems they had a shoot-out with a Midwestern guy who identified himself to the locals as 'Bob.' I figure that can only be one man."

"Really?"

"Yeah, really."

"I'm surprised, is all."

"Because?"

"Because Stone called, all kinds of pissed off. He wanted to know which one of us left a biker hogtied at a recent crime scene. Seems our target has specific ammo and left a shell behind."

Shit. That had been quick. "A necessary maneuver. I said I missed the shoot-out. Obviously, they didn't miss me. I had to beat it out of the guy who put a slug in my right shoulder."

"Huh." Clay could tell Fletcher didn't believe him. "Okay, then. And what did this hogtied biker tell you?"

"He confirmed the pastor's the key to finding Bob Singleton. I figured killing him would bring too much heat, and a biker ain't going to say shit to police."

Fletcher straightened up. He tossed the core of the apple over the balcony rail. It rattled into a tin garbage can below.

He took out a pack of non-filtered Lucky Strikes and lit one. He looked out at the city lights as he exhaled the first puff. "You've got an answer for everything, now, don't you?"

He took another puff and leaned on the railing, then cleared out his sinus before honking a ball of phlegm down to the parking lot.

Clay headed for the room door. He didn't say another word, but Fletcher could see from his expression that he was seething inside, angry enough to burn holes through it with his gaze.

39

D eacon Riggs sat on his motorcycle and watched the scene from three blocks away.

Lights flashed, uniforms strolled back and forth. Colbert Street teemed with police. It had been blocked off in two directions with temporary railings, a New Orleans police cruiser parked by each.

That was it, then.

There was no way they were going to meet Denny Roulette's target of Friday, no matter how important it was to his client. They couldn't get to multiple homes without being seen by the police, who had warned Paul Harris that anyone caught on the block who wasn't a resident would be arrested.

The explosion had made the papers, worsening his embarrassment. Four bikes, destroyed. Harris and Danny D had had to endure the humiliation that morning of renting a car until they could acquire real wheels.

He flexed his grip on the bike's throttle and clenched his teeth. The Damned MC were a national club. His chapter presidency could still be revoked, which sometimes was accompanied by winding up dead in a slough somewhere. Or maybe, given the availability, a swamp.

Behind him, he heard a car door slam. He checked over his shoulder and saw Harris walk his way.

"They're like ants, there are so many scurrying around," Harris said. "What now, boss?"

"Now? Now we're fucked. Now we prepare for Roulette's money man to unleash someone worse than 'Bob.' We spent his money setting up the new lab, and he has nothing to show for it," Riggs spat contemptuously. "How do you think he's going to react, Paul?"

Harris held up two hands in surrender. "Whoa! I'm not the fucking problem here, okay?"

Riggs nodded. Paul was right. He didn't deserve a shit-kicking because some outsider had messed everything up.

"We need to plan for the worst. We've got about twenty keys of meth already cooked and waiting for distribution. We get that dealt with first, recruit some new blood, replace the bikes. Keep our heads down and be ready for a fight."

"Okay," Harris said. "And the meth? We can't store it at the stash house."

"It's safe where it is."

"Are you sure?" Harris asked.

Riggs shot him a hard look. Paul never questioned his decisions. "Why are you asking?"

"It's just... the cooks don't make much money. It's a single padlock on a storage bunker. I mean, some of them must be tempted. And they've been done for days; normally we'd have moved it by now. But with this other job going on, it's just sitting there."

He was beginning to get on the biker boss's nerves. "You want us to go check it, make sure it's solid? It's two hours out of our fucking day, Paul, but if you're so goddamned nervous..."

"It wouldn't hurt," Harris argued. "Besides, it ain't like we can do a whole lot here anymore."

That was true, Riggs had to admit. There was no getting around the police presence. "Fine. Let's roll."

He fired up the bike's 1,746 CC engine as Harris walked back to the rental. They needed to deal with business, keep the bills paid. But then he was going to find the pastor's hospital, wait for Bob to show. Riggs figured he was due some payback.

THE SIGNAL WAS STRONG. Bob made sure the Honda stayed a half mile behind Deacon Riggs's bike, in case anything stopped them abruptly and he had to evade discovery.

The pain from the wound under his armpit helped him focus despite his growing fatigue.

The GPS beacon led him south again from Lakeville, back down through downtown to the Ninth Ward, along I-90 where it crossed Lake Saint Catherine to the north.

The freeway skimmed the shore of the lake, passing a tourist camp's fishing shacks and piers to his right, dense bayou swamp to his left, tall, narrow cypress trees in groves so thick the light between them seemed consumed by darkness.

Quite suddenly, in the middle of nowhere, the signal jumped to the left. But there was no road shown on the satellite map. Bob took quick note of where the position was relative to the tourist camp.

Three minutes later, he reached the trail they'd used. It was a single-lane track heading into the trees. That meant there had to be more solid ground ahead of it, somewhere to go to other than swamp water.

He pulled over at the gates to the camp's main office. Turning around and heading back was an option.

But it made more sense to leave the car there and walk back, Bob figured. Judging by the map, a canal ran just parallel to the road, with the trail the bikers had used being the only crossing point. If he drove in there, he knew he could turn the first bend and find himself surrounded by them – or on a track so narrow he couldn't turn around. There wasn't much room for error when he couldn't see where he was going.

Staying on foot gave him easy egress and an easier time avoiding detection. He began to trudge back the quarter mile to the trail.

THROUGH A SMALL GAP in the twisted vines and bulrushes, Diesel watched the biker pull up outside the cookhouse, followed by a gold Toyota.

A car!? Were they planning on moving the stuff already? *They'd use a truck or van.*

Riggs got off his bike and walked over to the long wooden steps up to the cookhouse porch. The long, rectangular structure had contained bunks for a kids' fishing camp, once upon a time.

He unlocked the doors and headed in, not waiting for the others. A moment later, he headed back out. "Everything's stored away until they cook the next batch in November," he announced to the men by the car. "No point cooking more until the twenty Ks are distributed."

"Nobody around for miles," Paul Harris said.

Diesel's eyes narrowed. It figured that Harris would be acting as muscle; it meant his brother, Booker, was still locked up.

"Let's check on the stash," Riggs said, making his way down the stairs. "We should be able to get a handle on how many vans would be best."

He rounded the corner of the building, the other men following. Diesel crept through the brush, parallel to them, until they reached it. He'd covered the pit again, and they spent thirty seconds clearing away mulch, wood chips and leaves.

Riggs unlocked the double steel doors and opened up the pit. For a moment, he said nothing. Then he looked back over his shoulder at Danny D. "You said you crunched the numbers and this would store exactly twenty keys. Right?"

Harris looked over his shoulder. "Doesn't look full to me. Looks like you could store another six or eight kilos in there, easy."

Danny D was frowning. "I checked the numbers twice. Maybe when they dug the hole, they overcompensated."

Riggs closed the doors and knelt down to shut the padlock. "I don't think so," he said. "You might've hit on something, Paul. They're skimming us."

To his right – he couldn't say how close – Diesel heard a twig snap. He turned that way. In his periphery, he saw the four men follow his gaze.

"You hear that?" Danny D asked.

Riggs nodded. "Go look."

The taller man nodded. He began to stride towards the bushes where Diesel was hidden.

.   .   .

BOB SPOTTED the camp from three hundred meters down the road. He moved off the trail and into the overgrown swamp. The swamp water was only held back by berms on each side of the road in, and his feet sank slightly in the mud. Within a few seconds, the murky water was up to his shins.

He moved slowly to avoid splashing and noise. It was hard going; tree limbs and tangles of mangrove blocked his path.

If they had perimeter guards, they'd be looking for people near the only way in. He stayed low, allowing him to duck and cover if absolutely necessary.

After about a hundred and fifty yards, the road ended at a clearing under cypress trees. He could make out the shape of a bunkhouse or camp house, with its low-slung A-frame roof and wraparound porch.

A car was parked about twenty yards from it. Four men were standing at each of its doors, looking at the camp house. Just ahead of them was Riggs's motorcycle.

The doors to the camp house swung open, and Riggs came out. He said something to them, gesturing towards the side of the building. Then he trotted down the stairs. The other men followed him as he walked towards the edge of the cleared, dirt area. He stopped about ten feet before it and began to clear debris away from the ground.

What the heck is this now? A bunker of some sort?

Riggs opened double steel doors. He looked down into the hole and said something, but Bob was too far away to make it out.

Need to get closer.

He took two steps that way. On the third, he stopped, foot suspended in midair.

The snake was red, black and pale yellow, as thick as a

man's wrist and about six feet long. It was eyeing him curiously, its neck and head off the ground, articulated joints holding it aloft even as it glided slightly from side to side.

He froze, muscles taut. It was in a striking position, he knew, ready to deal with any threat. The chances of him evading it were slight, at best.

He held his breath. His right leg was holding all his weight. He wasn't sure how long he could maintain it.

The snake lowered its head and neck back to the ground. It slithered towards him, sliding around the contours of his right ankle in slow, meandering coils.

A few moments later, it was gone. Bob watched it slither off. He turned and continued towards the men, crouching, moving his feet carefully, so as not to—

The snap might as well have been a gunshot; the twig cracked like a peal of lightning.

Bob winced and froze in place.

Then he was moving, scurrying low but quickly, farther into the swamp. They'd be moving immediately, he knew, trying to pinpoint the source of the sound. That meant they'd be making too much noise to hear him skitter away.

The water got deeper, up to his knees as his path verged toward the canal. The trees and mangrove bushes were thick, gnarled roots in bushy bunches, the odd thick mud bank to clamber over.

After a minute of moving, he found a small recess in a grove, where the bushes and reeds were nearly five feet tall. He crouched down, hidden from sight.

The place was probably full of alligators, Bob knew, and he'd been disturbing the water, announcing his presence to the wildlife for miles around. He tried to keep his breath regular: in through the nose, out through the mouth. If one came for him, he wasn't likely to see it, let alone stop it.

He could hear the men somewhere nearby, sloshing. They were moving quickly enough that the water must've still been shallow. That suggested they didn't want to venture deeper.

"You see anything?" a voice called out. It didn't sound like Riggs.

"Nah. Shit, man, there's probably a million things out here I wouldn't want to meet on a good night. Worrying about a branch breaking. Shiiitt..."

"Yeah, I guess."

The feet sloshed on. Bob remained completely still. After what seemed an eternity, it was silent again save the slight lapping of the water against the reeds.

He moved slowly and cautiously, staying low, circling back to close to where he'd trodden on the branch. He used a forefinger to gently pull aside the cluster of weeds blocking his view of the clearing.

They were closing the bunker up, the four heading back to the car. Riggs got back on his motorcycle and fired up the motor. A few moments later, they disappeared down the track.

Bob carefully pulled the branches aside and entered the clearing. He walked across the area where the door had been until his feet felt a change in the surface.

Here.

He swept the leaves and mulch aside with his feet.

The doors were padlocked, but it was a simple Master-style lock. He didn't want to shoot it; that would create too much noise, too much potential for attention. He wondered if he could pick it. It would be a five-pin mechanism, he suspected.

On the other hand...

He drew his .357 Magnum and flipped it around to hold it by the barrel. Then he hammered the lock once, twice, three times on its tip, near the metal loop.

It popped open on the third strike.

Modern Chinese craftsmanship, he thought dryly.

He opened the doors.

The pile of meth was deep, each package probably a quarter kilo. There was less than a foot between the top of the hole and the first layer.

The blow struck him from the right, a stinging shot to the temple with a heavy object, his head snapping to the left, slamming against the open metal door. The gun flew out of his hand and into the hole, coming to rest in the middle of the giant drug pile.

Bob rolled to his left instinctively, the branch coming down hard, clanging against the steel door where he'd just been.

His attacker turned his way immediately and swung it again. Bob blocked it with a forearm, the pain overtaken by adrenaline.

He kicked to his feet, but the man anticipated the move, the branch coming around full force, like a baseball player's line-drive swing, smashing into Bob's jaw.

The background bayou faded to a soft, muddled focus, and the lights grew dim as he slammed to the ground again.

The world faded to black.

40

B ob was dreaming, running through the woods in upstate New York, a deer in his sights. He didn't have a gun, but he knew he didn't need one.

He could hear the animal's heartbeat, smell the sweat as it ran past him in the darkened forest.

The dream disappeared. He snapped to consciousness, startled to be back in reality. He felt a hand holding his jacket, another digging through his right pocket.

He took a quick peek through one eye.

A blurry figure was moving just ahead of him.

Diesel.

The biker he'd left drifting on the lake.

He was going through Bob's pockets, doubtless looking for ID or some other rationale to explain the man's presence. Bob reached up suddenly, clapping both of the man's ears simultaneously, the pressure change nearly rupturing the eardrums.

The biker yelped and fell backwards, off him. Bob shot

out a heel, smashing him in the ankle, full force. He felt Diesel's leg bend at an odd angle, the biker squealing, falling over face-first, his knee slamming into the hard-packed dirt.

Bob leaped to his feet. The biker was already trying to rise from the awkward position when Bob spun on his left heel, right leg extended in a half-curl, like a ballerina, snapping outwards with whip strength as he completed the rotation, the foot slamming into Diesel's jaw and knocking him out cold.

The biker had made the mistake of assuming the guy he'd knocked out would stay out. Bob wasn't going to repeat it.

He pulled the wrist ties from his coat lining and restrained the burly gangster, hands behind his back.

It would take a minute or two for him to come around. He checked Diesel's pockets, confiscating a set of keys and a paring knife.

Missed the keys at the marina. Sloppy.

He gazed over at the doors to the camp house. Maybe...?

He jogged over and climbed the steps.

The third key opened the doors with a smooth turn of the lock.

Inside, the light was dim, the generator turned off. It looked like a giant high school chemistry lab; long wooden tables, each with three Bunsen burners. Stools for workers to sit for hours. Collection trays. Along the back wall, large collection jars and rubber tubing occupied most of the space.

This is their bread and butter.

Bob wandered the interior slowly. Diesel had probably figured out how to get to shore eventually, then walked to a familiar spot. From the number of tables, there were probably cots in the back of the building. Workers probably stayed there for days, which meant food and water.

But what about the other guy? He said he couldn't swim. Maybe...

Maybe Diesel just tossed him overboard. It wouldn't have surprised him.

Bob turned back towards the main doors. The long tables and the Bunsen burners caught his eye. He scratched under his chin absentmindedly, an idea forming.

He made his way back outside.

Diesel was awake and writhing about in the dirt in a futile attempt to get the wrist ties off.

"You can't leave me here like this, man!" Diesel wailed. "They come back and find me here, they'll kill me! And... and if they don't, some gator'll wander in here and—"

Bob walked over to him and crossed his arms, deliberately making a show of it. "Gator bait. That's an interesting prospect. I could copy James Bond in *Live and Let Die*, try to use your body as bait to lure gators into the camp. That'd cause all sorts of hell."

"Man... you can't be serious."

"Of course, they'd probably just grab you by the leg and drag you back into the swamp. They like to tenderize their meat," Bob explained, "drag it under the water, beat the life out of it, then store it down there under a log or rock. Hell of a way to go, drowning, waiting to be gator lunch."

"Dude... please!" Diesel wailed.

"Nahhh... I'm just messing with you," Bob said with a smile. He crouched down beside the other man. "Come on, get to your feet. We're going inside."

"Huh?"

"I had an idea that I figured a lying, cheating, murdering piece of shit like you is really going to love, Diesel. You're going to help send a message to your piece-of-shit colleagues about picking on old folks."

41

Denny Roulette hated the casino.

The flashing lights, the incredulous tourists, the zombie-eyed slot jockeys. None of it impressed him in the slightest.

For a man as seemingly wealthy and connected as Habsi, who was reputedly a cousin of the Saudi royal family, it all seemed a little crass and low-rent.

Basic. I think that's what they call it these days. God-danged basic. He climbed the plush, carpeted steps towards Habsi's second-floor office. Whatever he thought of the man, Roulette knew Habsi could be dangerous. The casual ease with which two of his men had nearly murdered the pastor was proof.

So it was a matter of telling him the right things, the things he wanted to hear.

Roulette had been billing the casino operator and would-be construction king a thousand dollars per hour for nearly two years of work. Most had been heavily padded. As much as he feared Habsi's temper, he was also fairly certain the man was a bit of a dope about the small details.

He opened the glass door to Habsi's office. A reception area greeted him, an aging receptionist with a blonde dye job busy typing something.

"Fortunes Casino, can I ask you to hold a moment?" she said into her headset. "Thank you! Well?"

Roulette realized she'd turned her attention his way. "Oh! Yeah, Denny Roulette. I have a five o'clock appointment..."

Her smile was plastered on and polished. "Go right on in, sir; he's expecting you."

Roulette opened the wide oak door and entered the room. Habsi's desk was along the glass back wall, giving him a view of the casino floor. A pair of leather armchairs studded with rivets sat ahead of the desk. Along the far wall, Habsi's mustachioed bodyguard, Molham, sat on a leather sofa in front of the bookshelves, one leg crossed over the other.

"Denny! Sit, sit," Habsi suggested, gesturing to the chairs ahead of him.

Roulette did as suggested.

Habsi rose from his chair behind the desk. He turned and looked out the tall window to the casino below. "Denny, do you know why I asked you to come and see me today?"

Great. We're playing twenty questions. Maybe for once he could get to the freaking point. "I can't say that I do, Sammy. Apologies. I'm sure it's necessary. I know how busy you are."

"Denny. Denny, Denny, Denny... what am I going to do with you?" Habsi asked, pacing. "I tell you six months ago that I am not happy with the speed of acquisitions on Colbert Street. I tell you to get your biker friends active again, impress upon them the need for impetus, speed and effort."

"They've been working real hard at it, Sammy."

Habsi turned abruptly, his face dark. "They've been fucking it up! If it's not the old people being defiant, it's this pastor who gets brave, or his friend you mentioned. I take care of this for you – my men take care of this for you – and even then, your 'muscle' makes a mess of things."

"Hey!" Roulette answered. "Now that's just unfair. They've got a lot to take care of. Yes, there have been a few complications. But we'll get it done, Sammy, don't you worry."

"But I do worry, Denny." Habsi turned and studied him, tilting his head slightly, like a bird considering a worm. "I worry that I picked the wrong man to handle my affairs. I worry that you're a lightweight, Denny, trying to slug it out with heavyweights. Most of all, I worry about any man who, having fucked up as much as you, would walk into my office as if he did not have a care in the world. As if he could, or should, ever talk back to me."

"Sammy—"

"No! Don't 'Sammy' this and 'Sammy' that. In my country, Denny, a man like you – a man who speaks with a tongue as smooth as velvet but as forked as a snake – he would not retain the power of speech for very long. Someone would grasp that tongue and cut it out, probably with him still alive to experience it."

Now he was getting creepy. Who did the little Arab think he was? In New Orleans, Roulette knew, his reputation carried weight. It carried water. He had friends in casino licensing, in construction. The problem with Habsi was that he didn't know his place, Denny figured. In his father's day, there was no way some foreigner mongrel would even dare request his services. The wrong kind of people got strung up by the righteous for that kind of insolent shit.

"I have given you plenty of chances, Denny," Habsi said. "Eventually, in a situation like this, when warriors fail, their leader must step forward and take control of the situation. Amends must be made. The right example must be set."

"Look," Roulette countered, "you just don't understand the nuances of business in—"

He didn't finish the sentence, the leather cord looping over his head and around his throat before he could react.

Behind him, Molham pulled the garrote tight, cutting off the lawyer's air, shutting down his windpipe.

Roulette grasped at the cord, trying to pull it away from his skin to no avail, the leather already cutting in. His face turned red, then purple, his eyes bulging as he tried to scramble to his feet. The bodyguard leaned forward, his full weight keeping the lawyer held down until he stopped kicking.

He gasped a last time, a tortured, strangled throat noise, before losing consciousness. Molham did not release the cord, instead pulling it tighter, ensuring he would not regain consciousness or the power to fight.

HABSI HELD UP A HAND. "STOP!"

"He's not dead yet, just unconscious."

"I don't want him dead yet. I want you to gag and bind him."

Molham frowned. "Why? I could just—"

"Because he is a piece of shit, and he has offended my good-natured patience. Take him out to the bayou and toss him to the alligators. Make sure it's shallow; I don't want him to drown before he feels them eating him alive."

While Molham got to work, Habsi took out his cell phone and dialed a number.

It took three rings for an answer.

"Yeah?"

"Deacon Riggs."

"Who wants to know?"

"You work for me, through Mr. Roulette. He is no longer employed by my company. If you want payments to continue, I need the problems on Colbert resolved immediately."

The biker would know exactly what "no longer employed" meant, Habsi knew.

"Look... we tried just about every damn thing so far. There's been complications."

"The pastor and his younger friend; yes, I know. I don't care. Get this right, or what happened to Denny will seem like a pleasant gator-watching tour to you."

"Look, man," Riggs sputtered, sounding flustered, "it ain't as easy as that. These people are entrenched. Some of them say they'd rather die than move."

"Then perhaps you should accommodate them."

"Roulette told us to keep the rough stuff to a minimum."

"Yes, and look how much good such sterling advice has done him. You want results, Mr. Riggs? Make it personal."

"Like what? Go after the wife? She's got cops around her twenty-four seven."

"Mr. Roulette's backgrounder on the street said the pastor has a niece, Denise. She is twenty years old, a college student. Surely, it would cause everyone great concern if something were to happen to her. When I suggested before that you assault the old women on the street, I was not making light banter; it is an effective dissuasion technique used by interrogators the world over."

"So you want me to—"

"Violate the girl. Leave her naked, somewhere public. In the street, perhaps. When they understand real fear, real pain, the rest will come easily."

"Leverage," Riggs replied. "I can dig that. Where is she?"

"She was staying with a neighbor; I do not know what the name is. But Roulette said it was another senior citizen. Surely that will not be too much for your brave men to handle."

There was a slight pause. Habsi knew hard men like Riggs. He was weighing whether to talk back. Eventually, instead, he muttered, "Okay, then. We'll get the girl."

"Serve me well, and you will be financially rewarded, Deacon Riggs. Fail me," Habsi suggested, "and you can go for a swim with Denny Roulette."

IT WAS JUST after six when the cloned phone on the coffee table began to ring again.

Bob had been in and out of sleep.

He'd stopped at the hospital, only to be told they were giving Wanda a special exemption to stay with her husband for a third day. They'd even arranged her a cot.

Back at the rental, he'd made a light dinner of an omelet and salad, thinking back to Diesel's shocked face when he'd left the camp. That trip had borne fruit. If he was lucky, the bikers would be permanently dealt with sooner rather than later.

He used the phone to access the bug in The Purple Bird.

It was designed to be triggered by sounds at human voice volume or below.

He plugged in an earpiece and listened for an hour. The recording was noisy, the mic often triggered by small actions like someone shuffling a chair. He watched the sound wave form in the app's display screen as he fast-forwarded through it, stopping whenever someone spoke.

It was all garbage, bragging about pool, about drinking exploits, about guys they beat up.

Deacon Riggs being his usual charming self.

"Deke." Bob had been listening for nearly two hours when he recognized the voice. But he couldn't immediately place it.

"What? I thought I told you not to come here."

"You did. And I thought I told you that cooperation is a two-way street. Besides, we've got too much history."

"Yeah... I don't need to hear your church bullshit, Pastor," Riggs said. "Your old man was the best screw in Angola, as far as any convict was concerned – but that doesn't mean I have to listen to holier-than-thou shit from his kid. What do you want?"

Pastor?

Derek Bevan. *The young man working for Don Green.*

"I want you guys to leave the street alone now that you've got what you want. You wanted Don out, I found out where he was hiding for you. Now you hold up your end; get out of Lakeville."

"I don't recall promising nothing like that," Riggs said. "I said we'd get things done more quickly if we knew where he was. I didn't say nothing about leaving."

"But... the whole point of helping you was I get my own congregation out of it. If they all flee Colbert Street terrified, there aren't going to be too many generous parishioners in St. Christopher's on Sunday morning. A few homes, okay, fine. But more than that—"

"Pastor, did I tell you at some point that I gave a shit about your problems?"

"But—"

"Because I don't. Sack up, Derek. Damn! Your old man would be ashamed! We have a job to do. You knew we were clearing folks out—"

"From ONE block! Now your men are visiting seniors all over Lakeville, blowing things up—"

"That was Pastor Green's carpetbagger buddy," Riggs growled. "You want us to go away quicker? Help me get rid of him."

"How?"

"The girl. Denise Green. She's perfect leverage."

"I won't—"

"Now, Pastor, don't kid a kidder, friend. You strike me as a fella who'll do whatever needs to be done to get what he wants. You want to be a big name in preaching, but you need a head start on your own church. I need an address. That's all. You ain't doing nothing worse than sharing information. You ain't deciding what I do with it, are you?"

There was a long pause. Bob wondered if the young pastor had rediscovered his conscience.

"She's with Mrs. Summerlea, next door to the Greens. Her parents live in the Ninth Ward, but that's all I know."

"It'll do just fine."

"Once he's out of the picture—"

"Then you do whatever you want to do, Pastor."

"But you won't hurt her, right? Okay?"

"We'll do whatever we want. We're The Damned."

The voices dropped, the recording ended. Bob put the phone down.

Derek Bevan was how the Saudis had known the motel and room the Greens were staying in. If Don died, he'd have been directly responsible.

And Denise was in terrible danger.

He got up and retrieved the .357 from under the coffee table. The recording was two hours old already. For all he knew, the bikers were already visiting Mrs. Summerlea.

He had to get moving.

42

The heat inside the Toyota Corolla was stifling, even at seven thirty at night. With the sun yet to go down, it made sense to leave the windows up, glare shielding them from view.

Danny D sat behind the wheel, sweating. He was a big man at six four, two hundred and twenty pounds. When he wasn't working on club business, he was the only member of Deacon's crew with a day job, as foreman of a construction company owned by his uncle.

He prided himself on being a hard man. He'd been a hard child, mean enough to smile back when his pappy whipped him with a golf club. But he'd have begged, borrowed, or stolen to have air conditioning in the moment.

He wiped the sweat away with a hairy, tattooed forearm. "Are these fucking guys going to fucking leave or what?" he complained.

In the passenger seat, Paul Harris looked even sweatier. He was rotund, over three hundred pounds, and beads of sweat were dropping from his bushy brown beard like raindrops off tree leaves. "Just be cool, brother. They shift change at eight o'clock; the new shift has been late for three straight days."

Ahead of them, four blocks away, one of the two police cruisers lurched forward a few feet before backing up, its tail end just about touching the crowd control barriers.

It sped past them a minute later. After twenty more seconds, the second police cruiser left in the opposite direction, heading south.

Harris checked his phone. "We've got thirty minutes, max, before the replacements show. Let's get this done."

The bikers clambered out of the car. Danny was glad they'd worn their rocker vests; it gave them an edge when it came to intimidation, and made up a little for them not having their bikes. At least the Toyota hadn't attracted attention.

He looked both ways as they crossed the street for any signs of trouble.

Mrs. Summerlea's porch was deserted. The whole street was quiet, front yards empty, the wind rustling the American flag on the pole next door.

Harris opened the gate, and they followed him up the wooden steps to the front door. He drew his Colt Defender 9 mm pistol from his waistband. Then he knocked on the door. "Mrs. Summerlea! You there, dear?" he barked.

It was silent.

"Keep an eye out, boys," Harris said. He turned back to the door and rapped three times again, his fist pounding the wooden obstruction. "Mrs. Summerlea! Come on out, dearie, and talk to your neighbors!"

He readied the Colt, balancing the butt on his left palm,

his right hand on the grip, finger drifting to the trigger. "I'm going to kick it in," he announced.

Harris raised his leg and thrust a mighty kick towards the door.

His foot didn't reach it.

The gunshot's force blew a hole the size of a potato through the plywood, the slug catching Harris center mass. He clutched at his chest and stumbled backwards two feet before tripping down the top step, slamming to the front-yard grass.

"Motherf—" Danny managed to get out, leg raised to repeat the kick. Animal grabbed him and threw them both to the left, off the front step, the second gunshot blowing another hole roughly where Danny's chest had just been.

They crouched low, to one side of the door. Danny looked over at Paul Harris. He lay still. "I think he's dead." He glanced back at the door. "Dirty bastard. It has to be—"

Animal called out, "That Bob?"

"It is," a voice answered. "Before you ask any more questions, you should know that anyone else who tries to enter this woman's house is going to die as quickly as your fat friend, there."

"Fuck this!" Danny snarled. He rose quickly and threw his considerable frame at the door. The lock gave, and it snapped inwards, wood splintering.

The pistol-whipped him across the temple before he could straighten up, knocking Danny to the home's hardwood floor, his pistol tumbling from his grasp.

He reached frantically for it, turning onto his back, finger on the trigger...

Three bullets slammed into his chest. His arm spread

wide, and he dropped the gun, his head lolling back, eyes turning glassy as the life began to ebb from his body.

On the other side of the door frame, Animal tried to contain his sense of panic. Both of his brothers had gone down instantly, recklessly. He was isolated, on his own. The cops would be back in minutes, and if he so much as moved, he'd probably be shot in the head and die next to Danny D and Paul.

Or...

"Hey!" he called out. "I give up! I surrender!"

"Throw your piece out in front of the door," Bob ordered. "Take a step out, then turn so that your back is to me."

Animal did as ordered, the gun bouncing twice off the warped old decking before coming to its rest. "You can't kill an unarmed man," he said, hands slightly raised in submission.

"First of all, I'm not a cop, and I can kill you pretty much whenever I feel like it. But I'm not going to," Bob said. "Your time on Colbert Street is done. I need to leave you with a reminder of that."

Animal felt his sweat turn icy. What did he mean by that?

"Reach back towards me with your left arm, please," Bob said.

"I don't... Reach back?"

"Just as it sounds. Stay where you are, but reach back with your left arm."

"Okay."

He did as ordered. The sensation of a man gripping his wrist lasted the barest of split seconds before a knee came down on his elbow joint, snapping the arm in two cleanly, the crack of bone audible.

Animal screamed and fell to his knees. A boot caught

him square in the back, pushing him face-first down the stairs, into the yard.

He lay on the grass, moaning with pain.

"When the next police shift shows, Mrs. Summerlea has kindly agreed to explain how she shot the intruders who tried to break into her home. Don't bother looking for Denise; she's already gone. If I were you, I wouldn't be here, either."

The biker's arm ached and throbbed, the pain radiating down to the bone. He got to his feet shakily. Then he stumbled out of the yard and across the road to the Toyota, one arm clutching the other.

He turned and looked back, his face white from pain. "I... don't have the fucking keys."

Bob sighed. He looked through Danny D's pockets and found the keys. He threw them from the porch into the road. "Go on, get out of here. Tell Riggs he's next."

The biker limped over and picked them up, whimpering slightly throughout. A moment later, the car pulled away from the curb.

"Oh Lord."

Bob turned. Mrs. Summerlea was staring at the corpse in her cloakroom. He expected an expression of horror and revulsion. But after eighty-six years, she'd seen death too many times for that.

She sighed and tsk'd, shaking her head. "I suppose I'll have to do some cleaning," she said.

43

Associate Pastor Derek Bevan moved frantically, shuffling to and fro between the small floor safe by the desk and the suitcase atop it.

By his count, the church's rainy-day fund, to be used for congregation emergencies, held just under nine hundred dollars.

It wasn't much. But he also had the church's ATM card, which gave him access to the capital repairs fund. That contained more money.

A lot more.

It was still likely less than twenty thousand, but it was enough to get out of Louisiana, make a new start.

He'd miscalculated terribly helping the bikers. Don was old, bound to retire soon enough. He could have just waited him out.

But his ambition had gotten the better of him.

Now he had to run.

He'd gone down the street a way with the binoculars his cousin had sold him for birding. He'd seen the men on Mrs.

Summerlea's porch, seen one of them go down, a gunshot ringing out a moment later.

He'd realized immediately that things were going wrong.

I shouldn't have told them. I shouldn't have told them about Denise. That was going too far.

I didn't have a choice, he told himself. *They'd have forced it out of me if I hadn't told them.*

It's not my fault.

He fished the last of the cash out of the safe and closed it behind him. He'd called Wanda, ensured Don was safe and wasn't going to die.

There was no point sticking around. Their friend Bob would realize eventually that he was the only other person who knew where the Greens were staying. He'd come asking questions.

He rose and zipped up the case. He'd so wanted to be a celebrity preacher, own his own megachurch with tens of thousands of followers. He wanted to feel the power of their lives being placed in his hands. The diamond tie studs and mansions wouldn't hurt either.

But that was over, for now.

"Going somewhere, Pastor?"

He turned slowly. The Greens' guest was standing in the doorway. He tried to slap on a genial smile.

"Bob! I wasn't aware you were still in town. I'm just getting a few things together for a business trip."

"Anything special? A healing circle in Hawaii, maybe? A prayer for peace in Punxsutawney?"

Bevan's hand drifted towards the top drawer of the desk. "No, no, just the usual parish business." He began to slowly slide the drawer open.

Bob took three steps forward, quickly. Bevan froze as the

bigger man reached over the desk and slammed the drawer shut on his hand.

He squealed, but Bob held the drawer shut, pinning his hand there. "Now, where did you say you were heading again?"

"Please..." the pastor pleaded.

"You didn't give Don Green a chance to beg for his life," Bob snarled. "You told them where to find him, and now he's clinging to life, with tubes up his nose, in an intensive care unit." He pushed against the drawer, feeling the small bones in the associate pastor's hand begin to snap.

"Aaiighgh!" Bevan screamed gutturally.

Bob yanked the drawer open. A dainty Beretta .32 pistol was inside it. He took it out. "I'm guessing he doesn't know you keep this here."

"The bikers..." the pastor panted, trying to formulate a lie that might stand up to scrutiny on the fly. "I needed protection."

Bob sprang the magazine and emptied it. He left one bullet in the pipe. "You can say what you want, but we both know what you did. Once he's recovered from surgery, Pastor Green's going to find out, too. In the meantime, shove all that money back in the safe."

The young man summoned his courage. This was Pastor Green's friend. This wasn't a man who was really going to hurt him. "And if I refuse?" he said.

"Well... it wasn't my intention to beat you senseless, but if that's the route we have to go..." Bob said. Before the pastor could react, he turned on his heel and pistol-whipped the traitorous preacher across the left temple.

Bevan collapsed to his knees. He began to sob. "I'm sorry."

"I don't care. Put the money back."

The associate pastor complied, grabbing loose handfuls of cash like so much debris, shoving it back into the floor safe.

"Lock it," Bob ordered.

Bevan complied.

"Hand me the key."

The pastor did so. Before he could step back, Bob hit him again, hard, smashing the pistol butt into the man's nose, breaking it. Blood streamed from his nostrils, and Bevan collapsed forward onto the desk. He moaned, grasping at his nose to staunch the flow. He grabbed a wad of tissues from a box on the corner of the desk.

"Don't tilt your head back. That's a myth," Bob said. "You'll just swallow and inhale blood by mistake. Sit down, lean forward, pinch the bridge below the break."

Bevan did as instructed.

"Now, here's what's going to happen," Bob said. "I'm going to let you live, because I want you to feel the scorn and disgust your behavior will receive from the congregation here once they've been told who and what you are."

"I didn't think they'd be seriously hurt," the young pastor tried to argue.

"Shut up and stop making excuses, dickwad, or I'll change my mind and end you right here and now. By tomorrow, every religious leader in this city – hell, probably in the South – will know the truth. The police will be looking for you, and you're going to go to jail. Or..."

"Or?"

"Or I can offer you another way out." He tossed the .32 Beretta back onto the desk, the weapon sliding halfway to Bevan. "There's one bullet still in there."

Bevan grasped it frantically and leveled it at Singleton. "You... you..."

"If you don't kill me, you're a dead man," Bob said. "So you could try it. But you'll only have one shot. And a pistol like that... it's mostly only deadly from very close range. That's also why you could use it: for that other way out I was talking about."

He turned and walked out the door, down the hallway.

Bevan stumbled to his feet, the gun still extended. He pointed it down the hall at the man's back. But he did not pull the trigger.

Everything he was saying was true. His theft, the attempt on Pastor Don. It was all going to come back on him. All of it. He'd be lucky just to rot in prison.

His career was ruined, his reputation. Everything was gone.

Everything.

Bob was halfway down the hall when the single gunshot sounded.

He didn't bother to turn back and look.

He exited through the nave of the church, walking between the rows of pews to the giant front doors.

Outside, the evening sky had darkened. It was humid, rain beginning to spatter the brickwork landing atop the church stairs.

The punch came out of nowhere, a rapid right cross that caught him flush in the side of the mouth. He went down, biting his tongue, the iron taste of blood in his mouth.

The other man was on him immediately, trying to pin him down and pound him mercilessly. Bob reacted on instinct, flinging his knees backwards and wrapping his lower legs around the man, using the leverage to throw him off.

He rolled to one side and came to his feet. The gun flashed into view, a Ruger American 8649, a powerful .45, seven in the mag. Instinct kicked in again. He grabbed the man's wrist, trying to lock up his arm, to shake the gun loose.

His attacker was a pro. The moment his wrist was restrained, the pistol shaken loose, the man flexed at the left knee, using the slight drop in height to hammer Bob's midsection with a right front kick.

Bob left his feet slightly as he crashed onto his back. He reached for the Ruger, but his attacker was on him again, this time more precise, knees trying to pin Bob's arms, punches raining down from both sides.

Before his right hand was immobilized, Bob managed to draw his FN 5.7 from his coat pocket. He tried to turn it inwards, but the other man spotted it, grabbing the barrel with one free hand, trying to rip it from his grasp.

Bob squeezed loose, rolling clear even as his gun flew from his fingers and clattered to the ground.

He rose again. His assailant was balanced on the balls of his feet. He snapped a high kick, and Bob blocked it with his forearm, dropping and pivoting on his right knee so that he could drive his other elbow into the meat of his opponent's thigh.

Fletcher Thibodeaux stumbled backwards. Bob tried to press the advantage, swinging his leg low, trying to sweep Thibodeaux's feet, the younger man jumping out of range.

The two men squared off, both panting slightly, the sudden, rapid conflict draining. It was warm. They'd attracted attention; thirty feet away, a handful of local kids were peering through the property's chain-link fence.

"You're quick for an old man." His assailant was grinning. "I figured a decade on the street would knock all the strength out of a guy, but maybe not. I can fix that real quick, though."

"The last guy I fought seemed to think the same thing. It didn't go well for him," Bob said.

"You mean Clay? Figured that was you. But he's yesterday's news. I'm the star attraction." The young man leapt ahead, two rapid steps followed by a flurry of straight, short punches.

Bob blocked them in patterns, his forearms moving with subconscious speed and accuracy, decades of practicing on the blocking dummy paying off. The man had skill, speed, style. He was mixing disciplines, like any good mixed martial artist.

He dropped low, sweeping his leg in a coffee grinder circle. Bob jumped over it and kicked back, low, feeling the man's ankle bend slightly. He threw his weight in that direction, the attacker's balance slightly off, the extra momentum forcing them both to crash to the ground.

They rolled away from each other, both men springing to their feet.

"So would I be right in guessing you're Eddie Stone's cleanup hitter?"

Thibodeaux smiled wickedly, a gold tooth glinting. "The police are blocks away. They're not going to help you. I'm younger, faster, and I don't quit. Give up now, and I'll make your death quick."

He had a point about the strength and speed advantage, Bob knew. If he couldn't overwhelm the young man with technique, he needed another edge. He circled the man slightly, Thibodeaux mirroring the movements, both men repositioned.

The front kick was fast, snapping towards his midsection. Bob let it catch him but rolled with it, going over backwards, rolling over on his shoulders and coming up on his feet.

Thibodeaux was already pressing the advantage, his hand dropping to his boot to retrieve the throwing knife, the onyx blade catching the light as he backhanded it Bob's way. Bob dropped backwards into a limbo duck, the blade millimeters from his face as it passed him.

He thudded to the brick pavement. His hand found the pistol, and he leveled it, the trigger pull timed in years of practice, the gun level with Thibodeaux's chest.

The gunshot caught the younger man square, stopping him dead in his tracks. He stumbled another half-foot forward, then dropped to his knees. He was losing blood quickly, panting. His pupils were already dancing about, confusion setting in.

Bob rose, fatigued. It had begun to rain hard, thick droplets coming down, obscuring his vision. He wiped the rain away as he stumbled, panting, over to the kneeling figure.

The young man was choking on blood. "Fug... fug-ing shot me..." he gargled.

They always said that. It was always a surprise, even though it almost never should've been. Bob stood over him. "You're done. Septicemia will get you if the punctured lung doesn't. I can end this quickly, or I can leave you and let it be slow and painful. How'd you find me?"

Thibodeaux grimaced, his eyes steadying as he stared up at the sky, rain coming down heavier, drops spattering his face, running down his torso. His body was convulsing gently, shaking from the combination of adrenaline and rapid blood loss. "Fucking... fucking traffic cam... in Slidell..."

When he'd been followed. He'd neglected to turn his head away at a red light, given the camera monitoring software a chance at facial recognition. The NSA had likely caught it on its surveillance network.

Sloppy.

Bob raised the pistol and fired twice.

Thibodeaux fell over sideways and stopped moving.

In the background, the kids across the street scattered. A car gunned its engine to get off the block.

Bob crouched beside him and checked his pockets, looking for anything useful, scraps of paper, life lint that might lead to something.

But there was nothing. His wallet contained a Florida driver's license and just under four hundred dollars in cash. He took the money and wiped down the wallet.

He tossed it beside the body and pocketed the Ruger, then retrieved his FN from ten feet away. He followed the path to the front gate and let himself out, jogging across the street.

It was a start.

But his wounded arm hurt like hell, as did his jaw. He needed painkillers, quickly and in no small dosage. He knew the night would be long and challenging.

44

D et. Lewis looked at the clock above the nearby window. It was eight minutes past eight o'clock... which was two hours past the end of his shift.

He'd hoped to get a call back from Washington. Instead, his former partner had gone silent.

Staying much later would mean explaining himself to Sondra. She put up with enough from him and the kids, he knew, and he'd promised to try to watch his overtime.

Time to go home, pick this up tomorrow. If he was lucky, he figured, he'd get home before his daughter Nadine was put to bed. He knew he'd see her before morning anyway, as she'd taken to climbing into bed with them in the middle of the night, the darkness and nightmares conspiring. But it wasn't the same.

The multi-line phone on the corner of Lewis's desk lit up, a surprise any time after eight o'clock at night. The clear plastic buttons for the first two lines began blinking near simultaneously.

He picked up the receiver and hit line one. "Detective Lewis."

"Detective... fine evening we're having."

"I've missed most of it, sir." Deputy Commander Irwin Leffle was neither an empathetic nor an attentive man.

"Hah! Still, the evening's loss is no doubt the department's gain," the division deputy said. "Working like a dog, Detective! Commendable, commendable."

It felt slightly like being complimented by Foghorn Leghorn, Lewis thought. "Thank you, sir."

"Still, don't want you working too hard, burning out your intellectual faculties, on account of all play and no work being a mite stressful."

"Sir?"

"You've been going real hard on this whole Colbert Street thing. Well now, I don't want you to worry no more. I've called Armitage and told him he's working it solo now. You just pass off what you've got to him, you hear?"

What the hell is going on? "But... sir, I've been making progress. We found a shell at the scene of the second—"

"Now, you know I've got the diabetes and blood pressure issues, so don't make me repeat myself on this here thing, boy, just get on home for the night, take a couple of days off on the department. Am I clear, Detective?"

"Yes, sir, of course."

"Well then, I shall thank you kindly again for all your good work. Take care now."

The deputy commander hung up. Lewis stared at the receiver, dumbstruck for a moment at the man's brazen interference. Then he realized the other line was still flashing.

"Detective Lewis."

"PT, it's Jerry Cross from Fire and Rescue. You left a note with our guys about getting a quick call on any first responder stuff around Colbert."

"Sure."

"Well, we've got some sort of bloodbath down here. We've got two dead bikers, maybe a third wounded, based on the blood trail. We've got a third unsub victim and what looks like a priest who has committed suicide."

"Jesus Christ."

"Yeah... He was not in the building at the time, would be my guess. I'm outside the Church right now and... Hang on, Armitage is here."

Lewis felt a gnawing in his gut. He heard the phone change hands. "Yeah, look, I guess Leffle was going to call you," Armitage said.

"He did, but—"

"Then why are we having this conversation?" the older detective said. "Go home, PT. If I need you, I'll call you."

Armitage ended the call.

Lewis stared at the receiver again.

All hell seemed to be breaking loose, yet he was being waved off.

He hung up the phone. He knew he should go home immediately, but something was bothering him, the sense that he'd missed something, maybe even something that could've justified him challenging the deputy commander's decision.

The evidence report sat on his computer screen, to his left. He turned his chair that way and used the mouse to scroll through it again. There was nothing obvious from the items found in the burned house. The Chapstick would give them DNA on someone, but it would take two days to get lab results; then they'd have to hope for a match.

Photos from the scene didn't help much. A sad backyard of burned and broken dreams; neighbors looking on – and likely knowing more than they would ever tell; the debris from what had been three motorcycles. A few street shots.

He backed up, conscious he'd seen something familiar.

There. His finger traced the screen momentarily. It was a shot facing north, taken a block south of the church. Parked just about ten feet in from the curb, on the west side of the adjoining side street, was a pale red Honda Civic.

That's the Greens' car.

It had been there at the time, but she'd been at the hospital, and he'd been in a hospital bed.

Their friend is still here.

And Wanda knows it.

He hastily dialed Second District Staff Sgt. Terry Cowan. "Terry? PT."

"What's up, amigo? Got you on the night shift, too?"

"Working late. Look... can you do me a solid? I've got a witness I'm a little worried about. She's staying in a condo in Harahan. Can you send a car over to the New Orleans East emergency, have a couple of guys pick her up, then keep an eye on the condo building doors for a few hours?"

He gave Cowan the weak description they had of Wanda's guest "Tyler Gaines." If they were lucky, maybe he was foolish enough to head there after Colbert.

THE CONDO BUILDING was hotter than a furnace.

A police cruiser was parked at the curb; a patrolman was waiting at the front door.

Bob watched from the driver's seat of the Civic, parked two blocks away. *They've brought Wanda here.*

He'd left his stuff stashed out of sight, so there would be no suspicion from whatever detective or officer was there helping her settle in. There had been no suggestion she was a target, which meant they were just there dropping her off.

Patience was required. He still had a lot of work to do, and Wanda didn't need any element of risk.

He turned the Honda back towards downtown New Orleans.

Twenty minutes later, he stood at the front desk of the youth hostel and paid $87 for a room. The lobby was busy, but everyone was young, happy; college kid travelers, there for the bargain.

He took the key from the earnest young clerk. A set of concrete stairs led to the second floor. Despite their reputation, hostels were generally dependable and safe in most cities.

The police would find the assassin's body. The coroner would identify him as a local hitter; the name would be flagged on law enforcement networks, maybe even be recognized quickly by Stone or whomever hired him.

But that would take a day or two, at least, to unfurl.

He unlocked the door to the tiny room and closed it behind him, slipping the bolt. The facilities were usually safe no matter what city you were in, but it paid to be cautious. Cheap temporary rooms were cheap temporary rooms.

He stored his bag in the bottom of the closet, its hangers permanently attached to the rod to avoid theft. The room was too small to hide anything effectively: just narrow whitewashed walls, a single cot-sized bed, a side table. A shared bathroom was down the hall.

It was nearly nine o'clock. After changing back into dark clothing, he checked his email.

Nick Velasco had forwarded an eyes-only FBI folder on Sammy Habsi.

Nicky, Nicky, Nicky. He was always a risk for sloppiness. If newly acquired from his source, the file was almost certain to have triggered a security inquiry.

But perhaps it had been stolen a while ago. The first page was stamped "Secret," the date listed at Nov. 19, 2018.

Bob scanned through it quickly. Habsi was a surprise; he was selling himself as a Saudi prince, a cousin of the king. But he was actually a former Egyptian political organizer, a bag man.

He'd raised millions in support for two popular political movements before being accused of plundering the donations. He'd fled to the US twenty-five years earlier. He had a brother in the Egyptian Secret Service, a cousin in the Egyptian education ministry and a cousin who worked for the US State Department, albeit with low security clearances.

Habsi had purchased Fortunes Casino when it was in disrepair and losing money for an older local family of some social standing.

He'd turned it around within two years, partly by winning a string of government contracts for official engagements and tourism excursions. The media attention had led to a flood of new customers, and the casino had become a license to print money, netting him more than $230 million in profits over the first five years.

He'd followed that by buying a string of tenement buildings with decent inherent land value, each suspiciously later being in the exact location of a city project, requiring them to purchase the undeveloped properties from Habsi.

So he's got politicians in his pocket. Figures.

There was a second sheet attached, for an associate, Molham Al-Maghrebi. His occupation was stated as "head of security" for Fortunes Casino. His CIA sheet said he was a former enforcer with Egypt's often-brutal State Security, now allegedly reformed.

He'd somehow gotten permission to enter the US and had been sponsored for employment by Habsi, who had taken citizenship a decade earlier.

"Al-Maghrebi is a superior hand-to-hand combatant, a superb marksman and an accomplished undercover operative. When with the Security Service, he showed a preference for inflicting pain upon his targets, and he is believed to have a penchant for injuring prostitutes. He exhibits little empathy, compassion, or remorse."

These were the men who wanted to become the construction kings of New Orleans?

That wasn't going to happen.

But first, he needed to stake out the casino, find out how the place ticked over, where its vulnerabilities lay.

Dinner and a drive. Sounds like an evening.

45

Deacon Riggs stood in the dimly lit office and watched as the doctor, under an overhead lamp, built the fiberglass cast around Animal's newly set arm.

"How is it, Doc? Is he going to be jacking it with the other hand for the rest of his life?"

"It'll heal, albeit with some potential problems. The bone was snapped at the joint, which will cause some fusing issue, some questions of mobility in the joint."

"Ohhhh..." Animal moaned.

"The painkillers should kick in soon."

"Oxy," Riggs said. "We got you the good stuff."

"Will... will I be able to ride my bike again, Doc?"

"Oh, I imagine so," the doctor said, peeling off his rubber gloves and tossing them into a silver flip-top bin by the sink. "You'll never pitch in the majors again, though."

Riggs had never seen Animal reduced to whimpering. He'd always thought the burly biker was impervious to pain, scared of nothing and nobody. But he had a look of genuine fear in his eye.

Maybe that was it. Maybe they'd been secure for too long, controlled a quarter of the city for too long. Everyone else was afraid of them, especially the other criminals who made up most of their dance card.

But "Bob" wasn't like that. If it was the last thing he did, Riggs vowed, he was going to kill that son of a bitch.

"Give us a minute, okay, Doc?"

"Hrmpph..." the doc grumbled as he wandered out of the room.

"So what happened?" Riggs asked.

"He had the drop on us. He knew we were coming somehow, or he guessed. Paul drew his piece and knocked on the door... and that was it. He shot him through the door. Danny D and I got into cover, but he tagged Danny nonetheless. He had the drop on me, and he could've killed me, but he broke my arm instead. He... he told me to tell you that he was coming for you, and that he's going to kill you."

That just about fit. Riggs figured he understood how the man felt. "Plenty men tried; plenty men died," he muttered. "Danny and Paul, both." He didn't try to hide the numbness he felt at the news.

Doesn't seem right. Doesn't seem fair.

With Animal out, there were only three of them left. Dozer and Terry were good soldiers, but not as tough as the men already taken down.

"Deacon... Look... maybe we should get out of town for a while," Animal said. "We could hide out until this dude fucks off..."

Riggs shook his head. "Let him come. A man can't outrun his problems. Dude doesn't scare me."

His phone rang.

An accented voice said, "I hear things went poorly once again on Colbert Street."

It was Roulette's employer, Habsi.

"He killed two of my boys. Look, man, this dude faces up to me, he's going to die. But we're not looking for him no more. We're not going to turn this into some vendetta thing, because this dude has already made two of my men disappear, jailed a third, shot a fourth and fifth and put another in hospital. So, it's over, man. If we don't get no more of your money and no more houses, that's something I'll have to live with."

"Will you?" Habsi said bluntly. "Perhaps I will decide you no longer deserve to live, given how much of my money you have already spent. You work for me, Mr. Riggs. You would do well to remember it before I lose my patience."

Riggs mulled it for a few moments. He knew this guy was connected to the Saudi royal family or something. He had bodyguards and hundreds of millions of dollars. Taking him on, it seemed, was even stupider than attempting to track down and kill Bob.

Jesus H... Rock and a damn hard place.

"What do you want?" he eventually asked.

"I need protection from this lunatic 'Bob' until my men have made an example of him," Habsi said. "You will join my men here at the casino. My security chief expects that he has identified me by now as the source of his issues, and will attempt to assault the business."

"Man... knowing this guy, he's already inside playing blackjack," Riggs muttered quietly.

"Excuse me? I didn't catch that."

"Nothing important. When?"

"As soon as you can get here. With the killings today, he seems to have escalated matters. He is no longer leaving his targets alive, which means he has run out of patience. He will attempt to 'go to source,' Molham informs me. You will come here and act as a wall of protection, ahead of my men."

"We're supposed to be your cannon fodder, that about it?"

"Now or later, Mr. Riggs. At least my way gives you the odds on your side, a chance to win. The alternative is you and your men joining Denny Roulette in his new occupation as friend of the animals."

"We'll be there in an hour."

"I look forward to it." Habsi hung up.

"Who was that?" Animal asked weakly.

"That was the devil we know." He patted his friend gently on his good shoulder. "Rest easy, big man. We'll get things squared away by the time you're back on your feet."

There were just three of them left. He'd have to leave the decision to a vote, let Terry and Dozer decide whether to stick around or head for the hills. But he'd make sure they knew the consequences of leaving.

Once on the enemies list of a guy like Habsi, they'd never be safe in New Orleans again.

46

So far, the Big Easy was full of surprises.

As he stood on the docks and looked up at the top deck of the four-story riverboat, high above, Bob had a slight sense that fate was messing with his head.

"The casino is a freaking boat," he muttered. "Great. Just great."

It was ornate, in an old-timey way, wraparound iron latticework painted white and surrounding each deck level, each roof supported by lattice arches; a giant paddle wheel on the back end; two giant black steam chimneys to vent the boilers that would power the wheel if the boat was moving.

A man and woman walked by, drunk and swaying, giggling. The man heard Bob's comment and checked out his grimace. "Hey, man... only gamble what you can never afford to lose," he offered nonsensically. "Wait... did I get that right?"

They stumbled on past him, arm in arm.

His brain should've been focused on more important matters. Instead, the pair made him feel jealous. *Oh, to be drunk right now*, he thought. *Just... oblivious to all of this shit. To all of it.*

Get your head in the game.

He strode the length of the vessel, getting a good look at it. It had a fixed gangway to the dock at each end, sloped and made of metal. A guard stood at each, the man at the bow of the ship letting them on board, the one at the stern letting them disembark.

The easiest way in would be to pretend to be a customer. They came and went up and down the gangways at a reasonable rate. But after Colbert Street, they'd be looking for him. His size and frame would make him easy to spot.

The timing was a problem, too. Even if he could figure out a discreet way on board, it would have to be in the early morning, when the fewest customers were around. He had to minimize the chance of collateral damage.

It was nearly midnight. There were two ways in, and that was it. There was nothing at water level, no sign of any other entrance.

"She's pretty big, ain't she?"

Bob turned his head towards the voice. An elderly man was sitting on a bench nearby, drinking a coffee. "I'm not really a ship guy or a gambler," he replied.

"That's okay, then. It ain't much of a casino," the old man said. "Sure rakes in the suckers, though."

"You're here a lot, then?"

He nodded. He leaned forward on an umbrella that stood on its tip, perched between his knees. "I always liked the smell of brackish water and gasoline. Did a pair of tours in the Navy when I was a kid, spent a lot of time around harbors. Still... used to get a whole bunch of different cruise vessels at that slip. For the past decade, that ugly hulk has just sat there."

The conversation gave Bob an idea. "You ever see the guy who owns it, Habsi? He come and go?"

The old man shook his head. "He doesn't leave the ship much. I heard the staff talking one day; said he has a luxury suite looking out over the casino, thousands of square feet. Must be nice."

"Sure. Still... surrounded by customers and staff twenty-four seven?"

"I mean, he's off in his own little corner of it. Probably never sees them unless he wants. I had a sandwich about... oh, ten days ago, maybe... with one of the young cleaners who go in each morning..."

"Cleaners?" Bob interrupted. "They bring in a crew?"

"They have to! Place runs twenty-four seven. By four or five in the morning, there's trash everywhere. So a crew comes in for three hours, works around the hardcores who won't go to bed."

Now that had prospects. Bob checked his watch.

"Am I keeping you, young feller?" the old guy asked.

"Nah... just a night of work ahead still."

"Well, good luck to you. I am retired, twenty-three years ago last Thursday. People told me day in and out how bored I'd be with nothing to do. But I'll tell you, friend: sometimes doing nothing sure beats doing something."

Bob wasn't sure if the notion was wise, or just alluring. For now, he was going to do nothing. He'd come back at four, check out the cleaners, see if they held opportunity.

Then, perhaps, he'd do something.

. . .

DEACON RIGGS PACED the atrium by the rear elevator, the brown marble floor reflecting the tube lights overhead.

The atrium was effectively the back entrance to Sammy Habsi's apartment – although at more than three thousand square feet, it was more like a floating mansion, Riggs figured.

He'd been guarding the elevator for three hours. Habsi's quiet, disconcerting giant of a bodyguard had made it clear nobody was allowed to leave until dawn, when the bulk of the customers would return. Based on his behavior so far, Bob would try to hit them with as few collateral casualties as possible, Molham had suggested.

That meant another six hours of waiting to do... what? Probably nothing. Riggs figured Habsi was being paranoid. Bob had been careful with The Damned, either isolating them and taking them out when they couldn't get help, or striking first, taking them by surprise.

The casino was the opposite of both. Molham had three more gunmen on his team, plus two rent-a-guard security personnel in uniforms – although they were really there for the regulars. Riggs doubted either man – both were elderly – would stick around if shooting started.

His earpiece crackled. "You there, boss?"

"What's up, Dozer?" Dozer was Diesel's first cousin. Riggs hadn't thought it possible to find someone dumber who could still tie his own shoelaces. The cousin had set that straight.

"Nothing, I guess."

"So... why are you calling me?"

"Just bored. This is boring, dude. We've been here for hours, and nothing has happened. Nothing's going to happen. There are eight gunmen waiting for him. He ain't that stupid."

"Nine."

"Eh? No, I counted. The four Arabs, the two security guards, you and Terry. That's eight."

"You forgot to count yourself." Damn, he was dumb.

"Oh. Oh, yeah! Okay. Still... Can't figure as Terry matters. Dude couldn't hit the broad side of an eighteen-wheeler with a shotgun from five feet."

That was true. But based on where they were positioned – Riggs ahead of the back doors to the apartment, the other two bikers where the elevator exited on the bottom floor – they were as much cannon fodder as Habsi had promised.

They were there to slow him down if he decided to go through the back of the casino somehow.

Riggs wondered where everything had gone wrong. It felt like the world had opened up under them. They'd gone from feeling like kings to feeling like losers in less than a week. All because of one man.

Bob.

He didn't care if he ever learned the man's last name. If he had his way, the dude would be dead and dumped in the bayou long before then.

He just prayed he was the one who got to pull the trigger.

Then he'd go back, visit that pastor again. He'd correct his original error; he'd goad the man back onto his property again, and when he came through the gate, Deacon would draw that .357 and blow the fool's damn head off.

THE INTERNET MADE the job easier.

When he'd entered the trade eighteen years earlier, the

online world had been in a fledgling state, nothing organized. Now, it was a treasure trove of databases, personal
information and archived material.

He sat on the edge of the single bed at the hostel, his
phone on speaker as he tapped on the laptop keyboard.
"Okay, the Tor browser is loaded. What now?"

Nick's voice echoed from the tinny speaker. "Okay, copy
and paste the address I sent you into the address bar."

"Okay... annnndd... done," Bob said. "It's a negative-
image picture of file cabinets against a black background.
Oh... and thank you for the laptop, by the way. Same
provider as the condo?"

"Uh-huh." Velasco made mushing noises. He'd always
had a sweet spot for sour candies. "Want to know how I
scammed his credit?"

"Not really."

"The granddaughter of a hotel magnate worth more than
fourteen billion has a charge card to one of his department
store chains that offers cash advances," Nick said, ignoring
him completely. "The cash is withdrawn by a JavaScript
routine and deposited via an online-only bank, then trans-
ferred to another, then another. After each transaction, the
software closes the first two accounts and opens new ones,
repeating the cycle. Voila, auto money laundering."

"That's—"

"Pretty damn ingenious. I mean, you couldn't do it every
day, as all sorts of flags would go off in the banking industry,
but... yeah, pretty damn ingenious."

"I was going to go with 'diabolical,' but... thank you, all
the same."

"Oh, it's going on the favor tote board, which last time I
checked, was up to three. You do realize," he said, putting on

a Don Corleone accent, "that these aren't going to be small things, these things I ask of you."

"Yeah, yeah. Focus, Nicky. The file cabinets?"

"Oh! Yeah, just click on that. This is a Dark Web information brokerage. These dudes gather high-level intel on everything from parent-teacher politics to global commerce to nuclear policy. They charge a LOT of money for it."

"Great. One thing I don't have much of."

"But, as we just discussed, I have in abundance. I sort of enjoy this, Bob. I sort of enjoy getting my hooks into the great Bob Singleton, Team Seven Alpha."

"You're appreciating my absence of computer knowledge waaay too much, Nicky."

"Heh. Okay, see that box labeled 'request' at the bottom?"

"Yep."

"Plug in what you need there. The more complex the file they gather together, the more the quoted cost."

"This is vanilla stuff. I just need it quickly."

"Great," Nicky enthused, through the cheap speaker. "That should save us some money."

Bob typed in "Cleaning company, New Orleans, Fortunes Casino."

A white-on-black search bar appeared under his request. It began to creep up, to one percent after a few seconds, to four percent after twenty more.

"How long...?"

"About five minutes for something simple. What was your request?"

Bob told him.

"Really? I'm paying good money for a Dark Web file on a cleaning company?" He didn't sound impressed.

"Like I said, I need it quickly. Plus... it's someone else's money, Nicky. Not that I'm ungrateful or anything."

Nick was wrong. It took ten minutes.

But the file was extensive. Nicky shared Bob's screen as he guided the former agent through it. Delahunt Commercial Cleaners had contracts all over the city, many for various levels of government.

They had a crew of six at the casino each night. The crew membership rotated. It appeared the owner, Vaughan Delahunt, also managed the business, along with his son. Staff all wore the same gray jumpsuits; they were close to those worn by mechanics, Bob noted.

"So... I'm guessing you need to find a gray jumpsuit at midnight, in New Orleans."

"That would help, yeah," Bob said.

"Hmm..." Nicky went silent, but Bob could hear the faint sounds of keys being tapped. About a minute later, he returned to the line. "Okay... there are a surprising number of twenty-four-hour stores there, including Walmart. A cross-check of their website says they have one-piece gray jumpsuits in the auto parts section."

"Any ID?"

"They use a simple name tag. I can send you a file, but you'll need to take it to a copy shop and get it laminated. Most of them hang the badge from their neck on a chain or cord."

That covered looking the part. But with only one way in and one way out, getting on board was another matter.

Nick was reading his mind. "The cleaning firm uses a common piece of scheduling software for staff shifts. I can see what their site security is like, possibly add a name to the next crew rotation."

"How long will that take?" It was nearly two in the

morning already, three on Nicky's east-coast clock. "We've got maybe two hours."

"I can't say for sure. The best I can offer is, you head down there, and I'll let you know. But you might have to try to bluff your way through. Tell the shift boss the owner... what was his name again?... tell them the shift manager, 'Vaughan,' took you off a later schedule because they were expecting a busy night. Something like that."

"Sure... something like that."

And if it doesn't work, I'm in a shoot-out with a guard on an open dock at 5 a.m. Fan-freaking-tastic.

THE OVERALLS WERE A DECENT MATCH, a forty-dollar purchase at Walmart. The laminated name tag had required a stop at a copy center.

Bob parked far enough away from the ship to remain inconspicuous, waiting until the first member of the cleaning crew showed up, dropped off by a battered Nissan Altima.

As he'd suspected, the man didn't go aboard alone. He stood and waited in the lot, sitting on a guardrail until a second car showed and he could join a co-worker, sitting on the back bumper of the second man's car.

They doubtless had a set starting time, probably five o'clock, and would go aboard as a crew. At least going aboard in a group provided a chance to spin a bogus story if Nicky didn't come through.

He checked his watch. It was ten minutes to the hour, daylight beginning to intrude on the morning gloom. The new overalls and name tag had taken less than an hour to get together, but the gray jumpsuit pinched at the groin.

He got out of the Honda and crossed the street to the dockside, a strip of gray-white concrete fronted by palm trees that ran parallel to Lakeshore Drive for about a mile.

The workers were waiting about ten feet from the gangway. Two more men in gray coveralls were heading that way.

They arrived together. Bob nodded at the other men. His earpiece was well concealed, but so far, silent. If Nick had managed to hack the cleaning company, he wasn't sharing it.

Five minutes. Come on, Nicky.

A guy parked thirty yards away got out of his old pickup and headed their way. He was taller, with glasses taped in the middle to repair a break. He frowned when he saw Bob.

He stopped a few parking spaces from his car beside a dark minivan. A man in an identical jumpsuit got out and opened the side sliding door. They began to remove two large carts. Each featured storage bays for mops, buckets and a pair of industrial vacuums.

The men rolled the carts over to the group, their worn plastic wheels scraping a bass-heavy tone on the asphalt.

"Who're you?" he asked Bob bluntly.

"Bob."

"And...? What are you doing here? We're a six-man crew."

Bob shrugged. "Mr. Delahunt said he needed me here today. Something about them having more customers last night or something."

The dude looked at his name tag. "Hmm. Bob. Okay, Bob, I'm Richard, and I'm your supervisor." Then he frowned. "I've been supervising this shift for five years. I can't remember us ever adding a body. I figure maybe I should give him a call, make sure you're at the right place."

He took out a phone and began to tap the screen.

47

The cleaning shift supervisor scrolled through a list of numbers.

"You're going to wake up Mr. Delahunt at five in the morning?" Bob needed to sow doubt.

The supervisor kept scrolling.

"Okay... I mean, I want it on the record that I thought this was a bad idea. I mean, I'm the one he's probably going to shitcan if you do that. Jesus." Bob rubbed his scalp, making his anxiety obvious. "I can't lose this job."

Richard lowered the phone slightly and gave him a doubtful look. "He's not going to shitcan you just for that."

"He might," Bob said. "You know what the man can be like." That was just a guess, a gamble that most people hated their wealthy boss.

"Yeah... yeah, that's true. Okay. Just keep your head down for today. I mean, we're not knocking the extra help. Y'all are most certainly welcome."

Bob gave him a smile and nod.

"Just stick to the assigned tasks; focus on the work. Mr.

Delahunt wouldn't send you over if you didn't know the rules already. And in case you didn't realize it, you get new-guy shift duty... which means the latrines."

Bob nodded twice but kept silent. There was no point trying the guy's patience.

He could feel the weight of the extra FN magazines in his overall's side pockets, the pistol in a lower leg holster for both concealment and quick access. The fanny pack held a couple more surprises. The Ruger was in his left side pocket, for good measure.

By the gangplank, the gate attendant nodded towards the group.

"Right, guys, let's have a good day and look out for each other, okay?" Richard said. They began to roll the carts up the gangplank.

AT THE TOP of a set of winding stairs that began on the second floor and led to the riverboat casino's upper deck, Molham Al-Maghrebi watched the cleaning crew go to work three floors below.

Each level of the vessel was open to the rectangular central gaming area, railed balconies protruding from rooms rented out for parties and conferences, as well as private gaming rooms for poker and blackjack.

The staircase offered an even better view; it began on the second floor, stretching up and around to the fourth. Molham liked to sit at the top step during the two hours after he rose, at five, for prayers. That was also when Habsi usually appeared, silk-suited, after eating his breakfast.

It was always the same view, but that was comforting to a

security professional. Changes weren't appreciated. Changes meant unforeseen circumstances.

And something had changed on this particular morning. Despite his cool exterior, emotionless and stoic, he was seething inside. Something was off; in his three decades of security and intelligence work, he could not remember a time when he had been so sure something wasn't right... but in which he could see no sign of anything wrong.

He scolded himself. *In other words, you're having a bad feeling. But that's probably all it is. Stop worrying so much, you big child.*

The cleaners seemed to be about their normal business, vacuuming between roulette tables, picking up loose snacks, wrappers, brochures. They would usually find a few dozen dollars in loose change and bills, which, as he understood, they divided evenly after their shift.

He turned his attention to the front door. The rented security guard was stationed there.

A few feet to the door's right, at a raised two-person café table, his assistant, Ibrahim, was in cover, reading a paperback, pretending to be just another patron having a coffee. He was keeping an eye on each person entering, looking for anyone immediately heading for the main steps, ahead of the doors, to the second level.

Hani, his younger brother, was guarding Habsi. Mohammed was at the apartment back door, with the biker boss, Riggs.

If he is coming, now would be the time. There are few patrons; the city sleeps. He checked his watch; it was almost six a.m.

As much out of nervous energy as anything, he reached for his waistband, under his suit jacket, and unholstered the .44 Smith & Wesson Model 629 revolver. He liked its shorter four-inch barrel for how easily it cleared his jacket, even if it did mean a small sacrifice in accuracy. It also had stopping power; someone shot at close range didn't generally get up.

He opened the cylinder to make sure it was fully loaded. He'd never believed that nonsense about leaving an empty chamber under the hammer to avoid a misfire. He preferred to simply never make stupid mistakes.

Killing the lawyer had been... energizing. He hadn't strangled a man in years, just the odd prostitute, duly dumped into the Gulf of Mexico. Feeling Roulette's weight as he kicked and struggled, the heels of his dress shoes splashing against the bank of the lake, had somehow made it more exciting.

But the Good Samaritan – "Bob" still had no last name that they could determine – was another matter. He'd shown considerable guile and skill already.

The two he'd sent to the motel – ex-Saudi foreign service hit men recommended by his brother – had stupidly not thought to take Bob's picture. It would have given them something more than Riggs's pathetic attempts at a description to work with.

Both men were now at the bottom of the harbor with concrete blocks chained to their ankles, a message to the rest of their trade for their abject failure to kill the pastor or his man.

They would manage without them. They outnumbered this individual nine to one.

Sammy was not a strong man. But he had saved Molham's life, giving him the necessary employment and resources to escape prosecution in Egypt and move to America. He owed him everything.

He snapped the cylinder closed.

Let this man come. I will be ready. And like so many other irritants to have interfered in our plans, he will die screaming.

BOB WATCHED the casino floor from the men's room, the door propped open by his mostly full bucket of water.

He held the mop in hand, but the position of the washrooms, under the second-floor balconies, meant he was not easy to spot and follow from above.

Those on the casino floor certainly weren't paying much attention.

He'd clocked the undercover muscle at the third table as soon as they'd walked in. The wiry young man was reading a paperback but looking over the top of the pages, gauging each of them as they entered.

There'd been another figure looking down from the regal second-floor staircase, he'd noticed. He wasn't close enough to be sure at a glance, but given his position at the top of the stairs, that was probably the bodyguard and head of security, Molham Al-Maghrebi.

The man's positioning was tactically sound, if nothing else. There was only one approach, up the stairs, and anyone rounding the final corner to the top flight would be a sitting duck. If they felt threatened, they would bar themselves inside.

He scanned the rest of the casino floor. The slot machines, against the far wall and in rows ahead of it, were nearly all occupied, with a few hangers-on beside. The blackjack tables were nearly empty, the Texas Hold'em and baccarat completely so. *Card players aren't up this early, I guess.*

The bar, which ran across the back wall, had just three

patrons on stools, two of them slumped in a manner that suggested they'd need help getting up.

It wasn't going to get much quieter.

But so far, Habsi hadn't made an appearance. It seemed likely he had a panic room or strong security within his apartment. He might be able to hide, unreachable in any reasonable amount of time.

So Bob had to be careful. He needed sight of the man before things kicked into higher gear.

There was no sign of the bikers, either. But Habsi was paying their way, which meant he was calling the shots. They'd be inside the apartment, or possibly by the rear staff service elevator. It was down the back-side corridor, however, out of sight.

Assume at least one there, possibly two. He'll use them as a first line of defense, in case you try the back way in. If you go up the front stairs, he'll use them to flank you.

He checked his watch. It was five minutes past six.

SAMMY HABSI ADMIRED the half-Windsor knot on his crimson silk tie in the mirror by the suite's front doors.

It was immaculate, with a gold, centered stick pin and a small diamond stud. His pale gray suit was silk, handmade for him on Savile Row in London, England. His mostly bald head was smooth, the crown of graying hair shaved short.

If it were up to Molham, of course, he would not leave the suite until this man "Bob" was dead. But that suggested fear, and he did not believe in leaving his leadership open to question.

It was his custom to walk the casino floor each morning at six fifteen. It was the quietest time of the day, a perfect opportunity to greet staff and say a quick hello to patrons without risking confrontation or being mobbed with requests.

That was the price of wealth and power, he supposed, small limitations on the day-to-day. But he was not going to end his custom completely, not for Molham or anyone.

A few minutes, a coffee with the front-of-house. That's all that is required to make my presence felt.

"Hani, I'm ready," he said.

Hani Al-Maghrebi approached from the corridor to the living room. He was smaller than his brother and less experienced, but every bit as loyal.

"Okay," Habsi said. "Let's go and greet the money."

Hani stepped ahead of him and opened the left double door. He looked outside to the landing, seeing his brother at the top of the stairs. The bodyguard exited, Habsi behind him.

The sounds of the casino floor echoed from down below, bell chimes and whistles from the slots, the clack of the metal ball circling a roulette table.

"It's slow," Molham said before being asked.

"No sign of anyone out of the ordinary?" Habsi asked cautiously. "Perhaps our assessment was incorrect. It's past six already; in an hour, it will be busy again."

"He will come," Molham intoned solemnly. "Everything about him says this is a matter as much of honor as safety. Perhaps more so; he must know he will be completely outgunned."

The casino boss lifted his chin, his expression haughty. This was beneath him, all of it. On top of that, this man "Bob" would be suicidal to take on nine paid guns.

"I am going to take my tour of the floor," he said.

Molham backed away from the rail and straightened up. "What? No! Sammy, this is not a good idea..."

Habsi gave him a cold stare. "You are my most trusted advisor, Molham. But do not question my intelligence. I do not accept that from you."

"I do not. I question your passion for maintaining normalcy. I doubt Ibrahim would miss this man entering the premises; I highly doubt it. He is good at his job, I think. But we cannot put you directly in the line of fire."

"It will be five minutes, no more," Habsi said.

"It will be your last five minutes if he's already in the casino. You have trusted me for ten years to protect you, Sammy. Listen to me now on this, okay?"

Bob was on pause. Habsi had walked out of the front door of the suite and up to the upper rail, next to the mountainous security chief.

But he'd gone no farther. He'd briefly approached the steps, and Bob had contemplated trying to wing him from there. The FN was so accurate a pistol that in an expert's hands, a stationary target wasn't entirely safe inside a hundred yards.

Habsi was perhaps half that distance, or slightly more. But a killing shot from that distance was still down to chance. He knew he might not get more than one opportunity. He needed to be close to the man.

Come on, come on. Come down the stairs, you little weasel.

The file had included an excerpt from a local business magazine, which claimed he toured the casino floor every morning to greet staff.

So why isn't he moving?

A moment later, the bodyguard sidled up to the casino owner and said something. Habsi looked animated, as if they were arguing. Then Habsi shrugged, looking away for just long enough to express distaste.

Then he walked back past the taller man and leaned against the adjacent railing.

He's staying on the fourth floor. They're isolating him to better protect him.

The file had pegged his head of security, Molham Al-Maghrebi, as former Egyptian intelligence. That suggested he would think tactically. Keeping Habsi back made sense. Even if Bob managed to breach the front entrance, they had a back door to flee through. He could only cover one route unless he stayed on the ground floor... and then Habsi was unreachable.

Which is all pretty much what you expected. So why are you so damn twitchy?

The truth was, he hadn't had a drink in weeks, hadn't had enough sleep in days. He hadn't been truly operational in more than a decade. The flesh wound under his arm burned and stung.

He was nervous.

You don't get nervous, remember? That's why you're... that's why you were Alpha.

He checked his watch again; it was ten past six in the morning.

Okay, that's as good a look as you're going to get. Time to go to work.

48

K elvin Smith hated his job.

Sitting on a stool at the casino doors in his gray security guard uniform was the dullest he'd ever found life could be.

No prolonged church service, no wait at the Department of Motor Vehicles, no rehab from a broken limb could be as tedious as watching depressed gambling addicts lose their money, day after day, with nothing else to occupy his time.

He wasn't allowed to use his phone on shift, and he wasn't allowed to read a book. In fact, all distractions were out, because he was supposed to be guarding the place.

It was a joke. The Arab feller who owned Fortunes had at least two bodyguards and a bunch of other shifty-looking foreigners on the payroll, at least two of whom seemed to be members of a bike gang, judging by the denim jackets on the guys near the elevator.

He'd never drawn his pistol, a Glock 19, at work, although he was an okay shot at the range on weekends. They had occasional troublemakers that he or Steve – the guy on the exits – had to help with. But they just tasered whichever troublemaker was that night's headache, then banned them from re-entering.

Still, it paid enough to make his half of the bills while he went to night school.

He turned slightly in his chair, shifting his attention from the door to the casino floor. There was precious little traffic at six in the morning.

Three tables past the doors, along the front windows, one of the owner's guards was in civilian clothing, ostensibly reading a book. They'd been told there could be particular trouble that morning that they were worried about... what had Sammy Habsi called it? A "vexatious individual" who might try to harm the casino boss.

He'd have to be a complete wack job. This place is armed to the teeth.

Just past the inconspicuous guard, one of the cleaning staff was rolling a mop bucket down the aisle, toward him. Kelvin frowned. He didn't recognize the man. Still... they probably had to replace cleaners all the time because they paid them shit money.

Big dude, though.

There was something strange about him, but Kelvin couldn't put his finger on it. He was staring straight ahead, head up, as if deep in thought and not really paying attention to his surroundings.

About a foot before reaching the guard's table, with the seated man's back to him, he stopped rolling the bucket. But he kept walking, leaving the bucket and mop in place.

That is even weirder. Is he walking out or something? It wouldn't have surprised Kelvin. His late mom had been a school custodian and had warned him how hard the work was, for how little pay.

Cleaners were so unappreciated.

The blast shocked him, an explosive, bass-heavy pop near the man at the table that almost made him fall over backwards. A cloud of gray smoke spread outwards from where the bucket had been, enveloping the area.

A figure emerged from the smoke, walking quickly straight towards him.

Kelvin reached for his holster.

THE SMOKE GRENADE had done its job, visibility around the seated bodyguard's table reduced to nothing.

Bob had timed the maneuver perfectly, stepping behind the unwitting gunman and grabbing him by the head and chin at the exact moment the grenade blew, twisting hard, closing his eyes at the crunch of the man's neck breaking.

He let the body slump to the table, on top of the paperback the man had been reading.

Bob kept his eyes closed and took one pace to the right, then walked calmly through the smoke. He opened his eyes. Patrons were screaming, running for the doors.

Twenty feet ahead of him, a security guard rose from his stool, scrambling, panicked. He was tall and young, fumbling to try to unclip the holster carrying his sidearm.

Glock 19, Bob thought as the gun came clear. *Nerves too much for him, hands shaking.* By the time the gun was level, he'd reached him, left hand blocking the barrel down, towards the ground, right hand punching the wrist, the man's fingers unable to hold a grip, the gun flying.

The boy was brave. In the moment, he forgot the danger

and tried to fight back, swinging his free hand in a round-house punch. Bob bobbed backwards slightly, using the man's momentum to stick out a foot and trip him up.

He fell face-first, then tried to right himself.

Bob leaned down and hit him twice, hard, on the point of the chin. The second shot made sure he was out.

Patrons were streaming by them and through the exit at the other end of the floor. A bullet cracked the window nearest him, a gunshot echoing from the rear of the casino floor. Bob stayed low, pivoting on one knee. From the corner of his right eye, he saw the second security guard flee through the exit.

Ahead, a man in a cream sport coat and brown slacks ran towards him from the rear corridor, in the back corner of the room, gun raised. He squeezed off two futile rounds, his movement guaranteeing inaccuracy. Just past him, Bob could see a pair of heads ducking in and out of cover, around the corridor's corner.

Bob drew the FN smoothly and stayed low, turning shoulder-on to lower his target profile. The man was thirty feet away when Bob raised the pistol, a deadly accurate and light weapon that more than justified the sticker price. Bob squeezed the six-pound trigger smoothly, letting the mild recoil surprise him.

The running man kept running even as the bullet struck him mid-forehead. A second later, his co-ordination seemed to desert him, legs becoming spastic, stumbling, crashing face-first to the ground. He tried to get up, his face covered in blood, but only made it as far as his knees. Blood was streaming from the bullet hole. He waved the gun around, as if confused or blinded.

Bob looked up at the stairwell high above. He could just

make out the top of the double door to Habsi's apartment as it swung shut.

So they're opting for a standoff.

It made a perverse sort of sense. Neither party wanted police involved, but the fleeing guests would have already called about the gunfire.

A priority call would see men dispatched from Third District station, just a couple of miles away, or those already rolling. Average response times would be slowed by morning traffic somewhat, but it still meant he had all of fifteen minutes to kill Habsi somehow and get out of there.

There were two men on the back door, at least – but possibly more. Going through the front meant dealing with Al-Maghrebi and one other man, at least.

Six of one, half a dozen of the other.

Front door it is.

He ran for the stairs, ignoring the flailing man in his peripheral vision. By the time he was up the first flight, the guard had pitched over sideways, lying still.

49

Bob ran up the staircase, reaching into his fanny pack in mid-stride to remove the grenade. It was a low-yield explosive, but would do the trick.

On the second floor, he ran around the balconied corridor overlooking the casino floor. It had cleared completely, the smoke and haze his only company as the fire alarms droned on.

The smoke bomb had worked perfectly, obscuring his first attack, his approach to the entrance guard. It had also panicked the customers into fleeing, getting them out of harm's way.

He spotted the sign he was looking for, a rectangular black placard extending from the wall with small white lettering that read "Security."

Gaming establishments had to protect against cheaters. That meant the first floor was lined with cameras, recording to a central stack of computer servers.

The door was ajar. He peeked inside. The room was

empty save for the server stack and two rows of computer desks. Staff had clearly fled with the rest of the guests.

He pulled the grenade pin and tossed it into the small room, then closed the door and jogged towards the main stairwell. The explosion came a moment later, the security office's window glass blown out.

The device had enough power – and a thermite sub-charge for good measure – to destroy much of the room's contents on explosion. He heard a *thunk* followed by a hissing sound, growing fainter as he neared the main stairs.

Sprinklers kicking in. They'd prevent the fire from spreading, but add damage to any stored footage.

He reached the foot of the stairs, water coming down from high above in a firm shower. Bob peeked around the end of the banister and up the twisting marble steps. It remained still, no one else around.

He took the steps quickly but quietly, eyes raised, head on a swivel as he reached the third floor, judging sight lines for anyone sniping from distance.

Bob checked his watch.

Response time down to ten minutes. Shit. Need to get moving.

He'd anticipated them entrenching themselves, which was why he'd brought the handful of extras. Habsi's apartment could only be entered through the front doors or via the private rear elevator, which would be locked off and guarded.

He climbed the last flight, stopping at the halfway landing to check around the corner. The top of the stairs remained clear. He withdrew the folded mini-binoculars from his pouch and scanned the door for signs of danger.

The glass on either side of it was narrow, but appeared to be thick-cut blocks, artistic but unable to be opened. That lowered the risk of them picking him off as he tried to breach.

Bob crept up the final flight.

In the vast living room that made up one of the top floor's four wings, Habsi was pacing nervously.

Nearby, Hani Al-Maghrebi stood by the main door, which was ajar just a crack. Beyond it, a long corridor fronted guest rooms, with the corridor to the atrium and dining room just past them. He had twenty feet of open space, with no cover for anyone to hide behind.

He considered himself an excellent shot, even at moving targets.

His older brother sat on the white Italian leather sofa, one leg crossed over the other, trying to maintain a façade of calm.

Molham Al-Maghrebi felt like giving Sammy a slap, telling him to get himself together. Then he realized such a reaction meant he was way too agitated.

Calm yourself. He is just one man.

"Why have they not radioed that he is dead?" Habsi asked. He had the forlorn look of a flood victim. "Why has Ibrahim not informed us of what is going on?"

"Because Ibrahim is dead. This was never going to be easy, even if he is only one man," his bodyguard informed him.

Habsi, for all his bravado and lizard coldness towards the lawyer, looked aghast. "Ibrahim... dead."

"He knew the risks."

Habsi shot him a look that hovered between anger and sorrow. "I knew him a long time, since he was a boy begging for scraps from tourists on the streets of Giza." He frowned. "And Mohamed?"

"We must assume the same. Your bikers possibly as well, other than..." He nodded over his shoulder towards the back door. Riggs was on the other side.

"Two explosions! He is a madman! He will kill us all, and himself along with us!"

"He is a professional." Molham added an edge to his voice. The man was becoming panicky and needed to pull himself together. "He used a distraction to take out two of our men and the door guards. He probably came in with the cleaning staff."

That was it, he realized. That was what he'd noticed. There had been one body too many. *Damn it.*

"The doors," Habsi said, gesturing wildly towards the entrance. "What if he shoots off the lock or something..."

"The lock mechanism is made of two-inch thick titanium and effectively bulletproof. If he decides to come that way, he will not shoot any—"

His sentence was cut off by another loud explosion, this one closer, the floor seeming to vibrate slightly.

"That would be the doors," the bodyguard explained. "He will have used a C-4 charge."

"Allah most merciful... who is this man?"

"A soldier or ex-soldier would be my guess. With a few more days, I could probably know for sure. But we do not have a few more days." Molham rose and strode over to the main doors, standing by his brother.

Hani nodded past him to Habsi, who was pacing back and forth. "Is he going to lose it, or what? His fidgeting is distracting."

"Just pay attention to the hall," his brother warned. "He

will be using small arms only unless he was prepared far enough in advance to pack something into a cleaning cart."

He strode over to the wall unit full of books. At its midpoint, he pushed gently, and a spring-loaded latch gave way. Molham opened the bookshelf "door." Behind it, a handful of weapons were secured in a recess, each suspended on a pair of hooks. He took down an Ingram machine pistol and tossed it to Hani, followed by a pair of magazines.

There was another Ingram and an auto-converted Chinese AR-15 knockoff. Molham gave them a moment's thought, then closed the secret locker. In close quarters, accuracy and caliber would count less than rate of fire.

"He's here!" Hani yelled from the door.

BOB POKED his head around the corner. The next corridor was half the length of the others, double doors at the end open a crack.

A sliver of a man's face appeared in the narrow gap.

He ducked back into cover. He'd only fired two shots, but he ejected the magazine on the FN 5.7 and replaced it, pocketing the mostly full reject. The twenty-shot mag gave him plenty of extra chances, but he was probably going to need all of them

He was also banking on them being predictable. *"Molham Al-Maghrebi!"* he yelled.

It was silent for a moment. He heard a faint creak, perhaps the door crack widening slightly. *"You know my name, my friend, but I do not know yours!"* someone bellowed back.

"Just Bob. That's enough for you."

"*Let me see the man with whom I speak!*" Al-Maghrebi bellowed.

Oh, sure. I'll just pop out of cover, then...

Then a thought occurred. "*Okay, give me a second to holster my weapon!*" he yelled back.

He knew Al-Maghrebi would not believe him, but in the moment the man took to consider whether he was doing just that, Bob poked his head around the corner quickly and stayed put for a moment, to assess.

The tiny black barrel and square stock of the Ingram poked out of the gap in the doorway. Bob ducked back into cover, jumping backwards to ensure anything stray that went through the wall didn't hit him. The machine pistol blared, spitting out the equivalent of a thousand rounds a minute, its extended clip emptied in seconds, bullets lodging in every part of the hallway.

Bob heard the slight *clunk* of its breach mechanism slamming to a halt. He looked around the corner, the FN at eye level. The corridor had been raked with rounds, bullet holes in the ceiling, the walls and the floor.

The door was still a crack ajar, his assailant pulling his arm back in before just about closing it. Bob lined up the crack and guessed at the second man's height, aiming center mass. He squeezed the trigger once, the crack of the shot near deafening.

His hearing was already compromised by the earlier blasts, much of it replaced with a high-pitched, constant whine. He didn't hear the slight yelp of pain from the other side.

But whoever was there pulled away from the gap.

.   .   .

HANI AL-MAGHREBI STUMBLED away from the door, clutching the side of his neck, blood streaming between his fingers.

"*Laqad taearadt lildarb!*" *I'm hit!* he bellowed in Arabic.

Molham moved quickly to his side and pulled Hani's hand clear. "Shit. Your earlobe on this side is mostly gone. Stay still." He pulled his handkerchief from his inside jacket pocket and gave it to his shorter sibling. "Hold this to it. Put pressure above the wound with your one hand."

He turned his attention back to the door, moving over to take his brother's place. Molham trained his revolver on the far corner of the corridor, where "Bob" had to be hiding in cover.

"*I bet that hurt,*" the other man yelled.

"*We are fine. Give yourself up, American. You cannot possibly take us all. Police will be here soon.*"

Molham tapped his earpiece with his free hand. "Riggs, get in here!" he demanded.

"I'm covering the elevator," the biker replied.

"He is at our front door! Get in here now and cover Sammy!"

He leaned back to the crack and saw a shadow by the corner. He sprayed it with a quick burst from the Ingram. He couldn't hit the man in cover, but he could keep him honest until the biker got there from the other end of the massive apartment.

AT THE REAR EXIT, Deacon Riggs stood soaking wet from the sprinklers between the back door and the elevators. The first explosion had been ten minutes earlier, but he still knew nothing.

Terry Beauchesne had tried to call him, but Molham had

interrupted, ordered them to keep the line clear except to speak with him.

That meant something big was up. A second explosion three minutes after the first, and closer, made it clear that it was Bob.

Fuck this. I'm not flying blind on this thing. He took out his phone and called Terry's cell.

"Hello?" a quiet voice asked.

"What the fuck is going on?" Riggs hissed.

"He's here," Terry practically whispered.

Terry was nearly three hundred pounds of mean. But he sounded like a frightened child. "What the fuck you mean 'he's here'? *Where?*"

"I think he went up the main stairs," Terry said. "The guy who was ordering us around, Mohammed, charged out at him and emptied a mag. But the dude just took him down from fifty-plus feet with a single shot."

Damn, son.

Riggs knew he wasn't much of a shooter, but that was ridiculous. The dude was relentless. He was heading up the main stairs, coming through the front, which meant they were last on his menu.

Habsi would kill them if they cut and run. But Habsi probably didn't have much longer to live himself.

"We're getting the fuck out of here," he declared. "Go! This place'll be crawling with cops soon anyhow."

"Just run?" Terry asked.

"Just fucking run. *Now! Do it!*"

He ended the call. Riggs used a damp forearm to wipe the water from his face as he jogged over to the private elevator. He hit the down button.

Nothing happened.

He hit it again, then twice more, frantically.

He looked up.

The sprinklers. The safety system. It automatically shut down the elevators for a fire evacuation.

Fuck.

Riggs was trapped. The only other option...

He looked to his left where a glass-panel side door led to the exterior upper deck and open air.

He ran over and opened it, running out and looking over the edge. He could hear sirens blaring, getting closer. The water was about forty feet below, but it seemed so much farther. *You hit that wrong and you'll break every bone in your body.*

He ran over to the stern. The giant paddle wheel sat unmoving, fifteen feet below. As far as he knew, the casino was semi-permanently moored. Riggs climbed over the rail and used the metal scrollwork for handholds as he tried to lower himself to the third deck.

His feet found the rail... and then he slipped, his grip giving way as he fell...

His flailing hands found the third-level railing and he clung on for dear life, but his body's momentum was too great, slamming him into the iron rail posts. His grip gone, he fell backwards, slamming back-first, ten feet below, into one of the giant paddles.

He lay there, still, for a moment, the morning sky above a blue-black haze.

The paddle blade began to dip downwards ever so slightly, slowly, rotating around the wheel's axis, his weight barely enough to affect it. He looked around frantically. To its right, he could see the very top of an emergency ladder.

It was attached to the boat's stern. It ended just above the waterline. He scrambled to his hands and knees, crawling frantically to it, grabbing the sides of the ladder as the slowly turning wheel rejected his weight.

Riggs scrambled down the ladder. It ended ten feet above the water. He dove into the lake's murky depths.

He wasn't a strong swimmer, but the nearest ladder to the dock wasn't far. He just prayed the others had been as lucky.

50

From his corner cover, Bob could barely hear the man yelling, even though he was only twenty feet away.

But he caught the word "police."

The man had a point. Bob checked his watch.

Response time in four minutes.

He poked his head around the corner quickly one more time. The Ingram spat fire, forcing him back into hiding.

The door looked thick, probably oak or walnut. The FN 5.7 had about eighteen inches of guaranteed penetration against a human target, despite the relatively small 28 mm slug, and enough muzzle velocity to ensure a nice big entry wound.

But the door wasn't a human. Hardwood wouldn't stop a slug, but it would misdirect it, slow it, minimize the threat, particularly using a slug that "tumbled" end over end after penetration.

Still...

It wouldn't take anyone out.

But it could shift the tactical playing field.

He crouched low. Then he sprang to his feet and rounded the corner simultaneously, pistol leveled as he emptied the twenty-shot clip at the door.

MOLHAM AL-MAGHREBI SAW the figure rising as it rounded the corner. He turned that way with the Ingram but saw the pistol leveled and knew he was too late.

He threw himself sideways, taking his brother down with him. *"Down!"* he screamed as bullets blew splinters of wood into the living space.

The ajar door swung inwards, nearly fully open.

From the corner of his eye, he saw Habsi scurrying on his hands and knees towards the far side of the room. He was whimpering loudly.

Molham rolled over onto his back and sprayed the doors with bullets, the Ingram barking out its metallic chorus. The magazine empty, he threw it to one side as he regained his feet and joined Hani behind the sofa, his .44 Magnum in hand.

The furniture wouldn't even slow a bullet, but it would offer visual cover, giving him a chance to get a drop on the man.

It was quiet for a moment save for the sound of the shell casings rolling on the hardwood floor and the hallway sprinklers raining down.

Behind him, he heard the solid *clunk* of a lock opening, then closing.

Sammy's going into the panic room. That's good.

"Hani, head for the back door; check what's keeping Riggs," he ordered.

There was no reply.

He glanced over his shoulder.

His brother was sitting in a growing pool of blood, eyes staring ahead lifelessly, body still trembling slightly as his brain function slowly ceased.

"Hani!" he screamed.

He began to turn towards his sibling, his only friend in the world. They had been together forever.

Before he could complete the move, a figure leaned around the still closed right-hand door and opened fire.

Molham ducked as bullets slammed into his surroundings, the man obviously firing blind, trying to lead a potential moving target before spotting him.

Behind the other door. He's...

He realized the implication at the same moment he remembered how powerful his revolver was. He leaned over the sofa and opened fire.

BOB LEANED AROUND THE DOORWAY, hoping one of them would break cover and run, strafing the room with bullets.

The room seemed empty except for the motionless top of a man's head peeking out from behind the sofa. Just past the end of the white leather splotch, a puddle of blood had begun to pool.

Okay, that's why he's not finding cover. One more down.

The second man popped up suddenly, gun at the ready. Bob scoped the size of the muzzle and dropped immediately behind the still-closed second door, trying to get as small as possible. The .44 slugs tore through the door like it was cardboard – one, two, three, four huge holes blown where he'd just been standing.

Bob used one to his advantage, aiming through it. The man was behind cover. He shifted his head slightly so he could see a sharper angle, to the left, of the room's interior. A steel door set into the north wall slammed shut.

Panic room, as I expected. He checked his watch. *Time's up. Police will be here imminently.*

The panic room would take some finesse. First, he needed to deal with Molham, assuming he was the one guy left still shooting.

The guy was the only person close to a pro he'd encountered in days, outside of the young man at the church. He would be using the moment to reload. But even with a speedloader...

Go NOW, the little voice said.

He lowered his shoulder and burst through the second door. His aim found the sofa, and he opened fire, six shots thumping through it, feathers and stuffing flying into the air.

His target popped up out of cover, unscathed, and shot back. Bob threw himself sideways, returning fire even as Molham used his last two shots.

Bob's finger yanked the trigger one more time, but it held firm, the slide back, the gun empty.

That was expected. He rolled over and rose, dropping the FN even as he drew the Ruger pistol. He sprinted forward, firing, reaching the other man before Molham could latch a new cylinder into place.

Molham dove to one side, the unloaded .44 Magnum flying from his grip, as Bob fired twice more with the Ruger. The big Egyptian swung a foot out, hard, catching Bob's ankle and throwing him off balance.

Bob went down on one side, his gun arm striking the

hardwood floor, his grip lost. The pistol flew out of his hand and slid across the floor, stopping between them.

The pause was a split second, but felt like an eternity.

Then both men scrambled, diving for the unclaimed weapon.

51

M olham's fingers found the Ruger's cross-hatched plastic grip. He thrust his hand out, punching the other man hard in the face with the weapon, both prone on the floor.

The bodyguard rolled sideways and found his feet. Bob was up almost as quickly, charging at him, trying to take him down before he could aim. Molham raised the Ruger and fired twice, the slide back and mag empty. Bob stumbled forward, collapsing at his feet.

The Egyptian leaped backwards. His opponent lay still, unmoving, a puddle of blood growing outwards from underneath him.

He glanced at the safe room door, nodding to the camera above it. Sammy would be watching the closed-circuit monitor.

A few moments later, the safe room door swung open.

Habsi stepped out cautiously. "Is he..."

"He is."

Habsi looked at his old colleague. He clapped a hand

upon his shoulder. "Once again, old friend, you have protected me when it was most important. Now, we need to..."

He did not get a chance to finish the thought. Ahead of them, the body on the floor lurched forward suddenly, a hand thrust out. By the time Molham realized it was holding a stun gun, it was already touching his leg, the current coursing through him.

Habsi's hand was still on the other man's shoulder; it carried the current. Both men spasmed in place for a few seconds until Bob pulled his hand away.

They both dropped to the hardwood, muscles paralyzed by lactic acid production.

Through gritted teeth, Molham muttered, "How?"

Bob rose from the floor. "Blood pack. Blanks in the Ruger. They were fifteen bucks a pop, but it was worth it."

"Blanks..." Molham moaned. "Why would you...?"

"I figured a place like this, with the top floor isolated? He could be cornered unless he had some way to wall himself in. A panic room made the most sense. Some trickery was necessary to get him to expose himself."

He walked over to the FN 5.7 and picked it up, replacing the magazine with a fresh one from his fanny pack. He walked over to Molham, his overalls smeared with fake blood. "If it's any consolation, I take no enjoyment in this," Bob said.

He raised the pistol and fired twice, both bullets striking the bodyguard in the head. He lowered the muzzle slightly and shot him once more, in the heart. Al-Maghrebi lay motionless, eyes wide open, blood pouring from the wounds.

Bob turned to the other man.

Habsi was struggling, his limbs beginning to wake, the paralysis receding. "Please... I'll give you everything..." he pleaded. "I am a big man in this town. I have power, money. I can get you anything. I... I'll give you everything. All of my riches, all of my properties..."

"You have nothing I want. When you sent those men after Pastor Green, you lost any chance at redemption," Bob said coldly. "But I'd say whatever chances you had in life to make amends, to be a decent human... they ran out long ago. You're just finding out about it now, is all."

He raised the gun and shot Habsi in the head twice. He lowered it slightly and put a bullet through the man's heart.

He paused, a sound catching his ear.

Sirens. The police are here.

They would come through the main doors, which made the back exit the best route. Riggs hadn't made an appearance, which meant it was possible the bikers lay in wait.

But he doubted it. He headed for the other end of the apartment. The Damned's members had proven themselves self-interested, disorganized. He suspected they'd fled at the first opportunity.

He walked the back corridor. At the end of it, he opened the door and found himself on the rear upper deck. The morning air was cooler than usual. There were more sirens approaching, from a distance.

He jogged over to the dock-side rail. Three squad cars were parked, the pair of officers from each crouching in cover, behind open car doors.

Bob ran over to the other side and looked down. It was at least a forty-foot drop to the lake below. He ran back ten steps, then sprinted ahead, leaping forward, pushing off the rail with one foot, tucking into a dive, hands turned together to knife through the water tension.

He plunged into the cool, brackish water, water slapping his forearms with stinging intensity. He allowed his momentum to carry him down, holding his breath, then kicked eastward.

There were other vessels moored farther down the shore, near the New Canal Lighthouse, ladders to help him climb out. By the time the police rushed Habsi's office, he would be long gone.

52

B ob drove back to the hostel at a leisurely pace, his clothing and gear sodden, reeking of brackish water in the morning heat of the car's cab.

The bikers would be demoralized, disorganized. By his count, Riggs's gang only had three or four members left to face him.

Their paymaster was gone, their mission to destroy Pastor Green's neighborhood over.

Now he needed to be sure they didn't come back for retribution.

He stopped at a Starbucks and bought an extra-large coffee. He avoided caffeine, typically, but two days with little sleep – and none in the night prior – made stimulation necessary.

On the way, he turned on the car radio; 99.5 FM's hosts were discussing the big story of the morning, a fire raging aboard the Fortunes Casino paddle wheeler, reports of shots fired and people killed.

Don and Wanda wouldn't get any details from him. They

didn't need the stress, the worry of knowing they were connected to such bloodshed. They didn't need to know.

By the time Don got out of the hospital, if everything went to plan, Colbert Street would be back to its quiet, normal, middle-class self.

At the hostel, he tossed his bag onto the bed. Bob sat down on the edge and took out his phone, tapping the recording app to check on the bug at The Purple Bird.

It was a mostly empty sound file, just the odd movement triggering the recording function. As he sat and listened, he stripped the FN down to its component parts, drying each with bathroom tissue before reassembling it.

Five minutes from the file's end, the .wav file indicated voices.

He forwarded to it. The time stamp suggested it was only ten minutes old.

"... time to eat! Get your head in gear!" Riggs was dressing someone down. "There's three of us still. The other chapters will help us start over. And we've got the meth."

"So we hide out for a while until this dude is gone?" Terry Beauchesne suggested. "Then we rebuild?"

"Exactly," Riggs insisted.

"Huh. Don't much like the idea of hiding," Terry grumbled.

The recording was dead for a moment. Then Riggs chimed back in, "You want to go back there? You want to fight that guy, you're more than welcome to it. There's brave, and there's stupid. He's either dead, and Sammy Habsi wants to kill us... or Sammy Habsi is dead, and that means he ain't paying us no more. This ain't our fight, dumbass!"

"But the houses..."

"We didn't buy them to get into real estate. They served their purpose. Now that purpose is done."

A third voice chimed in. "Look, you want to give up your cut and stay in New Orleans until he finds you..." Dozer suggested. "I mean... you do you, Ter, but I'm getting the fuck out of here with Deacon."

Terry must've been thinking about things, the audio momentarily cutting out. "Okay," he said. "I'm in."

"We go home, we clean up and pack some stuff for a road trip, then we head to the cookhouse until we can figure out if it's all clear to come back. We meet out there this afternoon at four o'clock. Got it? Good."

The recording ended.

Bob let out a deep breath, shaking off some of his fatigue. He had to take a shower and change the dressing on his wound. The Damned could wait until he'd had a few hours' sleep.

DET. Pullman Lewis sat in the hospital parking lot, watching the main entrance.

He munched on the egg salad sandwich his wife had prepared for him.

He'd been sure that morning. It had struck him as a moment of inspiration, and he'd told his wife, Sondra. She'd been serving up pancakes at the time and had stopped, pancake and spatula in hand.

"You were taken off that case, I thought," she'd said.

"The Green shooting, uh-huh. This is different... this is something else."

She'd been skeptical, staring at him warily over her fork

as they ate breakfast. They still had twelve years left on the mortgage, a daughter heading to college.

Now, hours later, he was wondering if she'd been the more astute on the matter. Even if Wanda Green was lying about Tyler Gaines's involvement, what could he do? Arrest someone based on a solid description and suspicion?

But at least you'll know who you're after... if not why. Whoever he was, Gaines had been present at the scenes of at least three homicides. Lewis was sure of it.

He'll want to see them again. No one has visited them since the weekend. It just makes sense for him to try. There was only one officer guarding the nurses' station, and the bloodbath from that morning guaranteed most other officers, plain-clothes or otherwise, were tied up for the day.

Ahead, just past the sidewalk dividing the lot from the road, a bicycle messenger cruised up to the doors, standing on his pedals as his momentum took him up to the bike rack. He locked up his ride, fetched a package from his bag and headed inside.

Lewis looked at his watch again. *But... how long do I wait?* He'd been there for four hours without a sign. There were other entrances and exits; he might even have tried another route in.

Wait until the official visiting hours are over at 9 p.m. Then go home to your wife, idiot.

WANDA GREEN RUSHED DOWN the hall of New Orleans East Hospital. She would have sprinted, but at fifty-nine and after years of walking and standing, her arches wouldn't allow it.

She made good time anyway. The call had come in less

than an hour earlier. She'd practically whipped the taxi driver like a thoroughbred to get him to drive faster.

Don's room door was ajar. She pushed past it forcefully. Dr. Bhardwaj was standing by Don's bed, smiling.

Don was smiling even wider.

Wanda ran over and threw herself on him, hugging his prone body through the blankets. "Oh baby!"

"Whoa... don't squeeze me too hard, my love. They just patched that part up."

She turned and stared at the surgeon. Then she hugged him, hard. Dr. Bhardwaj looked momentarily taken aback before nervously giving her a little hug back. "He's going to be just fine," he said.

Wanda moved over to Don's side again. "I prayed day and night," she said. "I knew the Lord was listening, Don. I felt it. I never feared." She leaned over and put her head on his chest.

"I know, sweetheart, I know." He patted her back. Then he'd frowned, looking past her. "Is Bob...?"

"He can't be here," she said. "The police have been here on and off all the time."

"I'll just give you two some privacy," the surgeon said tactfully, heading for the door.

Wanda hugged her husband again. "Everything went so crazy. I haven't been so scared since Jon died."

"The men at the motel..."

"Bob has been... well, he's decided to settle things."

The pastor frowned. "I was kind of afraid of that."

"They burned our house down, Don. Everything. Gone."

He closed his eyes and held them tight for a moment as the magnitude of it hit home. Then he steeled himself. "House was insured. As long as nobody was hurt..."

"Not at that point. But judging by the news reports, Bob's been... well, he's been busy. There ain't too many of those bikers left. They attacked Denise – don't worry!" She read his concern. "Don't worry, she's fine, back home with her folks. But he killed two of them at Mrs. Summerlea's place, saving her."

"Good Lord."

"I just don't know quite what to think, Don. I know he's trying to do right by us, but Jon's friend... he's an angry man inside. There's something very dangerous there."

"We know what they did for the government now," the pastor said. "Can't say as I'm that surprised."

On cue, a nurse entered the room. "Mrs. Green?"

"Yes?"

"A courier just left this for you at the nursing station." She handed her a brown manila envelope.

"Oh! Thank you kindly, dear..."

The nurse departed. Wanda tore open the envelope.

Inside was a cell phone.

"Well now, what on Earth..."

The phone began to ring.

"I don't think that's supposed to be turned on in here," Don said.

She looked around quickly to ensure no one was near, then answered it. "Hello?"

"Wanda? It's me."

"Bob! Bob, oh my goodness! Where *are* you? When I didn't hear—"

"Is Don okay?" he asked, ignoring the question.

"He's fine! He's awake!"

"Hey, Bob!" Don said, raising his voice a little to be heard.

"Can you put me on the speaker, Wanda? It's the top right button on the lock screen, there..."

She tapped it. "Go ahead."

"Hey! There we go," Bob said. "Can you both hear me?"

"Yeah, I'm here, young man," Green said. "Hear you've been creating a little havoc out there."

"Things escalated," Bob said. "But that's why I'm calling. I just wanted you both to know you're not going to have to worry about the blockbusters anymore, or The Damned MC."

"It's over?" Wanda said.

"Yeah, inasmuch as most of the problem no longer exists. You can read into that what you want, but it's better if I leave out the details."

"That's... well, that's welcome news," the pastor said. "We'll pray for those men, assuming that's appropriate."

"Eh... up to you. I can't say they deserve it," Bob said. "Anyway, it's time for me to get moving. The heat around here is getting considerable."

"It would be good to see you again before you go, son," Pastor Green said.

"Yeah... not a great idea. Wanda can fill you in, but there are a lot of different people looking for me. But we'll see each other again, eventually. I'm sorry about your home, Don. I tried..."

"Son... please. You saved my life. You saved my niece."

Wanda knew better than to tell him about Derek Bevan just then, his horrible choice. That could wait for later. "You ever need help in New Orleans, you know you can call on us, okay, hon? Just knowing that Jon's work was important... that meant the world to me."

"Well... good," Bob said. "You're good people. You two

take care, okay? Oh... and do me a favor: if anyone shows up asking after me, I don't exist."

"Who doesn't exist?" Wanda said.

"Well, exactly."

The line went silent.

After a moment, Don said, "I hope he finds something that will make him happy. The pain radiates off that man in waves."

"Maybe that's what it takes," Wanda said. "Maybe to do the kinds of things he just did, a man has to hate himself just a little bit. Maybe taking that hate out on someone who seems to have earned it helps him cope."

Don remembered what Bob had said in the bikers' front yard, that he knew he was already dead. "Maybe. Maybe so."

53

Deacon Riggs felt strangely at peace.

It had come upon him suddenly as his Harley chewed up the miles on the I-90, heading out to St. Catherine Island and the chance for a new start.

The vibration of the road under his wheels was a sort of white noise. He'd learned after a few long trips how it could numb a man, make his legs go to sleep, if he rode too long.

The rented Toyota was just ahead of him, Terry and Dozer in the front seats.

If he dwelled on it, how badly everything had gone wrong ever since that pastor crossed the street, he figured it'd drive him nuts.

Instead, he was going to count the death of Sammy Habsi – confirmed by news radio an hour earlier – and Denny Roulette as warnings, signs the chapter needed a reboot. He'd seen a lot of other outlaws come and go since his time in prison.

He'd learned not to get too attached.

The car turned left, onto the short wooden bridge.

Across it, Riggs dropped back slightly to prevent the dirt from the car's tires from flying into his face.

At the camp, they were already getting out of the car when he arrived. He parked his bike and shut off the engine.

He nodded their way, then frowned. Something seemed different about the cookhouse, but he couldn't place it. He got off the bike.

Riggs walked over to the pair. "Let's check the stash, just for peace of mind," he suggested.

They walked around the right side of the building, towards the edge of the swamp. After moving the table, brush and debris away, Riggs unlocked the double steel doors while Dozer and Terry each pulled a side open.

The three men froze, stunned.

"What the fuck," Riggs muttered.

"At least half of it's gone," Dozer said.

Riggs peered over his shoulder at him. "You don't fucking say. Do you have any more helpful observations?"

Dozer gestured past him. "There's a note."

Riggs reached down and picked up the folded piece of paper.

THE REST IS IN THE COOKHOUSE had been scrawled in blue ballpoint pen ink.

Riggs had a sinking feeling. As he rose, he removed the .357 from the speed holster clipped to his belt. "Look alive. Whoever pulled this might still be here."

The other two men drew their guns. They followed Riggs to the stairs and up them, to the front door. He inserted his key to open it, then realized he didn't need to do so. "It's unlocked," he said.

He depressed the latch and pushed the door open.

The smell of rotten eggs swamped them. It was dark

inside, and he realized what had been off visually when they arrived. Someone had shut all the exterior wooden shutters on the old cookhouse.

Dozer reached for the light switch.

"*Don't!*" Riggs yelled. He dove sideways as the beefy biker's fingers found the switch, knocking his arm down and away.

"Deacon, what the fuck!?" Dozer said.

"Can't you smell it, you idiot! The room's full of gas. Someone's breached the propane lines to the Bunsen burners. Don't turn on any lights; don't use any electronics. This place could blow sky-high."

Terry tapped him on the shoulder. "Uh, Deke..."

The gang leader looked behind them, towards the far wall.

Diesel.

The missing biker was bound with rope to a steel office chair pushed up against the wall. Mini towers of methamphetamine were stacked on either side of him, like garish drug pillars.

They hurried over to him. His wrists were bound to the chair arms, his ankles to the legs. He had duct tape across his mouth. Terry leaned down to begin untying him.

Riggs ripped the tape off his mouth.

"*Don't...* Don't... touch the rope," Diesel gasped. He sounded like his tongue was swollen. In fact, it seemed to be partly sticking out of his mouth, as if so parched he could no longer control it. "There's a bomb under me."

The three men shrank away. "Jesus Christ," Terry muttered.

It was visible now that they were looking for it. It didn't look large, just a rectangular block of grayish material, a couple of coiled electrical leads, a cell phone plugged into a small black box. On top, a small red light blipped consistently.

"Well, now..." Riggs licked his top lip. "What the hell do we do with this now?"

"Deacon..." Diesel began to say.

"*Just...* Just shush right now; I'm thinking," Riggs replied.

"Deacon, you've got to get me out of this."

"We have to save him somehow," Dozer said. "Can't leave him to die."

"That thing goes off, this whole place goes with it," Terry countered. "You know how to disarm a bomb? I sure as shit don't."

"*Just... let me think!*" Riggs barked.

They were silent.

"Good. Now, here's what we're going to do: first, we're going to move the meth out of here. Then we're going to figure out how to handle this mess here."

"Please, Deacon..."

"How'd you end up like this, anyway?"

"The dude... Bob. He knows about this place," Diesel said. "He said he can call the phone underneath me and..."

Riggs straightened up again. There was no telling when he might decide to act. "We need to move quickly."

They each grabbed four kilos of meth at a time and began to haul it outside. "Trunk of the car," Riggs suggested.

They opened it and began packing the sedan.

BOB PARKED at the fishing camp, less than a mile from the cookhouse turnoff. It was the same spot he'd used for surveillance two days earlier.

He couldn't see anything through the brush and trees on the other side of the small bridge. But he suspected he wasn't going to need to.

The tracking beacon on Riggs's bike was parked outside the cookhouse, according to the map on his phone.

Give them... what, fifteen minutes to load up most of that meth?

He'd hoped leaving the cookhouse to fill with gas and the lights off would be enough. Closing the shutters made it dark enough in there, after all. But they'd taken the exit five minutes earlier, and he hadn't heard a bang or seen a column of smoke yet.

He wondered how significant a blast that cookhouse would cause. The propane tank behind the building seemed big, but he didn't really have a frame of reference.

He checked his watch.

Twelve minutes.

IT TOOK four more trips before the trunk was full. Riggs nodded to the storage bunker. "We'll grab the rest from the bunkhouse, put that stuff on the back seat. I think it'll all fit."

They headed back into the cookhouse.

Diesel had begun to weep softly. "Jesus friggin' hell, Deacon, *please!* Get me out of here."

Terry and Dozer began to fetch the last few stray keys. "Now, you just hold on tight a few more minutes. We'll get you squared away," Riggs said.

When they were a few feet from Diesel, he turned to the other men, keeping his voice low. "Boys, once we're out of here, I want you two to start packing the rest. I'll come back in here alone, try to take a crack at that thing."

Terry frowned. "You sure, boss?"

"Better only one of us is at risk, and it's my responsibility," he said.

His men nodded solemnly.

They seemed convinced, Riggs thought. *It's going to be tough saying goodbye to Diesel. He was a good soldier.*

They began to walk back to the exit.

The double doors flew open, the figure bursting inside forcefully enough that each door slammed into the adjacent wall.

"Dieesell!" the figure bellowed. He was barely visible in the darkened room, his outline framed by the light streaming through the doors. The man was mud-caked, blood smeared across his forehead like he'd dipped his head in paint.

Riggs gasped. *"Dirty Carl?"*

"I'm coming for you, Diesel, you double-crosser!" the bedraggled figure yelled. He took a halting step forward, slowed by two days in the swamp. "Left me for dead! Hit me and left me for dead. Walked in circles for hours. But I found you... dirty, backstabbing bastard!"

"Oh shit," Diesel mumbled.

Dirty Carl paused. "Why's it so damned dark in here?" he muttered. He reached for the light switch.

"Nooo!" Riggs and Dozer screamed, diving forward to try to stop him, neither man close enough, the muddy finger clicking the switch to the on position.

A MILE AWAY, the explosion made the ground shake slightly, the mushroom cloud of smoke and fire that shot out of the bayou catching Bob slightly off guard.

"Damn!" He leaned back reflexively at the force of the thing as he watched through the binoculars, a black pillar streaming into the cloudy blue.

Well, that answers the question of how much C-4 was too much, he decided. *Probably could have done with half that.*

Still, it paid to be thorough.

He put the binoculars into the fanny pack and started the car. He had to drop the Honda off, but Colbert Street would still be crawling with police. He had Denise Green's address in the Ninth Ward.

It would have to do.

He could finally head west.

The Greens were safe, and he needed to get his trip back on track. He had a package to pick up in Memphis, a little walking-around money stashed long ago.

He pulled the car out onto I-90. As it passed the turnoff, flames were still billowing above the treetops. They seemed even larger up close.

Ultimately, sometimes, that was what it took to do the right thing: to get up close and personal.

And when things didn't go perfectly to plan, there was always his father's advice, borrowed from a hunting trip that seemed very long ago: when you can't avoid a problem... sometimes it's best just to blow that sucker up.

He stepped on the accelerator.

It was time to get the hell out of New Orleans.

EPILOGUE

He parked the red Honda at Denise's house in the Ninth Ward and took a cab back downtown, to the bus station.

It wasn't as if he wanted to cut and run on the Greens, leaving them with so much to figure out. But the heat would be on after Habsi's death. Even despicable men left allies behind, family, dependents.

Not to mention the fact that the local police had to do something right eventually.

Bob paid $54 for a nonrefundable one-way ticket to Memphis, via Jackson, Mississippi.

He checked the departure boards. He had a five-minute wait until they left.

Cutting it close. That's probably a good thing.

Had it all been avoidable? Had wading into the pastor's problems betrayed his quest for some humility, for redemption from the sins of his past? *What's the measure of a man? That he accomplishes great things? Or that he is honest and sincere in the effort? That he's loved for what he does... or that he does what's right regardless?*

Maybe life wasn't something to "get right." Maybe it was just about the balance. Between effort and outcome, sure, but also the steps between, the journey leading to something new, whether it's what was wanted or expected... or maybe just what was necessary.

How would Nurse Dawn put it? As long as you keep trying, you might actually accomplish something. Giving up accomplishes nothing. So... don't give up.

When he got to Memphis, he could track down his old go bag, pay back John Butcher for his timely help. Then, maybe, find somewhere to lie low for a while, a smaller city where his past was unlikely to catch up with him.

A man sat down in the seat next to him. He was well dressed, in an olive patterned three-piece suit, steel-framed spectacles. His brown dress shoes gleamed.

"I thought I might find you here. You don't own a car, after all."

Bob didn't look back right away. He paused for a few seconds for dramatic effect. Then he glanced over at the man. "Sorry? Are you talking to me?"

"I am indeed. In the end, the description wasn't far off. Six two, dark hair, angular features, fit but thin. I'm Detective Pullman Lewis, with the Memphis Police Department."

Bob glanced around the room quickly. He was alone. "Are... you sure you mean me, sir? I think maybe you're confusing me—"

"I don't think so. I heard the dispatchers on that explosion in the county, and I figured that between that and the waterfront bloodbath last night, your business here might be concluded. I waited for you at the hospital initially. I figured against you stealing or renting a car. Too much of a trail. That routine with the phone and the bike courier was clever, by the way."

Bob leaned back, eyebrows raised, selling it. "I have no idea what the heck... I mean, with all due respect to you being a policeman and all... but I don't know what you're talking about. I'm heading to Memphis for some R and R—"

The man had come alone, which meant it was a guess. More than that, it meant he had something preventing him from bringing backup.

He's flying solo, playing a hunch. Damn it. Should've used another town as my destination, just in case.

"No, you're a former member of the military who worked with the now-deceased son of Wanda Green, when she was known by the surname 'Rice.' And I'm going to need you to come down to the Criminal Investigations Division with me and answer some questions."

Bob's eyes flitted over the detective's shoulder, judging the distance to the exit. "Look, I don't know who any of those people are, or who you think I'm supposed to be."

"I know exactly who you are, and you can stop eyeing the doors. You're not going anywhere. Let's see some ID."

Bob fished for his wallet. "I'm telling you—"

"And I'm telling *you* that I've had enough nonsense since you rode into town, Mr. Gaines. As I told your friend Mrs. Green, I'm a tenacious man. I don't leave loose ends."

Huh? What did he call me? "Excuse me?"

"ID, please!"

"My name is Bob Welling—"

"Your name is Tyler Gaines, you were friends with Jon Rice, and you stayed with his parents on Colbert..."

Bob passed him the New York State driver's license, and he stared at it.

"Robert Welling, aged forty-two, of Hudson, New York. Well..." The detective looked embarrassed. He turned the license over. It looked legit. "It appears I've made a mistake, Mr. Welling. I am... profoundly apologetic."

Lewis rose to leave.

"I'm confused," Bob said.

"It's going around," the detective said. "Sorry to have bothered you."

Bob felt his heart race slightly as he watched Lewis disappear out the side doors to the bus station. He slowed his breathing. Above, a chime sounded, a woman's voice announcing the departure in English and Spanish.

He got up and retrieved his soft-sided bag. The bus was never much fun, but he'd picked up a paperback to kill time on the journey.

New Orleans had been a trip gone wrong. But at least he'd managed to give Wanda some peace of mind about her boy. That was a form of redemption, Bob figured, some small measure of penance.

Once he had some cash once again, he'd head south, look for somewhere quiet to hole up for a while. He had to lie low, let the heat die down.

Maybe head to Arizona, slip anonymously into the background in Tucson or Yuma. Arizona was quiet.

Quiet would be good for a while.

ABOUT THE AUTHOR

Did you enjoy *Blood Debt*? Please consider leaving a review on Amazon to help other readers discover the book.

Ian Loome writes thrillers and mysteries. His books have been downloaded more than a half-million times on Amazon.com and have regularly featured on the Kindle best-seller lists for more than a decade. For 24 years, Ian was a multi-award-winning newspaper reporter, editor and columnist in Canada. When he's not figuring out innovative ways to snuff his characters, he plays blues guitar and occasionally fronts bands. He lives in Sherwood Park, Alberta, with his partner Lori, a pugnacious bulldog named Ferdinand, a confused mostly Great Dane puppy named Ollie, and some cats for good measure.

ALSO BY IAN LOOME

A Rogue Warrior Thriller Series

Code Red

Blood Debt

Made in the USA
Las Vegas, NV
20 December 2023

82709996R00215